Cow Creek

Richard Gehrman

ISBN: 0692267182
ISBN 13: 9780692267189
Library of Congress Control Number: 2014914153
Richard Gehrman, Wahoo, NE

In memory of LaVerne Nelson, who encouraged me to do this.

ACKNOWLEDGMENTS

John G. Neihardt Center
Bancroft, NE

Heritage Museum of Thurston County
Pender, NE

Fergie Nelson

Memories
by Irene Nelson Gehrman

PROLOGUE

My mother's name was Irene Nelson. She was from Oakland, Nebraska. She was the granddaughter of Olaf Nelson. She was one of five children born to Emil and Ellen Nelson.

While it's not wise to play favorites where family is concerned, I couldn't help it. Mom's brother LaVerne, nicknamed Fergie, was such a special person. He was short—I'm guessing five-four—and plump. He married Aunt Vivian, who was over six feet tall. They had two children, Jane and Sam. Vivian passed away in 1968. Jane and Sam married and moved away from Oakland. Fergie was never lonesome. Oakland was his family. He ate three meals a day at the Corner Café and never missed an event in town. While he has been gone for eight years now, anyone who is from, or ever was from Oakland, knew Fergie.

Fergie had a way with people. I mean, he could strike up a conversation with the banker or the town drunk. He would tell stories, joke, or gossip. He had bought a strip of abandoned railroad right-of-way just east of Oakland and moved in an old country school-house and made it into a home. Behind the house

was an array of old sheds he either dragged home or
built. He loved pigeons and fancy chickens. After his
death, the Burt County Fair Board named the poultry
barn in his honor. The fairgrounds are in Oakland,
and when the fair was on, he all but lived there. He
served as poultry superintendent.

Fergie loved the birds, but his great talent and
love was his dogs. The first dog I remember was Bozo.
Bozo was some kind of sheepdog, black with patches
of white. He had Bozo when he still farmed. He would
tell Bozo to bring in the cows, and he would do it.
Later he gave up farming and went to work at a large
dairy nearby.

I visited him at the dairy, and he laughingly said,
"They hired me, but Bozo does all the work."

The next dog was Lizza, I think a rat terrier mix
mutt. This dog could put on a fifteen-minute circus
act. After Lizza came Rambo. Fergie told me he was at
the fair and a boy had a puppy in a box to sell. Since
Lizza had just died, he thought he might take the
puppy. He asked the boy if the puppy had a name.

The boy said, "Rambo."

"Why do you call him that?"

The boy replied, "'Cause he's a mean sombitch!"

Rambo was not mean at all, and soon learned all
of Lizza's tricks, and was a longtime companion to
Fergie.

Speaking of mean dogs, Fergie once told me, "If
you ever pull into a place and you're greeted by a
mean dog, don't expect much from the person who
answers the door."

In fact, I'm also a dog lover and an avid bird hunter. For years I have had my beloved English setters and am an excellent wing shot. In the fall of the year, I would hunt the hill country north of Oakland. If I could, I would try to get to Oakland in time for lunch with Fergie. I would meet him at the Corner Café. Once inside the café, I would be introduced to every patron. He was so glad to have his nephew come, and of course, for a free lunch.

There is one day in particular that sticks out in my mind. It was a story I was trying my best to figure out how to share. I thought about it all the way home. Then, it was nearly forgotten as I went on to other pressing matters of day-to-day life.

My love of bird dogs and hunting led me to subscribe to *Gun Dog* magazine. I read it faithfully every month. After reading an article on problems with training dogs, the light bulb clicked: *I should share my story of that afternoon with Fergie.* I sat down and wrote a full-page feature story and submitted it. Two months later I was disappointed to find that they edited my story and put it in the Letters to the Editor column. They did a good job, it still made sense, but it was not the full story. I cannot find the manuscript of the full story, so here goes from memory.

There is nothing like a frosty morning to give a bird hunter a great feeling of optimism, and this was one of those glistening mornings. Elsie, my setter, woke from her sleep beside me and sat up on the seat as soon as the truck turned off the highway and onto the gravel. She was so excited! By the time we went the four miles to our first spot, she was trembling with excitement. I pulled off the road, got out, loaded the gun, and let her out. She worked her way up a patch of thick grass about fifty yards and froze stiff. What a beautiful sight, the light breeze blowing the long hair on her stiff tail. I walked up to her, gun ready, kicked in front of her, and a hen pheasant exploded from the grass. Elsie was after her like a rocket, and I yelled to no avail. This was terrible. All morning was the same. She had become uncontrollable. She had shown so much promise last year. Now this year she was terrible, flushing birds instead of pointing them. I shot a couple of roosters by chance, no help from Elsie, so by eleven,oclock I gave up and headed to Oakland for lunch with Uncle Fergie.

My uncle LaVerne, nicknamed Fergie, always ate lunch at the Corner Café in Oakland, Nebraska. Everyone in town knew him. He was quite a jokester. After lunch I followed him a mile east of town to his place. Elsie was content to sleep on the truck seat, so I got out to visit with Fergie. As I got out, I was greeted by a border collie pup that followed as we walked and talked. He told me his old dog got run over, so he got this new pup. I told him of my frustrating morning with Elsie. He never commented.

We continued walking and talking and ended up by the basement door.

He said, "Come in and have a fresh apple."

He got me a nice Jonathan apple from Grandpa's old GE refrigerator. As I stood there eating my apple, the pup sat next to his master. Soon he asked the dog to sit up, shake hands, roll over, play dead. The dog did it all! He surely could teach a dog to do tricks. As if on cue, a cat jumped down off a ledge, walked over to me, and began to rub its head on my ankles, as cats do.

At this, Fergie said to the pup, "Isn't that a nice cat? Go pet the cat."

I couldn't believe it. The pup walked over, raised a paw, and petted the cat. I can't tell what would have been harder, teaching the pup or the cat.

"Oh my God, I couldn't even get Elsie to 'come here,' and you can get a pup to do all this," I said.

His answer, "You can teach a puppy a lot until they are eighteen to twenty months old. After that, you think they forgot everything, and you can't teach them much. If you figure it in dog years, they are teenagers. They are just like people. If you bring them up right, they can survive the teenage years, and by three, you'll be surprised how much they'll remember."

When the magazine came out, I ordered an extra copy. I noticed in the paper that the Burt County Fair was going to be the next week. So I got up the next Saturday and went to Oakland and found Fergie in the poultry barn. We chitchatted for a while, and I pulled out his copy of the magazine and showed him the article. He was so proud he wept. Then he smiled and grabbed everyone he saw all day and showed them the article. We had a fun day.

A year or two later, after a hunting trip north of Oakland I stopped for lunch and a visit with Fergie. He asked me how Elsie was doing. Elsie was a Crockett-bred setter. These were bred to be hunted off horse-back. We had come to an agreement: I would let her run free for a half hour or so to hunt her way. Then she would come and hunt close and hunt my way, and we would get a lot of birds.

"Ya, you're right," Fergie answered, "breeding is important. If they are bred for one thing, it's hard to expect them to do something that goes against their bred-in instincts. You can't train a bird dog to guard the hen house."

We visited between ourselves and other patrons for some time. Then he asked me a question, and it has bothered me for years, until now, I finally am ready to sit down and write the story that this sweet man challenged me to write. It is a story that no one in the family had heard. I didn't think it true at first because Fergie could stretch the truth. But I have found no historical references to prove that it couldn't have happened. Nor have I found any historical facts that it didn't happen.

"Where were you hunting today?" Fergie asked.

"Oh, I was up at Dick Hartman's, west of Winnebago."

He sat there staring into space for a couple of minutes. Then he looked straight into my eyes and said, "I know where his place is. It's north of Cow Creek. Years ago that area was called the Indian Nations before it was called the Omaha and Winnebago Reservation. Pa [Emil] and Uncle Able went up there and worked on a cattle ranch one summer. Something terrible must have happened up there. Pa never talked about it even if you'd ask him."

Fergie's gaze softened. "Richard, you tell a good story, and I'll bet this is a good story to tell."

ONE

A noise woke me. I rolled to the window that faced east and saw through sleepy eyes a dim golden light on the horizon. The smell of bacon and cinnamon rolls baking was filling our little house. A moment later Pa opened the door to the boys' room, as we called it.

"Ya boyz git up. Vee gots lots ov verk today and a goot day to do it."

Gilbert, Able, and Erdie began to stir. Erdie pulled the covers over his head for a minute, then jumped from bed and pulled on his overalls, slipped on his shoes, and flew out of the room. A couple of seconds later, the back door slammed. He must have had to pee awful bad. The rest of us slowly got up and dressed. I was first out of the room. I always liked to take a second and stand over the register grate in the hallway floor, feel the warmth of the cookstove, and smell the breakfast cooking. As I tread down the steps and out the door, Erdie came in. The air outside felt cool but still had a balmy feeling to it, not like it was just six weeks ago. A quick trip to the outhouse, and opening

1

the door, I found Gilbert waiting his turn. Back in the house, the kitchen felt warm and cozy. Pa was at the table with a cup of coffee. Erdie was waiting for Ma to finish breakfast.

Ma turned from the stove. "Ya sleep gud, Emil?"

"Ya, Ma."

Soon the other boys and sisters, Nellie and Nora, were at the table. Ma put a bowl of oatmeal, a platter of eggs and bacon, and a pan of cinnamon rolls on the table and sat. Pa looked up from his coffee and folded his hands.

He glanced around the table. "Nellie."

She looked up, and he gestured with his folded hands.

"Dear God, tank you for dis goot day and des strong hands to vork. Keep da boyz and horses safe, and tank you for dis food."

As Pa finished, everyone started filling their plates. Gilbert took six pieces of bacon.

Ma said, "Gilbert, da bacon is from da pig, not for da pig."

We'd heard that before, but we still all laughed.

This was my family. Ma and Pa were born in Sweden and came to America with their parents when they were about my age. They came here to Oakland to be by other Swedes. I think everyone in Oakland was Swedish, and all the old folks spoke Swedish. Pa worked with his pa farming until he could get this place and marry Ma. Ma and Pa made us children speak English, and we all spoke English well. But, if we went to another town, people all seemed to know we were Swedes. Gilbert was eighteen. Pa wanted him to be a farmer, but he told Able and me he didn't want to be a farmer. But he worked hard on the farm because Pa needed the help, and he didn't want to tell Pa that he didn't want to be a farmer. Brother Able and I wanted to be farmers. Able was sixteen, and I was just a year younger. Then there were the little ones, Nellie, Erdie, and Nora.

Soon breakfast was over. Nora went over by the door and got the pan, brought it to the table, and Ma scraped all the plates. Nora took the pan out the door, where Willie, our dog, was waiting. The sun was coming up as we went outside. Pa and Gilbert went to the corral to get Sam and Charlie, the draft mules. Willie was running to catch up with his tail wagging. Able and I went to the barn to start our chores.

Soon Pa and Gilbert were by the barn door with Sam and Charlie, putting on the heavy harnesses and hooking them to the new riding plow.

Pa stuck his head in the door and said, "Vhen yu boyz finish chores, start shelling seed corn."

He slid onto the seat of the plow and headed out to the field with Willie running behind. Hanna and Sara were waiting by the pasture door chewing their cuds. I finished filling the feed trough with corn and oats and let them in. The two brown Swiss went right to their stanchions, and I hooked them in. I washed their udders and started milking. Able was filling buckets from the slop barrel and hauling them out to the pigs. Gilbert was harnessing Pete and Ida, the horses. The little ones were tending to the hens and ducks. A cat came down from the haymow to beg a squirt of milk. I was sitting on the milk stool milking Hanna and thinking of the summer ahead. It was May 1, 1888. The day before was the last day of school, and this was May Day. That evening, some neighbors with May baskets might come by. I knew I was getting too old for that. Some days, I wished I wasn't getting older, and at the same time, wished I was grown up complete. Milking was a good quiet time to think. I moved over to milk Sara and thought of all the corn we had to shell, May baskets, my own horses and farm, and soon I was done milking. Hanna and Sara went back out the door to the pasture. I dumped some milk in the calf bucket, took the rest to the house, and brought back yesterday's skim for the slop barrel. Able was feeding calves, and Gilbert was filling water buckets for the teams. Everyone was working.

The farm was so much work, but Pa said, "Vork for yourself and da Lord, and you vill be a happy man."

We all had our jobs to do, and if everyone did their share, we would all be happy together.

Chores were done, so Able and I started shelling seed corn. Pa said that we should only take kernels from the biggest ears for seed. I guess he knew what he was doing. We always had the best crop in the area.

After we worked awhile, Ma called, "Yu boyz take lunch out to Pa and Gilbert."

Able and I went to the house and each grabbed a pail. One had leftover cinnamon rolls, the other cups and a jar of coffee with cream and sugar wrapped in a towel to keep it warm. The sun was warming, so we

4

left our jackets at the house and headed for the cornfield. Near the house was a garden, then the hayfield
of fifteen acres, and next, the wheat field of twenty
acres. Across from the yard, hayfields, and wheat fields
lay the pasture going north forty acres. Next, on the
south, were twenty acres of oats, and the whole west
of the place, the cornfield. Pa had turned the last ten
acres of prairie last year, so we would farm the whole
160 acres this year, with sixty acres of corn.

Pa saw us coming, finished his furrow, and brought
the mule team over to the wagon. As we neared, Pa was
dipping water for the team. By the time we got to the
wagon, Pa was putting on the feed bags with oats, and
Gilbert pulled up with Pete and Ida dragging a harrow.
Pa sat down in the shade of the wagon as Gilbert watered
the horses. Soon we were all sitting in the shade of the
wagon, eating rolls and drinking coffee.

Pa said, "I hope da Lord grants us a goot year
dis year. Ve should have some corn to sell dis year.
Ankerson at da bank vill vant plenty dis year, what
with the new plow and sheller, an da mortgage dat ve
didn't cover last year."

Willie snuggled in next to Pa and got a morsel of a
roll and his ears scratched. The warming sun and the
sweet, musty smell of fresh-turned earth filled us all
with optimism.

"Dis sur feels goot after las' vinter, don't it, boyz?"
Pa quieted. "Let's go to verk."

Able and I got up, grabbed the lunch pails, and
headed back to the corncrib. Pa and Gilbert tended to
the teams and got back to tilling the cornfield.

The rest of the morning, Able and I took turns sorting corn and turning the corn sheller. When we got the grain wagon full, and all the bushel baskets, we would be ready to plant.

Able said, "I bet we can be done shelling by tomorrow night."

"Ya," I answered. "If we can move our arms tomorrow." The morning passed, and soon Erdie came by and said he was heading out to get Pa and Gilbert for dinner.

"Come on, Able. Let's get two more bushels done before they get in."

I turned the crank on the sheller as fast as I could, and the few kernels that flew off to the side were gobbled by the scavenging hens and ducks. We dumped the second bushel into the wagon as Pa, Erdie, and Gilbert were nearing the place. We headed for the pump to clean up and took turns pumping for each other. I noticed Pa slip over to the corncrib and peek into the grain wagon. He stepped on one of the spokes of the wheel, pulling himself up, looked in, and hopped down with a little grin and a nod. Able hit me on the back and said, "Pa looks satisfied. We did good this morning."

The kitchen was warmer than cozy now, but a cool breeze was coming in the screen door only to die from the heat of the cookstove. We prayed, and dug into pork steaks, mashed potatoes, gravy, and green beans. As we ate, Pa talked of how the soil was working, and Ma talked about making candy and May baskets. As we were eating our dessert cobbler,

Willie started barking, and soon we could hear this tinkling noise.

Pa looked up and seemed to be straining his ears. "Dat's da tinman."

Pa finished his dessert, got up, and went out the door. We all followed behind in the yard, and Pa yelled to Willie to shut up.

"Smithy, ya come at a goot time, before I gut back in da field!" Pa shouted.

I don't know what his name was, but everyone called him Smithy, and he came around twice a year selling buckets, washtubs, strainers, and the like. He climbed down from his now-quiet wagon. It looked like a buckboard with racks built up and buckets and utensils tied on that clanked as it would go down the rutted road.

"Olaf, Anna," he greeted Ma and Pa, "are you needing some tinware?"

Ma said she figured he would be coming soon and had a list in the house, and sent Nellie to fetch it. Ma could speak English but only wrote in Swedish, but she could translate it. Smithy got in the back of the wagon and handed down buckets, pans, utensils, cups, and a washtub. He got a tin box from under his wagon seat, got a statement book, and wrote down all the items and added the total. Ma took the statement and went to the house to get his money. Pa and Smithy were talking while Ma was in the house, and as Ma came out, Smithy raised his voice.

"Olaf, I almost forgot to tell you. The other day I was at Winnebago agency and ran into Tom Ryan.

He has a big ranch north of Cow Creek, in the Indian Nations. He told me he was looking for some big, strong boys to work the summer on his ranch. He said he would be paying a dollar a day plus room and board. He also said he would send any boy packing that didn't work worth a day's pay. That's good pay, but they have to have a horse and saddle."

Pa stood there thinking while Ma settled up with Smithy. Smithy asked if we were sure we didn't need anything else, and as he turned to climb up on his wagon, Pa turned to me and Able.

"Do ya boyz vant to be cowboyz?"

Able and I looked at each other, grinned ear to ear, and answered, "Ya," in harmony.

Pa asked Smithy for Mr. Ryan's address.

He got back in his tin box and wrote it on a piece of paper, handed it to Pa, slid into the wagon seat, and shouted, "See you next time!" and clanked away.

Pa, Gilbert, Able, and I headed to the back of the yard, where the field lane turned off to the fields.

Pa stopped, still clutching the paper from Smithy. "Dis is da answer to my prayers."

Pa went on to explain that the banker would get all the money from the wheat harvest, and that he would have to borrow from Ulmquist against some of the corn crop, unless we could sell some pigs.

"If dat grain dealer Ulmquist has a note on yur crops, he pays lower, and ya can't do nuttin' bot it. Vee need da money, boyz. Dis would git us by till vinter, vin I can go to Ashland and cut ice."

Gilbert spoke up. "Pa, can I go?"

"No."

Pa explained that after the corn was planted, Erdie could start doing more chores, and he and Gilbert could keep up with hay and wheat and oat harvest. You could tell Gilbert wasn't happy, but Pa had made his decision.

"Able and Emil vill go. Ve vill write Mr. Ryan tonight."

Pa and Gilbert headed out the field lane, and Able and I headed back to the corn shelling.

All afternoon we worked as hard as we could, talking about getting the corn planted and heading to the Indian Nations to be cowboys, visions of all things we had read in the dime novels about cowboys and Indians running through our heads. Nellie brought us lemonade and cookies, then carried them out to Pa and Gilbert.

When she got back, she joined Ma and the other little ones putting up a Maypole. Pa and Gilbert came in about three thirty and put the teams out to pasture.

Pa yelled, "Enough seed corn today Let's do chores so Ma can have supper before da neighbors come."

Pa helped me milk and joked about having cowboy sons. We finished chores, cleaned up, and put on Sunday clothes for supper.

Pa started supper prayers. "Tank ya, Lord, for dis chance for Able and Emil to help da family. And give Mr. Ryan goot guidance to choose dese boyz."

After supper, Ma hurried dishes with all of us helping so she could put on her dress and comb her hair. Pa and Gilbert sat on the porch, Willie by Pa's feet, sound asleep. We all joined them, and soon Willie's ears perked up, and he jumped off the porch, looked up the road, and started barking.

"I bet ve got company coming," Pa said as the little ones ran to look too.

Soon two buggies pulled in the lane. The Larsons and Johnsons came from town. It was only a mile and a half from Oakland to our farm, but it seemed so far sometimes. Mr. Larson worked at the grain elevator, and they had four children maybe a little younger than our little ones. Mr. Johnson worked for Ankerson the banker, and their oldest was Johnny. He was in my class at school. They also had two girls, about the same age as Nellie and Nora. It was great to see Johnny. It had been only a day since school, but I missed him already. Able and I told Johnny about being cowboys, while the little ones danced around the Maypole. The women talked. Gilbert joined the men talking crops, weather, and church. Able and I took Johnny out by the pasture to show him our horses and tell him how good they would be on a cow ranch. We talked of everything as the evening went on, which boy liked which girl, and what all was going on in town. As the sun was starting to set, they got into their buggies to head home.

"See ya at church Sunday!" they seemed to say in unison.

As we headed for the house, Ma put her arm around me. "Ya miss being a little one, Emil?"

"Ya, Ma, I do, and at the same time, I like being grown-up."

Ma laughed, and when we got in the house, she gave Gilbert, Able, and me our own May baskets.

Ma went through the house and lit the gas lamps. Pa was upstairs and came down with a piece of paper, envelope, and postage stamp. He put them on the table and took the piece of paper out of his pocket that Smithy had given him with the rancher's address.

"Able, Emil, come. Let's write dis nice man a letter. You tell him how strong you boyz are and how you can do hard vork. Able, you write da letter."

Able went up to the boys' room and got his pen and bottle of ink. When he came back down he sat for a few minutes to think of what to write.

Pa couldn't write English, so he said, "Tell me vat ya write."

Able opened the ink jar and began to write.

> Mr. Tom Ryan   May 1, 1888
> Cow Creek Ranch
> Winnebago Agency, Nebraska

> Dear Mr. Ryan,
> I would like to introduce myself. I am Able Nelson. I am from Oakland, Nebraska, and I have worked with livestock my whole life. My brother Emil and myself would like to apply for jobs for the summer. We were told that you are looking for summer help by Smithy the tinman. While I am only sixteen and Emil is fifteen, we are full-size men. Pa says that people in our family get their size early. Pa says that we

11

should be done planting corn in two or three weeks, so by the time we hear back from you, we should be ready to come.

Cordially,
Able Nelson

Able read the letter back to Pa, addressed the envelope, sealed it with wax, and put a stamp on it.

"We can put it in the mailbox tomorrow. That should be Oly's day to run our mail route."

I asked Pa how he would get by without the horses. He told us that if we were done planting corn, the mules could keep up and could pull the buggy to church for the summer.

"Ve might have to borrow a saddle from Grandpa. He never rides horseback anymore."

I asked Pa if he thought we'd see Indians.

"Oh ya, yul see Indians. Do ya remember ven da Indians came here?"

"Ya," Able and I answered.

Nellie was a baby, and Gilbert, Able, and I were little boys. We didn't have Willie to bark then, and Pa was in the barn. We heard a knock on the door, and Ma opened it with shock to see two Indians standing there. We huddled by her skirt and saw the Indians motioning hand to mouth. Ma said she wanted to send Gilbert out for Pa but was afraid it would scare the Indians. Ma motioned for them to stay there, and she went back to the kitchen, grabbed a loaf of bread and some pork, wrapped it in a towel, and handed it to them. By this time, Pa had seen them and was coming across the yard. The one Indian grabbed the food, and they kind of bowed as they turned to go. They saw Pa coming, and they gave him a bow, got on their ponies, and left. When Pa got to the door, he brought his hand from around his back and revealed a corn knife. Pa said it was all he could find in the barn, and he said he prayed all the way to the house that he would not have to use it.

Pa said, "Oh ya, yul see Indians up der, but dey don't come down here no more. Da Catholic priests are helping dem and are making dem Christians."

From the kitchen Ma interjected, "Better Catholic than pagans, but not much better."

Pa cracked back, "Dey will learn of Jesus and be good people. Dey don't come down here begging anymore."

Pa picked up his Bible and began to read. Able and I began playing checkers and eating sweets from our May baskets. Ma sat in a rocker mending clothes and humming some hymns. So the evening passed, and it was time for bed. I started to doze. The thought of being a cowboy kept me awake for a while, but soon I fell sound asleep.

***

The next thing I heard was Pa. "Come on, boyz. Ve got a lot of verk to do and a goot day to do it."

We all got up, did our morning rituals, and had breakfast. As we started out the door to start chores, Able grabbed the letter to Mr. Ryan.

I asked, "Do you have our return address correct?"

He looked down. "Ya," he said, and walked out to the road, put it in the mailbox, and raised the flag.

Out in the barn the daily routine commenced. As the milk tingled as it hit the side of the tin pail, my mind drifted off. What would it be like to work on a ranch?

Able must have been thinking the same. As I finished milking Sara and was about to start on Hanna, he came in to get more slop for the pigs and said, "Won't it be nice to not have to do chores for three months?"

I hadn't thought of that, but I supposed that there were chores on a ranch also.

Chores went smoothly that morning, and soon Able and I were back at the corn sheller. As we worked away, I would notice Able looking up every so often to see if Oly had been by the mailbox yet. Oly Olson was our rural mail carrier. He did our half of the route one day and the other half the next day. We kept on sorting and shelling corn as the morning sun grew warmer. Then Able let go of the sheller handle and raced across the yard. I could see the mail buggy pulling up to the mailbox, and Able was almost there. I watched as he talked to Oly. Oly handed a couple of letters and took our letter to Mr. Ryan. Able took the mail in the house and came out with the lunch pails. He motioned for me, and we headed out for the cornfield to have lunch with Pa and Gilbert.

"Oly said it would take at least two weeks for the letter to get there and for us to get a reply," Able said.

14

"I hope we can get the corn planted. I hope it don't rain too much so we can't finish on time."

Able was grinning from ear to ear, and I guess I was too. Pa and Gilbert saw us coming and were starting to tend to the teams as we neared them. Soon we were sitting in the shade of the buckboard having coffee and rolls. Able told Pa that Oly had come and he thought it would take two weeks before we would hear back.

"Oh," Able said, "you got a letter from your cousin Pontus from Sweden."

Pa grinned. "Oh, I can't vait till dinner to read news from da old country."

Gilbert asked Pa if he was sure he couldn't go work on the ranch and leave Able or me home.

"No," Pa answered. "Ya can help da family dis winter vin da men go to Ashland and cut ice."

Pa got up to fill the feed bags for the team, and Gilbert told us of Ashland. He had gone with some of the men from Oakland last winter.

"Men come from all over and cut ice," he said. "There is an icehouse as big as all of Oakland, and the men cut and haul ice into it. It's cold, hard work. Trains come and get ice, then go to the packinghouses in Omaha and haul meat back east. The Christian men all stay in one bunkhouse, but in the other bunkhouses, some of the men drink and gamble. On Saturday night, they have dances in town. And don't you guys tell Ma, 'cause Pa said Ma's never to find out, but Pa lets me go to the dances with some of the young fellows."

Pa came back to the buckboard. "Ya boyz have da seed corn done by evening. Ve start planting tomorrow. Ve von't be ready if ve sit here all day."

Able and I headed back to the yard. I got to thinking. I thought my arms would be stiff this morning from cranking the sheller yesterday.

"Able, are your arms stiff today from the sheller yesterday?"

"No, but I bet our backs will be stiff after we start planting corn."

By midafternoon we had the grain wagon filled and covered it and tied down the oilcloth to keep it dry. We were using two bushel baskets to shell corn. I went into the barn and found four more empties. Able went down in the fruit cellar and found five empties that had had potatoes in them. We had to leave one basket for shelling slop corn for the pigs, so we had ten bushels to fill and stack in the barn.

"I think we can be done by supper," Able said, "so keep sorting and shelling." He looked up and saw Ma hanging laundry on the line across the yard. "Isn't not telling Ma that Gilbert went to a dance like lying?" he asked in a quiet voice.

I answered back, "Pa said, 'Don't tell Ma.' He knows best. If Ma found out, Pa, Gilbert, and now us would all be in trouble. You know how Ma says dancing is for heathens. I'm surprised Pa would let Gilbert go. I guess he remembers being a young man himself."

We worked quietly for a while. Then Able said, "I get Pete and our saddle."

But I wanted Pete.

"He's faster. I'm the oldest," Able said. "And besides, last night I came out and rubbed some harness oil on our saddle."

Oh well, I thought. *Able is the oldest. I guess he gets his choice. And besides, I will get to go and ask Grandpa for his saddle and tell him about getting to work on a ranch.*

We had two more bushels left to fill as Pa came driving the buckboard with Pete and Ida into the yard. Gilbert was right behind with the team of mules. Gilbert was up on Charlie's back, Sam followed side by side, step for step. Pa got down from the buckboard, and Gilbert jumped down from Charlie, and they brought the team of mules over to the grain wagon and hitched them up. Pa got on the wagon and drove them out to the cornfield to leave the seed corn for morning. We were putting away the last two bushels when Pa came back with the team. Able and I started chores as Pa and Gilbert tended to the teams. After supper, Pa and Gilbert pulled the cultivator over by the barn door. Pa started changing the shovels on the machine and stretching out the wheels to the end of the axles.

"Eighteen inches from da veel to da shovel. Tirty-six inches to da odder shovel and eighteen inches to da odder veel." Pa loved planting time. "Dis da time of optimism!" he would say.

"Pa, can I go ask Grandpa if I can borrow his saddle and tell him about working on the ranch?" I asked.

Pa quipped back, "You can vait till Sunday and ask Grandpa at church. And who says ya vill hear from Mr. Ryan anyvays?"

17

Able was standing next to me, and we looked at each other. I could tell by the look on his face that he hadn't thought that we may not hear back from Mr. Ryan either.

As we walked back to the pasture to look at the horses, Able said, "We'll get the jobs. I just know it. I just know it."

As we walked back to the yard, Erdie came and asked if we would play hide-and-seek with the little ones. Able and I looked at each other, and I could tell Able was thinking the same as me. We were at the age that we thought we were too old, but it was so much fun when we were little, and besides, none of our friends from school were here to see us.

Able answered back "Ya, we'll play!"

So Erdie and the others ran to hide, and I counted five, ten, fifteen to a hundred and started looking. It was pretty easy. Each one had only two or three places to hide. As I came around the side of the house, I could see Nora's foot sticking out from under a bush. I reached down quietly and grabbed her, picked her up, and threw her over my shoulder. It surprised her, and she screamed in shock.

Then she started laughing. "Emil, this is so much more fun when you play."

We were still playing, and you could see the glow of the gaslights coming from the windows, and the red glow of the sunset framing Oakland in the west.

Pa and Gilbert came to the house, and Pa yelled, "Ya all come in before da bugs eat ya."

18

As we entered the house, I could smell popcorn. Ma hadn't made us popcorn for some time.

"Popcorn and lemonade, anyvun?" Ma shouted as the screen door slammed.

After Pa had lemonade and a bowl of popcorn, he went to his chair and picked up the letter from his cousin Pontus. At dinner he picked it up and looked at it and put it back on the table. He did the same thing at supper. Now he picked it up, looked at it, and broke the seal. It looked to be a long letter, three or four pages written on both sides. Pa started reading with all of us watching him. Sometimes he would grin. When he was all done, he read it again.

"Anna, you vant to read dis letter from Pontus?"

Ma took the letter from him and read it. As she finished a page, she would set it down, and I would look at it. I could make out a word here and there, but I could not read Swedish.

Pa said, "It is goot to hear from da old country. I vill write back on Sunday or a rainy day."

The evening routine continued, Pa and Gilbert reading Bibles, Ma mending and humming hymns, Able and I joining the little ones playing pickup sticks. I fell into bed that night with my arms aching, and heart aching that we might not hear from Mr. Ryan.

***

The next thing I knew, Pa was yelling, "Dis is a goot day. Vee plant corn."

At breakfast Pa prayed, "God bless dis planting, dat ve may have a goot crop and prosper in our lives and yor love. Amen."

After breakfast we started chores. Gilbert helped Pa harness the horses and hook them to the cultivator. Pa slid into the seat and headed for the cornfield with Willie following behind, wagging his tail. By the time Able and I finished chores, Gilbert had the water tubs on the buckboard filled and the mules hooked up. As he passed to get a couple pails of oats from the granary, he told us to get Erdie and Nellie, and he would be ready. We all climbed into the buckboard and headed for the cornfield. When we got there, we watched as Pa neared the west end of the field. At the end of the field, the horses spun about and came back toward us. In a few minutes, Pa was nearing us, and he motioned us out of the way. He got to the end, the horses spun, and he put the opposite wheel of the cultivator right on the same wheel track that he had just come down.

He dropped the shovels, went a few feet, and yelled, "Vo!"

The team stopped. He slid off the seat.

He went over a few rows and looked up the furrows. "Straight as an arrow. Ya can tell da vorth of a farmer by da straightness of his rows. Some of da fellows say der is a new planting machine dat cuts da furrow, drop da seed, cover it, and tamp it all at vonce. Two rows at a time. A farmer von't need so many children. But for now dis farmer needs dem."

Able and I went to the buckboard and got our seed bags, put them over our shoulders, went to the grain wagon and opened the little door on the back, and lifted our seed bags. Pa watched as Able and I each took a furrow and paced the right amount between seed drops. Then he showed Erdie and Nellie how to push the soil back into the furrow and press it with their feet.

After we had gone a way up the furrows, Pa yelled, "Dat looks gud!"

Pa helped Gilbert unhook the mules from the buckboard. Then they lead them over and hooked them to the plow. Gilbert went on to do more plowing, and Pa went to the cultivator and kept cutting furrows in the worked ground. Planting corn was slow and monotonous, and we kept looking back to the house, hoping to see Ma bringing lunch, even though it was too early for that. We would sing nursery rhymes or hymns, and it was kind of fun, but we soon realized how big a sixty-acre cornfield is.

Able said, "If you think it's big now, wait till we have to pick it all."

Soon we could see Ma and Nora coming with lunch, and we quit planting so we timed getting to the buckboard the same time she did. Ma put her arms around Erdie and Nellie and asked them how they liked planting corn. They both replied that it was fun.

"How about Able and Emil? Is it fun for you?"

"Ya," we both replied.

Pa and Gilbert came in, and there was not enough room in the shade from the buckboard for all of us to sit. We all laughed as Willie pushed Nellie out of the shade.

Pa said, "Vell, I tink I have enough furrows cut to last ya boyz and Nellie a few days. Gilbert, vill ve be done getting the field done in four more days?"

"Ya, Pa," Gilbert answered.

The field looked so big sitting there. *How will we ever be done in two weeks if Mr. Ryan writes back?* I thought to myself.

Ma said something to Pa in Swedish. Then she told Able and me to listen for her to clank pans together when dinner was ready. So we all got up, Able and I back to our seed sacks, Nellie and Erdie tamping, Pa and Gilbert back to tilling the field. As the morning wore on, Nellie and Erdie would fall back farther, and when Able and I would finish a row, we would have to go back and help them finish filling and tamping. Late in the morning, Nellie asked Able why we had to work so hard.

Able answered, "You know when Adam and Eve left the Garden of Eden, God told them they would have to toil in the soil to live."

"Well I would rather stay back in the yard and play," she snapped back.

Able told her, "I would, too, but we all have to work to keep the family strong."

It didn't help much. Each row they fell farther and farther behind. Finally we could hear a clanking noise, and we could see Ma at the edge of the yard. Able took his seed sack off his shoulder and swung it in the air so Ma could see it, and she turned and went toward the house. Able sent Erdie and Nellie to fetch Pa and Gilbert, and we went back covering and tamping furrows. As we all walked back to the house, Pa told Nellie and Erdie that they did a good job all morning, but Ma had work for them in the garden this afternoon. Then Pa turned and winked at Able and me.

After dinner, Able and I took turns, one of us putting seeds down, the other covering and tamping. Late in the afternoon, Pa and Gilbert came over to the buckboard. They walked over to where Able and I were finishing a row, and Pa told us that we were doing very good. I said it was so slow doing this field thirty-six inches at a time.

"Vell, I've been doing fourteen inches at a time plowing for days, and now I see da end in sight. Ya vill too in a couple of weeks," Pa said.

Gilbert unhooked the harrow, then hooked up the buckboard. We all got in and headed in for chores with the mules and Willie following.

The next two days were the same. By noon the little ones were not much help. In the afternoons, Able and I seemed to get a little more done, and by Friday evening, it seemed like the north end of the field was quite a ways away. The challenge of the field was the thing most on my mind right now, and only occasionally would I think of being a cowboy.

***

Saturday started as all others, with Pa opening our door and his familiar: "Vake up, boyz. Ve got a lot of verk to do and a goot day to do it."

As I rolled to the east window, the sky was glowing red. It was so pretty, but I knew what it meant. When we went out to start chores, the air felt a little warmer than it had the last few mornings, and wind was blowing fairly strong out of the southeast. Chores were soon finished, the buckboard loaded, and we headed for the cornfield. Pa had moved the grain wagon near the middle of the field, and the last couple days we had been using seed from the bushel baskets.

As we were going down the rows, the little ones started singing "Let It Rain." Able and I joined in, but I could tell from the look on his face that he didn't want to miss any planting time any more than I did. After dinner, Able and I were planting by ourselves again. We noticed the sky darkening in the west. By midafternoon we could hear the rumble of distant thunder. Pa and Gilbert stopped tilling, and Gilbert started hooking up the buckboard. Pa grabbed two steel rods from the back of the buckboard. He pushed one into the end of the row we were working on and came out to where we were.

"Emil, go back out to da udder end of da row. Stick dis rod deep. Ve haf to know vere ve been should da rain vash out da furrows."

I took the rod, put it in, and came back.

"Emil, go help Gilbert."

I ran to the east end of the row. Gilbert had grabbed a seed bag and was moving up the row faster than I could imagine. I started covering seeds, but I could not catch up. I looked up the row and saw Pa pulling away from Able. When Pa and Gilbert met, they turned and came back, covering till the row was done. Pa trotted over to check the oilcloth on the grain wagon, and we all piled on the buckboard and headed for the yard with the mules and Willie following. Gilbert backed the buckboard into the lean-to, and I helped Pa get the harness off the mules.

"Bring dem in da barn and git der feed bags."

Able and Gilbert were getting the harness off the horses, and they got them in and their feed bags on just as a big clap of lightning struck and the heavens opened up. We all stood in the barn door and watched the rain come down.

"Ve made it yust in time, boyz. I vas hoping da Lord would not forget dat ve needed rain. Vell, ve gots lots of rainy-day vork in here," Pa said.

We worked in the barn and got chores done in time for supper. The rain came down all afternoon and evening, sometimes hard, sometimes gentle. After supper we sat on the front porch and watched it rain while Ma was getting the little ones their baths.

Just as it was getting dark, Pa looked around the corner of the house to the west. "Hey, boyz, look, the rain is done."

We all looked. The sky was purplish red in a straight line parallel with the horizon. You could see the outlines of the buildings in Oakland. The sky was so red that it looked like the town was on fire.

Pa sighed, "Das a beautiful sight da Lord has made."

Saturday night we all had our baths. Ma had cookies and milk. Pa read his Bible as usual. Ma sat with the little ones and played Chinese checkers. Able and I played regular checkers. Gilbert was upstairs reading a dime novel he had hid from Ma.

As we were starting to get ready for bed, Pa looked up from his Bible. "Boyz, I tell ya, dose mules, day see da end of the field, an dey keep going faster. Sometime on Monday, if da field dries, I vill get done plowing. If it don't rain anymore, ya boyz vill be done planting by da end of next veek, an ya can go an be cowboyz."

Able and I looked at each other and grinned. Once in bed I lay there thinking. I rolled to look out the east window. There was a big round white moon. By the next time the moon would be full, I'd be seeing it from the ranch on the Indian Nations. This would be the adventure of a lifetime, and I would get paid for it.

***

The next thing I knew, Pa was at the door. "Its da Lord's day. Get up, boyz. Let's eat, do chores, go to da Lord's house, and give tanks for dis goot life."

After breakfast we started chores. Pa grained the teams, and I saw him walking out to the cornfield.

Soon Pa was back, and he stuck his head in the barn. "Da rain didn't wash out da furrows."

Pa and Gilbert pulled the buggy from the lean-to and harnessed Pete and Ida. Pa drove them up by the house and went in to get ready for church. Gilbert helped us finish chores, and we went in to get our church clothes on. Ma had her good dress and her best apron on. As we came in, she was pulling a pan of cinnamon rolls from the oven, and the smell filled the house. Soon we were all ready and climbing into the buggy.

Our buggy was not really a buggy but a buckboard. Pa had made seats and an oilcloth top with side curtains that rolled up. He said they didn't make buggies that hold eight people and a family should all ride together to the Lord's house. Ma put the rolls wrapped in towels under her seat.

Pa climbed up and yelled, "Villie, you stay home!" and pulled the buggy out onto the muddy road.

We were heading for our church, the First Baptist Church. We now had a church and a pastor in town, but Pa and Ma started the church in our house before they had us children. Pa still looked after the church as if it were his own, because it was.

"Look, boyz, da wheat and oats grew an inch overnight." Pa drove up the road, never looking at it but only at our fields.

Soon we pulled into the churchyard. I could tell by the tracks on the road that Grandpa and Grandma were ahead of us and their buggy was in the churchyard. They were standing in the yard talking to the Larsons. Abel and I jumped from the buggy and ran over to them.

Able asked Mr. Larson, "Did you tell Grandpa yet?"

Mr. Larson shook his head. "No."

I burst out, "Grandpa, Able and I are going to work on a ranch this summer, and I need to borrow your saddle."

Grandpa put his arms around us and said, "Mr. Larson didn't tell me, but Smithy da tinman said ya boyz might go verk on da ranch. Ya, you can borrow a saddle if you need it."

Pastor Nielson came out and rang the bell, and we all filed in.

Our family went in and sat in our pew, the front pew on the left side. We all filed in, and Pa was the last one in, sitting on the center-aisle side as usual. We sang some hymns, and Pastor Nielson took to the pulpit, read some scripture, and gave a sermon. I don't have any idea what he said. As soon as I'd told Grandpa about the ranch, I couldn't get it out of my head, and I sat there in my own world. In time, church was finally over, and we all went out to the churchyard. There was a big table in the yard, and the church ladies put rolls and pies on it. Mrs. Nielson had brought a big blue porcelain coffeepot from her kitchen. Pastor led us in another prayer, and we got in line to feast. The women laid blankets on the ground and sat and talked. The men stood by the buggies. The little ones ran all over the yard. Gilbert was talking to Anna Olson. Able and I met up with Johnny Johnson.

Johnny kind of looked over his shoulder to see if anyone was close. "Hey, I got a dime novel about cowboys hid out in the buggy barn. You guys want to read it?"

"Ya!" Able and I replied.

We knew we had plenty of time, so we ran up the street to the Johnsons'. Johnny pulled the tattered book from under some horse blankets, and Able and I thumbed through it. Then Able stuck it under his shirt and under his belt, and we headed back to the churchyard. When we got back, no one had missed us. We stood there talking, and Oly Olson came by on his way to get another cup of coffee.

"Ya, boyz, I'll get dat letter ta ya as soon as it comes in."

Able answered, "It can't come soon enough!"

Oly cackled a laugh and went to the coffeepot. In early afternoon, folks started heading for home, as did we. The sun had warmed the day, and a light north breeze had dried the top of the ruts on the road to a tannish-clay color. As we neared home, Willie ran out to greet us with his tail wagging so furiously, it twisted halfway up his back. Pa pulled the buggy up near the house.

Able said, "Emil and I will put the team away."

Pa answered, "Put da feed bags on dem and da mules too."

We led the team over to the barn, and Able ran in and hid the dime novel.

Sundays were the Lord's days. We did no work except for chores. This Sunday was a beautiful spring day, the sun so hot it felt hot on your skin, but the air cool and dry. Ma had put a big ham in the oven for supper and then joined Pa playing with the little ones. They were playing hopscotch and jump rope. Gilbert joined Able and me as we went out to play cowboys

29

and Indians in the haymow. We played while keeping an eye on Ma and Pa so we could take turns reading the dime novel. Gilbert said that he had read that one at least two years ago and, judging by the cover, it was probably the same one. Sundays were such special days, no work, special food, and fun.

Late in the afternoon, Pa came to the barn. "Let's do da chores, boyz. Supper vill be ready soon."

With chores finished, we went into the house and were greeted by the smell of baked ham and something familiar yet different.

"What's that, Ma?"

"Fresh rhubarb pie, Emil. Da rhubarb is jus' ready. Smells gut, don't it, Emil?"

"Ya."

We sat at the table, and Pa prayed extra long, as was the case on Sunday. I didn't think I could wait a second longer. When Pa said amen, we all started in. Sunday supper was the best.

After supper Pa said, "Yu children do da dishes so your mudder an' I can have some time."

Ma and Pa went out the screen door, and we could hear them talking Swedish. As I stood by the washtub, I looked out the west window and saw Ma and Pa walking out the field lane holding hands with Willie following.

When they returned, Pa announced, "Da cornfield is dry enough to verk tomorrow."

That night I lay in bed a long time thinking about corn planting, the ranch, and what I had read in the dime novel. Soon sleep crept in.

***

Monday started the same as all other workdays. At breakfast, Pa told Erdie and Nellie that this week they would have to come out and work after dinner, at least till afternoon cookie break. They whined, but Pa was already plowing. We set out the last two bushels of seed and started working. Since Erdie and Nellie knew they had to come back after dinner, they worked better all morning. After dinner they started lollygagging and fell behind. It was near midafternoon when we could see Pa riding the plow up to the buckboard. He got water for the team and waved us in for a cookie break.

As we neared the buckboard, Pa said boastfully, "Da plowing is done, and so is my butt."

After break, Gilbert went back to the harrow, Pa went to the yard on the plow with Erdie, Nellie, and Willie following, and Able and I back to planting.

The afternoon wore on, but Able and I were all alone, and we could talk now. We talked about getting done with planting, going to the ranch to work, and what we had read in the dime novel.

"What are we going to do," Able quizzed, "at night in the bunkhouse when the cowboys play guitars and sing songs? All we know is 'Let it Rain' and 'Rain, Rain, Go Away.' I don't think that the cowboys sing hymns."

I cracked back, "Oh, I'll bet that the cowboys sing hymns, and if they don't, we can teach them. I don't know if I can remember all the words. Maybe we can take a hymnal with us. I'll ask Pastor Nielson."

We could see Pa coming. "I can help ya boyz till Gilbert is dun harrowing."

Pa was kind of fun to work with. He told of farming in the old country and building the house and barn, cutting prairie with a big plow you had to walk behind. Some of the stories we'd heard before, others not. When we got downwind of Pa, we could smell the odor of kerosene that he'd used to clean his hands from putting up the new plow. We worked for a while and could see Gilbert pulling the harrow up to the buckboard.

Pa said, "Yu boyz finish dis row. I vill help Gilbert. Look at dat. Vee have tree furrows left. I had dat figured yust right."

We finished the row while Pa and Gilbert hooked the team to the buckboard and took the harrow apart and loaded it onto the buckboard. Able and I sat on the back of the buckboard on the way to the yard, feeling good knowing that planting would start going fast now that Pa and Gilbert were done tilling. Pa pulled the buckboard next to the lean-to, and they leaned the harrow sections against the building near the new plow. The new plow sat there with grease bulging from the axles and joints on the lift mechanism. And the plowshare that was once covered with green paint and then scoured by soil till it shined like a mirror was smeared with axle grease. I think Pete and Ida knew their hard spring work was nearly done because when Gilbert turned them into the pasture, they kicked up their heels.

After chores and supper, Able and I returned to the haymow for more cowboy-and-Indian play and reading. In bed that night, I lay there thinking.

In the book, the cowboys never go to church, but when one dies, they always pray over his grave. They must go to church. They all have guns. But we don't have any guns. Pa says we don't need a gun in our home. And I don't suppose that cowboys need a gun on Cow Creek because Pa said the Catholic priest is making the Indians Christians. Gilbert said he read this book two years ago, so who knows how old it is. Maybe times have changed since it was written.

***

Tuesday started the same as usual. The drudgery of corn planting was only brightened by thoughts of ranch life. The day passed.

Ma yelled as we came in for supper, "Take da table outside! It's too hot to eat da supper in here!"

So we sat in the shade of the trees that Pa planted the first year on the place, and had a good supper.

Pa looked up from his plate. "Ve vill be done planting before some of da neighbors even start, and ve vill have da biggest field. Ve can get a lot done vin ve all vork hard."

After supper, Able and I played cowboys and Indians and finished the dime novel. Ma had rhubarb pie when we came in, and the house was starting to cool off. Gilbert and Able played checkers, I played pickup sticks with the little ones, and soon we were off to bed. All the windows were open, and so were the doors, to get a breeze through the house. I lay there listening to Pa snore and thinking about how Mike the cowboy chased the Indians and married Millie, the rancher's daughter. What a good ending.

***

Wednesday and Thursday went much better with Pa and Gilbert helping with chores and planting. By Thursday we were getting closer to the road. About midmorning, Oly's buggy came down the road. Able dropped his seed sack and ran over to the road, then came walking back.

"He didn't stop."

Every so often we could see neighbors going back and forth from town.

Pa laughed, "No vonder Sam don't get nuttin' done. Das tree trips to town today."

We saw Grandpa and Grandma go by on the way to town and then come back. I was starting to feel like the mules. The closer we got to the end of the field, the faster it seemed like we were going. Seed by seed, the day went on.

At the end of the day, Pa looked in the grain wagon. "I tink I figured right. Ve should have enough seed to finish."

Then Pa picked up the tongue of the wagon, and Able, Gilbert, and I pushed it farther down the field. We headed in for chores, and when we entered the backyard, there was Grandpa's saddle sitting over a barrel. It had been recently oiled and was ready to go.

After supper, Able asked Pa if we could saddle the horses and go for a ride.

"Ya. Not too far, and don't run dem."

We ran from the house and got Pete and Ida from the pasture. We bridled and saddled them, and Able ran into the barn and got the dime novel, and we were off for town. If we rode horses we usually rode bareback, but not tonight. There is something about the squeak of the leather as you ride in a saddle. It makes you feel like you have such control. It makes you feel like a man. It makes you feel like you could go wherever you want. We trotted up to town. The horses seemed glad to be out. They had been in the pasture for two days, and trotting horseback probably felt so much better to them than being harnessed as a team pulling heavy loads. As we got into town, we could see some of the boys were on the south end playing baseball. We rode over to the vacant lot they were playing on. Johnny was in the outfield, and all the boys ran in as we rode up. Able gave Johnny the dime novel. All the boys looked at it. Some had read it before, and Linc Cull asked Johnny if he could read it next. So it was with dime novels. One dime would bring dollars' worth of enjoyment. I joined Johnny's team in the outfield, and Able, Linc's team. I could overhear Able telling the boys about the ranch job, and I was telling my team about it too. We played until near sunset, and then Able and I hopped into the saddles and started for home.

As we started to leave, Johnny yelled, "Hit the trail, cowboys!"

Then the other boys chimed in and kept repeating it till it faded in the distance. We trotted down the road to be met by Willie, then into our yard. As we unsaddled the horses, Pa and Gilbert were in the barn watching a sow have pigs.

Pa said, "Ya must have rode a long way."

Able answered and told him we were playing baseball.

Gilbert piped up, "Are the boys playing ball at the Larsons' lot now? Oh great, I suppose now if I want to go play ball, I got to ride a mule."

Pa laughed back, "Dat still beats shoe ledder."

We all watched as the sow finished up with eight pigs, two spotted, six white. Pa put out the lantern and hung it from the rafters. We walked across the yard with the last glow of the day faintly framing the house with gaslights glowing through the windows.

***

Friday morning started the same as other recent days, seed by seed. But the air was heavy, and the breeze was out of the east. Pa had said that if we didn't get rained out, we might get done by tomorrow night. About midmorning, Able and I looked up, and we could see Oly's buggy coming down the road.

Able looked at me and said, "This isn't his day for our route."

We could see Oly's arm sticking out of the wagon with an envelope in his hand. We dropped our seed sacks and ran for the road. Able pulled away from me.

"Dis vat yu boyz lookin' fur?" Oly said as he handed a blue-colored envelope with a red seal to Able. "I tawt ya boyz vud be excited."

Oly shouted as he turned his buggy and headed back toward town. We waved and yelled a thank-you and stood and stared at the letter.

To Able Nelson, Oakland, Nebraska

The return was printed from a printing press:

Cow Creek Ranch
Winnebago Agency
Nebraska, USA

By now Pa and all the others had gathered. "Open it! Open it!"

Able pulled out his pocketknife and broke the seal. A white folded paper was inside, and we could see as Able pulled it out that there was a map on the back side.

Dear Able,
Yes, I would be glad to hire you and your brother Emil for summer work on the ranch. I expect you to work hard and have a horse and saddle. In return for hard work, I will pay you

one dollar a day. If you fail to work to my expectations, I will send you home. I have drawn a map so you can find the ranch in the shortest distance. Should you have trouble finding the ranch, go to Winnebago Agency and ask directions. I will be looking for you in the shortest amount of time you can manage.

Tom Ryan

Able turned the letter over, and we studied the map. Pa looked at the map and pointed out where the high trail split from the low trail to Dakota City. The trail, or as some were calling it, the road, ran right through Oakland. At the bottom of the map, Mr. Ryan wrote "about 35 or 40 mi."

Pa said we may as well stop for lunch. We sat eating rolls and hardly warm sweet coffee, and Pa kept looking at us.

Finally he said, "Yu boyz told Mr. Ryan dat you vud have to finish planting corn before yu could come, an' dat's da vey it is."

Able fired back, "But don't you think we could be done tomorrow?"

Pa looked up at the sky. "Ya, if ve don't git rained out, and den it vill be Sunday, and ve don't work, man nor beast, on de Lord's day, and dat is dat."

We all got back up and started planting. Occasionally I would see Able pat his overall pocket to make sure the letter was still in there. The rest of the morning passed quickly, and soon we heard the pans clanking for us to come in for dinner.

Able ran into the house. "Ma! Ma! We got the letter. We got the jobs."

Able ran up and put the letter in our room and came down for dinner. During dinner, Ma and Pa talked in Swedish, and when we were ready to go back out to field, Pa told us to take Nora with us. Ma needed to go to the general store, and he was going to drive her.

We all walked back to the field with a cookie pail and a fresh jug of water. Nora played by the grain wagon while we went to work, and as Ma and Pa drove by, Pa yelled at Willie, and he came and sat under the grain wagon. The grain wagon was getting low, and Gilbert had to scoop the seed to the back so we could fill our seed sacks out the back door.

As he climbed from the wagon and covered it with the oilcloth, he yelled, "I think Pa is right. I think we have enough seed shelled."

Not that much time had passed when Willie jumped up and ran to the road. He stood there with his tail wagging, and when Ma and Pa passed, he followed them home. Before too long, Pa and Willie came walking out the field lane and called us in for a cookie break. Pa told us who all he saw in town.

Then he looked up. "Ve may have a short afternoon, boyz."

The sky was starting to darken in the west. The little ones went back to the house, and the four of us kept working. The sky kept getting darker off to the west, and we could hear the sound of distant thunder.

Pa started singing "Let It Rain" and laughing, and then Gilbert joined in with him. Able looked at me, and I knew what he had in his mind. We both started singing "Rain, Rain, Go Away." What a chorus, Pa and Gilbert singing one song and Able and I singing another.

We worked, sang, and watched the sky as the black cloud was coming at us. The cloud moved very slowly, and soon we could see a white line along its north end. Ever so slowly, the black cloud drifted southeast, and the white line looked like it was going to come over us. Then we could start to see blue sky behind the white line. Slowly the clouds drifted, and it seemed sure we were going to miss the rain. As the cloud moved, the sun came out. It made the cloud to the southeast look even blacker, and now we could smell the rain, it was that close.

Pa yelled over, "Yu boyz must be da better singers. But ve could use da rain."

When it was time to quit, I walked back counting rows to where I had stuck a stick first thing this morning. Then I went and counted the open furrows that were left. There were two more rows than we had done today. Able and I talked as we were doing chores, and after supper, we asked Pa if we could go out to the field and work till dark.

"Who am I to stop a man from verking?"

As we were heading out to the field, Gilbert came out and offered to help us. It was nice to have such a thoughtful brother. Gilbert told us on the way to the field that he wanted to get the corn planted as bad as we did so he could go and play ball in the evenings and maybe see Anna Olson.

"If that's what you want, fine, but I want to be a cowboy as soon as I can," I answered.

The air was much cooler now, and refreshed from supper, we got two and a half rows done by dusk. As we got ready for bed, Able got out the letter. We read it and turned it over, and we both ran our index fingers up the trail to Cow Creek.

TWO

As Pa woke us on Saturday, I rolled to look out the east window. A yellow-white glow in the east gave promise to a good day to finish corn planting. Out in the field, as the day passed, the road was getting closer and closer. We were so close now that we could shout greetings to the neighbors that passed.

Oly stopped on the road as he came by on his route. "Able, vas dat gut news?"

"Ya! Ya, it was," Able answered.

As we were going in for dinner, Erdie and Nellie asked Pa if they could stay out this afternoon till the last seed was planted. Pa put his arms around them and hugged them both. That afternoon when we were finished with cookie break, Pa told Gilbert to go get the team. When Gilbert got back and hooked the team to the grain wagon, we were coming down the last two rows. Gilbert came out and helped us, and soon Able and I were done with our row. Able started over to drop some seeds in the last row, and Pa yelled and told him not to. Pa got to the last place to put a seed and stopped. The little ones and Gilbert got to the last place and stopped. Pa grabbed a handful of seed from his sack, sorted through them, and picked the biggest one. He took that seed and kissed it and put it in Erdie's hand. Pa motioned, and we all put a hand on Erdie's shoulder.

"Put da seed in, Son."

Erdie put the seed in the ground, and Pa reached his foot over and pushed soil into the furrow and pressed it down. We all yelled and clapped. We all threw our seed sacks into the grain wagon, and Pa grabbed Pete's bridle and turned the team and wagon around. We walked nearly a quarter mile to the field lane. Pa jerked Pete's bridle, and the team stopped, but we kept walking another quarter mile to the end of the field where we started. It felt like forever ago.

When we got to the first few rows, it was plain to see that something was happening. Little yellowish-green shoots were pushing up in rows straight as an arrow. We all stood silent as Pa got on his knees, folded his hands, and prayed silently. He got up, and we walked back to the wagon in silence. Once back to the wagon, Pa grabbed Pete's bridle, turned down the field lane toward home, and started singing "I Know That My Redeemer Lives," and we all joined in.

Back at the barn, Able and I unharnessed Pete and Ida while Pa and Gilbert cleaned out the grain wagon.

"Von and a tird bushels left. I had dat figured close," Pa said as he swept out the wagon. We pushed the wagon over and into the lean-to. "Now da planting is done."

We did chores and went in for supper. Ma made an angel food cake for dessert to celebrate the end of planting.

While we were eating cake, Ma told Able and me to go up after we were finished and put our long johns on so she could finish our laundry.

"I don't vant to spend my Sunday vashing yur clothes."

Ma washed our clothes and gave baths to the little ones. Pa, Gilbert, Able, and I were on the front porch.

Ma opened the screen door and said, "Olaf," and nodded her head.

Pa said, "Let's go inside."

Ma was standing by the table, and Pa said, "Yu boyz know dat cowboys have to vork rain or shine."

Ma moved away from the table, and there were two new slickers stacked one on top of the other and two hats folded flat on top of them. Able and I looked at each other and grinned. I grabbed a hat. It had a cord and a slip bead so you could pull it tight. I grabbed a slicker and put it on.

Pa said, "Dis slicker has dese buttons on da back so yu can undo dem if you're on horseback. Den it vill open up to keep yur legs varm and dry."

Oh, we were a sight. Rain hats, slickers, long johns, and work shoes running around the house pulling imaginary reins on imaginary horses. Ma and Pa where laughing. We all were. After a while of play, Ma told us to take off the slickers and give them to her. She put them in a bag for me and a bag for Able. After baths, when we were getting ready for bed, both Able and I got out the letter and looked at the map. As I lay in bed, I thought of the day past. *Corn planting done, new slicker, bag being packed, it's really going to happen. We're going to be cowboys!* I lay there, looking at the stars through the window and thinking, until sleep overtook me.

***

I heard Pa say in a loud voice, "Dis is da Lord's day, an dis is da last day dat Able an Emil vill be going to da Lord's house vid us for a long time."

Pa left the room. Able and I looked at each other and grinned.

Ma yelled up, "Yu boyz do chores in your long johns so your clothes stay clean."

After breakfast and chores, we came in to put on our church clothes, and Ma had two rhubarb pies cooling by the window. Pa had harnessed Sam and Charlie and hitched them to the buggy. He told us that we should let the horses rest today. We were going to have to go to church all summer with mules. What was one more day? We were soon all ready and climbing into the buggy. Ma and Pa each brought a pie and put them under the seat, put a fruit crate over them, and covered it with a towel.

Out the lane and onto the road we went, with Pa yelling, "Villie, yu stay home!"

I was just like Pa this time, looking at the fields as we rode past and feeling proud. Pa claimed we had the biggest cornfield of any of our neighbors, and the first one planted. We pulled into the churchyard, and Grandpa and Grandma were there already. We had the usual chitchat. Then Pastor Nielson came out and rang the bell. We all filed into each family's pew and the spiritual comfort that it gave.

We started the service by singing hymns. I was singing, I think. I was reading the words, and sound was coming out of my mouth, but my mind was elsewhere. Then Pastor Nielson took the pulpit and started to read the scripture, and it caught my attention.

James 1:17–27

[17] Every generous act of giving, with every perfect gift, is from above, come down from the Father of lights, with whom there is no variation or shadow due to change. [18] In fulfillment of his own purpose he gave us birth by the word of truth, so that we would become a kind of first fruits of his creatures.

[19] You must understand this, my beloved: let everyone be quick to listen, slow to speak, slow to anger; [20] for your anger does not produce God's righteousness. [21] Therefore rid yourselves of all sordidness and rank growth of wickedness, and welcome with meekness the implanted word that has the power to save your souls.

[22] But be doers of the word, and not merely hearers who deceive themselves. [23] For if any are hearers of the word and not doers, they are like those who look at themselves in a mirror; [24]

for they look at themselves and, on going away, immediately forget what they were like. [25] But those who look into the perfect law, the law of liberty, and persevere, being not hearers who forget but doers who act—they will be blessed in their doing.

[26] If any think they are religious, and do not bridle their tongues but deceive their heart, their religion is worthless. [27] Religion that is pure and undefiled before God, the Father, is this: to care for orphans and widows in their distress, and to keep oneself unstained by the world.

After he read the scripture, he went on to say that as we came from our church community, we would be the first fruits of God's creatures, the ones to shine. How we acted was our mirror to the world. These things never mattered much when all you did after church was go back to the farm. But now I was going out into the world, and I must be a doer to witness that my faith in God was true. I sat and prayed for God to help me do what he wanted of me. I got so lost on these words that when I realized it, Pastor was on another scripture and lesson. And as he talked, I couldn't stay focused on what he was saying, but my mind kept going back to the first lesson. By the time the service was over, I felt good about myself. I knew I was not just a young man getting ready to go out into the world but a young Christian man ready to go out into the world.

As we got up from the pew, I turned to Able. "Boy, Pastor's sermon really hit home today, didn't it?"

He looked back to me. "I guess. I can't get my mind off tomorrow."

Well, I liked it, and it made me feel so good, so grown-up. Out in the churchyard, the ladies were setting out lunch, and everyone was talking and laughing. I'm sure that everyone at some time or another made a point to come and talk to Able and me. The little ones kept coming back asking questions about cowboys. Johnny asked me how far it was to the ranch, and I told him Mr. Ryan wrote on the map thirty-five to forty miles.

Johnny thought for a minute. "Don't that seem funny? That's about how far it is from here to Fremont, and it's the same, farms all over. But if you go northwest that far, it's a different world."

"Oh, it's the same world, just not so many farmers," Able cracked back, and we all laughed.

Pa was in the height of his glory. The word had got through the churchyard that we were done planting corn and how many acres we had. There were some skeptics in the crowd that we had planted too early.

Pa would answer them with, "My corn vill be big enough to have long roots dis July, vin it stops raining."

I saw Pastor Nielson talking to Able, then a short time later came up to me. "Emil, are you ready for your journey?"

"Yes, I am," I answered, "and your sermon this morning makes me realize that I am ready to go on this journey as a Christian, and to show that I am a Christian to the world."

Pastor put his arm on my shoulder, leaned close, and said softly, "That is wonderful, son. I always wonder if, after I go to all the work of preparing a sermon, anyone will get anything out of it. May the Lord protect you on your journey."

After noon, people started to depart, and we did too. As we pulled from the churchyard, I looked back at our church and felt comfort creep through my body. Oakland, our church, our friends and family—how lucky I was to be there. As it always was, Willie was coming up the road to greet us, and soon we were jumping out of the buggy.

Ma said to give her our church clothes and put on the clean clothes she had laid out. "And yu boyz keep dem clean 'cause dose vill be yur traveling clothes for tomorrow."

Able and I checked the horses and saddles probably every hour all day. The little ones wanted to play, so we played with them while Ma and Pa butchered some chickens.

"Oh boy, fried chicken."

Ma was going to fix my favorite for Sunday supper. Pa came out and played with us also. Sometimes Pa would be strict—"Dat's dat"—but he could be fun too.

Erdie held one end of the rope, and I held the other. As Pa jumped, he said, "No more corn to plant dis year."

Pa took my end of the rope, and Able and I jumped together holding hands. "We're gonna be cowboys."

Willie barked as Grandpa and Grandma's buggy pulled into the lane. Grandma went in the house to help Ma, and Grandpa joined in the games. The games were fun, but from time to time, my mind kept slipping away to what the summer would bring on Cow Creek.

Pa and Gilbert brought the table out into the yard. "If ve squeeze, ve can git Grandma and Grandpa at da table vid us."

Ma and Grandma came out and watched us play and brought us lemonade. The afternoon slowly passed. We were having fun, but the thoughts of our journey were starting to overwhelm me.

Pa came over and said, "Gilbert and I vill do chores. Yu boyz sit and talk to Grandpa and Grandma."

Pa and Gilbert went to the barn, and Ma went in the house to start frying chicken.

Grandpa called, "Hey der, all yu little vons. Come here. I vill tell ya a story."

We all gathered around the table to hear what Grandpa had to say. As he started to talk, Grandma put her hands on top of his.

"Able and Emil are going on a journey tomorrow, and dey vill hav an adventure. I feel so happy for dese boyz. Every man should have an adventure. "Dis vas mine. I vas a farmer near Skåne, Sweden. Yur pa vas about Gilbert's age and vas at an age vin he vould look for a vife and a piece of ground to start his own life. But der vere so many boyz his age dere dat da land vas so high dat he could not afford it. In da newspaper, der vas an ad dat told of a place in America dat vas fertile soil dat had never been turned, and all dis land vas reserved yust for Swedes. Dis land vas in Burt County, Nebraska, and da new Swedish town vould be called Oakland. Da land could be bought in forty-acre plots at six US dollars each acre. Vit da price of land in Sweden so high, I figured I could sell my land and livestock, pay da passage, and start in da new vorld and get my boyz a start. So dat's vat I did. Ve sold everyting except vat fit in a trunk.

"Ve vent to Stockholm and boarded a steamship. Dis boat vas not a fancy ship. Dis vas a freight ship vit room for immigrants. Da men slept in von room, and da vomen slept in anudder. Da sea made many of us sick. I vas sick. Ma vasn't, though. Some people got real sick, and dey died. Dey had to bury dem at sea. It vas a long journey, but soon ve got to America. Ven ve got off da ship, der vas ships from all over da vorld unloading people vit trunks coming to America. Dis vas New York City. Vell, not New York City but an island in da harbor. Ve stood in a long line, and dey checked our papers. Den dey checked us dat ve vern't sick. Den we got on a small boat and vent to New York City.

"Ve stayed in a hotel for a night. Dat vus so nice to have solid ground under me. Da next day, ve vent to da train station and found a man dat spoke Swedish, and he helped us to da train dat vould take us to Nebraska. Ve did not ride in da gut cars, but in da immigrant cars. Der vere people from all over Europe in dese cars, and dey vere going someplace vere dere people vere settling. Dis is a big country dis America. And it took us many days to get to Omaha. All dat vas left in da immigrant cars ver Germans and Czechs, and ve had no Swedes to talk to. Vin ve got to Omaha, ve got in a better car and got to Fremont. At Fremont ve got a ride in a freight vagon to Oakland.

"All dat vas here vas Ankerson da banker, Ulmquist Grain and Lumber, and a little general store dat Ankerson owned. Ve stayed in a room above da general store for a vile till ve got our land. Ve looked at da plot plan, den da land. Ve bought our place and put money down on your place and Uncle Jules's. We bought teams and vagons and plows. Ve cut sod and lived in a sod hut for two years. Every veek it seemed like another family vould come from Sweden, and Oakland started to have udder stores and houses, and farmland vas filling up vit Swedes. Dis vas yust like Sweden except da land vas cheap.

"Years later I found dat Ankerson and Ulmquist ver rich in Sweden and dey come to America and dey bought university scrib* for two dollars an acre. Dey sold it to us for six dollars an acre. Got money on da mortgage, money on da lumber, money on da grain. Dey got der money back. But dese men I respect. Because dey saved all dis land for us Swedes, and ve can live here in America vit da people ve love.

"Now, Abel and Emil, yu have yur journey, and someday yu can gadder yur grandchildren around and tell them yur story."

The University of Nebraska is a land-grant college. It was granted six to ten sections of land per county, called "scrib," to sell to finance the university.

Ma yelled for Grandma to help her, and they began carrying bowls and platters from the house. When everything was at the table, Pa nodded to Grandpa, and he said the supper prayer.

"Lord, tank you for da streng dat yu gave me to lead my family to dis great new land. May ve always prosper here. Look over Able and Emil as dey go on der journey. Tank yu for dis gut food and da women dat cooked it. Amen."

Ma made the best fried chicken and white gravy, and not one piece was left. Willie and the cats waited around the table for bones that were discarded as each piece was eaten.

After dinner, Pa drove a stake in the yard, paced off the proper amount, and drove another stake. The men pitched horseshoes all evening. Erdie tried, but he could not throw far enough to make it to the far stake, so he sat in the shade and watched. Over his many years, Grandpa had developed a style of throwing that was something to see. And the ringing sound of nearly every shoe that hit the stake, spun around, and landed at the base, even a blind man could tell Grandpa was pitching. The evening wore on, and at dusk, Grandpa and Grandma kissed us good-bye, got in their buggy, and went home.

The house had cooled down fairly well by the time we had gotten the horseshoes put away and headed in. The days are getting longer and the evenings shorter day by day, and this evening I spent at the table reading my Bible with Pa. Able and Gilbert were at the other end of the table playing checkers. Ma sat in her rocker reading aloud from a book of children's Bible stories, while the little ones sat on the floor in a semicircle around her listening intently. Pa announced bedtime, and we in turn made the day's final trip to the outhouse.

Pa looked at me and Able. "Yu boyz behave yourselves at dat ranch. Yu go to bed at a decent time so you can give Mr. Ryan a goot day's vork. And yu boyz stay clear da alcohol and da tobacco. Remember dis is vork for da family." Pa winked. "Yu should take time to have some fun, but remember yu are da Lord's children."

Later in bed I just looked out the window at the stars. Time passed, and I could hear that everyone else was asleep.

Then I heard Able say, "I can't sleep I'm so excited."

"I can't either." I lay there. It seemed like forever, but finally sleep overtook me.

***

"Vake up, boyz. Able and Emil have a journey today, and Gilbert, ve start on da new fence." Pa left the doorway with his clumpy steps.

As I strained to open my eyes, I found I had fallen asleep looking out the window. As I gazed out, I could see the stars were disappearing into a red glow in the eastern sky.

Able was up like a shot and out the door. "Come on, Emil. It's the day we have been waiting for."

I got up from bed and slowly dressed. Able was excited, but I had a melancholy feeling creeping into me: the last time in my bed for a long time, last meal with the family for a long time, last time at home for a long time.

I paused at the heat grate in the hallway floor and sniffed. I could pick it all out, coffee, sausage, and griddle cakes. Pa called griddle cakes "pan lops," and Ma made them good with brown-sugar syrup. As I headed out for the outhouse, I could feel a warm breeze coming from the southeast. I thought to myself, *I hope I don't need to use my slicker today.*

At the table, Pa said the Morning Prayer, and we dug in. As we finished breakfast, Pa told Able and me to stay in with Ma. He and Gilbert would do chores.

As Pa and Gilbert headed for the door, Pa looked back and said, "Erdie, yu come vid us. Today is da day yu learn to milk da cows."

Even though we were done eating, Ma kept making griddle cakes. She would take them off the stove, put them on a cookie sheet, sprinkle them with sugar, and roll them up. She had two paper sacks.

"I vill put plenty of dem in here so yu have plenty for today and for tonight, and tomorrow if ya don't make it der today."

When Ma finished filling the sacks, she rolled the tops down and set them on the table. "I vill get yur bags."

She went back around the corner in the kitchen and came out with two new saddlebags. We had watched her the last few days putting our stuff in flour sacks, and we thought that was what we were going to use. Somehow, while we were not watching, Ma had fashioned saddlebags out of oilcloth. The bags looked like real leather saddlebags, but they were black oil-cloth. She set them on the table, opened them, and showed us the contents.

"Here is yur church clothes. Ya vill need dem ven ya go to church. It might be a Catholic church, but you boyz go anyvey. Yu keep da Lord's day. Here are yur Bibles."

She pulled out Able's Bible and opened the front cover. "Der is paper and envelope. Ve put da stamps on dem, and yu have da same in yurs, Emil. I vant to hear from yu boyz. Der is a pencil in da bag also. Der is yur undervear and yur vork clothes and a bar of soap to clean dem. In dis udder bag ya got yur slickers and a roll of oilcloth in case you have to sleep on da ground."

Ma put the sacks of food in the bag with the slickers and closed mine. She looked at Able. "Yu got yur map?"

Able slapped himself on the head and ran upstairs and back in a heartbeat. He gave it to Ma, and she closed his bag.

Able looked up at Ma. "Don't you think Mr. Ryan will do our laundry, Ma?"

"It vould be proper if ya vere a guest, but yu vill be hired men, and dere vill be a lot of yu. So I vould be prepared to do yer own, and yu boyz vatched me do lots of laundry vin ya vas little ones."

Then Ma went back around the corner in the kitchen and brought out an old army canteen that we had seen at Grandpa's. "Ya boyz take dis out to da pump and fill it. Yu let da horses drink from da creeks, but yu boyz drink from clean home vater."

Able worked the pump handle, and I held the canteen under the spout, water burst by water burst, till it overflowed. I screwed the cap back on it as we went back in the house, then set it on the table next to our bags.

Ma walked up between us and put an arm around each of us. "Ya boyz behave yerselves vy yer gone. Don't you let dem cowboys talk you into alcohol and tobacco. And yu remember dat yur mudder loves yu." At that she gave us each a kiss. "Yu boyz go saddle dem horses."

When we got out to the barn, Pa had brought Pete and Ida in from the pasture and had their feed bags on them.

While they were finishing their feed bags, Pa told us, "I tink dat ya boyz can make it der in dis day if ya trot da horses a little each hour. Don't run dem up any hills. Let dem drink at any creek dey pass. But don't let dem drink too much at von time."

Pa took the feed bags and the halters off, and we started to put their bridles on and then their saddles. Pa watched.

"Yu boyz check dese saddle cinches as you travel. As da day goes by, da horses vill lose some belly. Yu boyz keep da cinches tight so dey don't get saddle sore. And vin dey stop to drink, loosen da cinch and tighten after dey drink."

Pa went over and grabbed a flour sack. The sack already had some oats in the bottom. Pa put in the feed bags, the halters, and two pieces of light rope for tie-outs. He gave me the sack and told me to tie it on my saddle horn. Once secure, we led the horses over to the front porch.

57

Gilbert and Erdie followed, teasing, "You cowboys sure look like farmers."

Ma and the little ones were on the front porch with our saddlebags and canteen. We tied the saddlebags on the backs of the saddles with the leather tie-down straps. Pa gestured, and we all stood in a circle and grabbed each other's hands. Pa bowed his head.

"Lord bless dese boyz dat are going out into da vorld to help dis family vit da money dey vill earn. Lord keep da boyz and da beast safe until dey come back home. Amen."

Pa gestured at the horses, and we mounted up, pulling the reins to turn them away from the porch, and started out the lane to the road. As we started up the road, we looked back, and they were all waving.

Pa was yelling, "Villie, yu stay home!"

We each gave a small wave, turned, looked ahead, and started trotting the horses west.

THREE

The sun was up now, and it felt warm on our backs.

As we slowed the horses for town, Able looked over. "No more chores, 'cept maybe laundry. Ma and Pa sure seem concerned that we'd take up smoking and drinking, don't they? Let's ride by Johnny's and show him how we look."

I answered back, "Ma and Pa just want us to act like good Christians as we go out into the world. Well, we have our first mile behind us."

We rode through town to no avail. Town people don't wake up early like farm people. We headed to the west side of town and turned north on the road that ran from Lincoln through Fremont to Dakota City.

We looked at each other and both said, "Here we go!"

As the road headed north from Oakland, it was easy to count the miles as section roads intersected the trail road. (The state of Nebraska is divided into sections one mile square, with a road or place for roads bounding each section.) We could see farmers tilling and planting, and an occasional freight wagon with big teams of mules or heavy draft horses or oxen pulling big wagons full of lumber or goods. Once in a while a buggy with a family or salesman would pass, and several men on horseback passed us. This road was sure busy.

Twelve miles north of Oakland, the section roads started to look more like two tracks from wagon wheels in the prairie. The farms were getting fewer and fewer. We stopped at a creek to water the horses and let them eat a little tall grass that was just maturing to seed-head stage, the best grass for the horses. We had loosened the cinches and grabbed the canteen and a sack of pan lop rolls. There were no trees around, so we sat in steaming-hot sun that was cooled by a wind blowing out of the east.

Able stood, and we tried to figure out from his shadow what time it was. Able said he thought it was ten,o'clock and I agreed. We had left home before seven, and we had come twelve miles.

Able picked up a stick and scratched in the dirt. "If we don't stop, we should get there by five o'clock. Add in the time we stop, and we should get there before dark."

We got up, tightened the cinches on the saddles, and mounted up. As we did, I looked at Able. "I hope my butt makes it in one day."

He grimaced and nodded back. A distant dust in front of us soon revealed a stagecoach coming at a good clip. It had seven people in it, with trunks and mailbags strapped on top, and six fine horses pulling it at near gallop. In a short time, the stagecoach was distant dust behind us, and a freight wagon was now in sight in front of us.

As the freight wagon passed, Able yelled, "How much further to Indian territory?"

The answer came back: "'Nuther hour."

The land was fairly flat, and we would trot the horses every so often like Pa said. When they started to breathe hard, we would go back to a walk. We hardly ever saw a farm anymore, and the section roads were hard to make out. Finally the section roads ended, and all we could see was waist-high prairie grass blowing half over in the wind, in huge waves that moved across the landscape as far as we could see. We looked at each other.

"We're here." We had both studied the map, and we knew we had only a few more miles to go to where the trails split.

As we kept traveling north, the wind from the east kept growing stronger. It was soon blowing so strong that it seemed like the horses were leaning into it to keep themselves upright. Able pointed to the west, and we could see a big black line in the sky in the far distance. The road seemed to go straight north, but now it was starting to curve east. We knew that we should soon see the high trail to Winnebago Agency. The wagon road headed east, near the Missouri River and flat terrain. It wound around the hills past the Omaha Agency, then back to the west to Winnebago Agency and north to Dakota City. The high trail went through the hills and was used by horseback travelers to save fifteen to twenty miles. In the distance we could make out a grove of trees. And just on the west side of the trees, we could see the high trail heading north up a gentle grade, and lots of hills to the west and north as far as we could see.

We could make out a Conestoga wagon by the grove of trees. As we got closer, we could see a man and woman and small children scurrying around. We noticed a creek by the trees. They were bringing their team up from the creek and staking them out. As we rode up, the wind suddenly stopped blowing.

The man yelled over at us, "Hello, boys! Bob Walsh is my name. You better get off them horses, and give us a hand. This is just the calm before the storm."

He raised his hand and pointed to the west. The clouds were coming closer now in a straight black line from horizon to horizon, with another white line of clouds parallel across the top of the black cloud.

Bob Walsh looked at Able. "You help me, and your partner can take care of the horses."

Able jumped down and went to the wagon with Mr. Walsh. He handed Able a shovel and instructed him to dig a trench around the wagon. He grabbed a heavy hammer and drove stakes at the corners of the wagon and tied it down. Able was digging as fast as he could, and I pulled the saddles off the horses and put them under the wagon. I got in the sack that Pa had packed, got the halters and tie ropes. I got the bridles off, the halters on, and led Pete and Ida to the creek for a drink and tied them to a tree.

By now the thunder was almost deafening, and the lightning was flashing horizontal across the clouds. Mr. Walsh was helping Able finish the trench, and then they dug some gutters to the south to get the water away from the trench. Mrs. Walsh and the little ones were under the wagon. We stood there watching. The cloud was nearly over us now, and it was starting to have a green cast. All of a sudden, the wind roared from the north.

"Let's get under, fellas."

As we got under the wagon, the wind went to the west, and we could see the rain coming. The rain hit for a minute or two, and then hail started pelting the wagon. The hail was not very big, but the wind was driving it so hard it was cutting the leaves off the trees in little square green pieces. It hailed so hard we could not see two feet from the wagon, and soon the ground was white. The hail was piled up an inch or two deep when suddenly it stopped and the rain came in buckets. The trenches worked. The rain came off the wagon and into the trench and away, and we stayed kind of dry. The wind blew a mist in on us, and the wagon shook but didn't tip over. Mr. Walsh was wise to dig trenches and tie the wagon down. It rained so hard we couldn't see the horses, and lightning bolts hit so close they hurt our ears.

"I hope we still have stock out there. I think there was a twister nearby the way it hailed. We are coming from South Dakota, and we get these kinds of storms several times a summer up there," Mr. Walsh said as we peeked out from under the wagon.

The rain and lightning kept coming for I bet two hours. The hail floated for a while, and then it slowly melted. The wind switched back to the north and slowly died down, and the rain slowed. Finally we could see the sky start to lighten in the west. We could see the horses now. They were all there. Pete and Ida were standing in a puddle up to their hocks. The rain finally stopped, and instead of thunder, we could hear a roar from the creek. The little creek I had to lead the horses down into before the storm was now a raging river. It was twenty foot wide and maybe five foot deep. It was running green with grass clippings. The trees were all but bare of foliage, and the ground was covered with little cut squares of leaves.

I got two stakes from the sack Pa packed, found a stone, and drove them in, in a place a short distance off that was well drained and had some nice grass. Able helped me move the horses, and we went back and looked at the creek. So much for getting to the ranch today. We couldn't make it across the creek.

Mr. Walsh came over and told us, "You fellas will be all right. You'll be able to spend the night with us, and by morning, you should be able to cross the creek. But I'm afraid it will be two days before the road is fit, and now we have no more shade trees."

Able and I turned to take a look at the road. The road was underwater going east, and looking southwest, two glistening ribbons of water filled the wagon ruts as far as we could see. Mrs. Walsh was up in the wagon surveying their belongings for damage. Sticking her head out, she informed us that everything stayed dry.

Mr. Walsh was looking around. "Bet it rained five to seven inches."

We went back and sat on the bank of the creek and watched the water run by all afternoon. Every now and then, a dead rabbit or possum would float by.

Able asked, "I wonder how far they float—to Omaha? St. Louis? Maybe even New Orleans?"

"No, they'll rot before they get to Omaha, and sink." I guess I had never just sat and watched water pass by. It was relaxing and peaceful, and the afternoon passed quickly.

Mrs. Walsh came up to us as we were sitting on the creek bank. "We are going to eat something for supper. I am sorry, but we have nothing to share with you."

Able told her our ma had sent food with us, and we went over by their wagon. They had two benches tied to the side of their wagon, and they had them down for us to sit on. Mrs. Walsh had a pail with a lid, opened it, and broke apart a piece of corn bread that looked dry and crumbly.

She said, "Even the road apples are too wet to burn. We can't even make coffee. Able got in our bags under the wagon and got out the sacks of pan lop rolls. We waited for Bob Walsh to say prayers, but he just started eating, so we did too. Ma had packed our bags full, and they only had one piece of corn bread to eat. I offered Mr. and Mrs. Walsh each a roll, Able offered some to the little ones, and they all gladly accepted.

Mr. Walsh said, "Your ma is a good cook."

And then the little ones nodded in approval. We left enough in our sacks for morning and put them away.

After supper Mr. Walsh told us, "We're lighting out from South Dakota. We tried farming up there, but we couldn't make a go of it. We either hailed out or dried out. We gave up. We'll go to Kansas and try there. We can get some ground to homestead down there and start over again."

We visited all evening and told them of our farm and our big cornfield and our ranch jobs for the summer. At dusk we put the feed bags on the horses, then led them to the creek for a drink. The creek was half the size it had been that afternoon. We tied the horses in a new area and went back to the wagon. We unrolled our oilcloths, set our saddles for pillows, and unfolded our saddle blankets for covers. We thanked the Walsh's for their hospitality and told them we would leave at first light. They climbed into the wagon, and we climbed under it.

We got under the covers, and Able looked over and said, "Look, we're sleeping out, saddles for pillows, just like the cowboys in the dime novels."

Lying there in the dark, and the steady sound of rushing water, made sleep come easy.

***

Able gave me a shake. "Come on. Let's get going. It's starting to get light."

We rolled up our oilcloths and quietly took our gear over by the horses and saddled up. As we started to ride away, one of Mr. Walsh's horses whinnied, and he stuck his head out of the Conestoga, saw us, and waved. We waved back and headed down the creek bank.

The creek was well down now, and you could tell from the way all the grass was flattened on the creek bank that the water would have been over the horses' backs after the storm. We climbed the north bank of the creek and followed the high trail. We had to move off the trail and go in the tall grass, as the yellow clay mud of the trail was slippery as axle grease. About a mile from the creek, you could see the hail line in the grass: one side all cut and torn, the other new and fresh. After an hour or so, we stopped and ate the last of our pan lop rolls.

"This is sure not like the road. The hills are steep, and we haven't seen a soul. I thought we would see some Indians by now."

We studied our map and figured we had about two hours to travel before we would come to the big valley that headed northwest, then two more hours.

Able grinned. "I hope we make it in time for dinner."

We rode for at least another hour up one hill and down and back up another, not seeing another soul or house or tepee. As we topped a hill, we could see something coming down the trail on a distant hill. When we drew closer, we could make it out: Indians!

We passed on the trail. There was a man and a woman. They were dressed in ragged white people's clothes with long black hair blowing in the breeze. They had a skinny spotted horse, with a home-fashioned harness of rawhide, pulling two poles dragging on the ground. Across the poles was fashioned a sort of seat with two children. We couldn't tell if they were boys or girls, as they both had long hair, and they had a worn-out blanket around them. Behind them on the seat was, I supposed, their few possessions wrapped in rags and old blankets.

As we passed them, we smiled, waved, and said, "Hello."

To our surprise they turned their heads and didn't even look at us. The bigger of the two children turned as their parents did, but the little one smiled at us.

I turned to Able. "They didn't seem friendly, did they? Maybe those ones aren't Christians yet."

That was the event of the morning. The only other thing we saw was grass and creeks with flattened grass on the banks. Finally we topped a hill, and there it was, a big valley running northwest to southeast with more hills on the other side. We descended the hill, stayed on the south side of the big creek, and turned northwest.

We grinned at each other. "We're getting close."

The big creek we followed was still really full, and when we had to cross a feeder creek, we sometimes had to go downstream a quarter mile to cross. This slowed our progress some, but we kept going.

We were starting to doubt if we had followed the map right, when Able yelled, "Look, something has been eating the grass here."

We realized that the grass was shorter, but we couldn't see any cows or ranch house.

"Look, Able!" I pointed to a distant hill that was dotted with reddish-brown cows. "We're here!"

The big creek turned north, and there was a feeder creek running into it from the west. We followed the creek west a ways to find a place to cross. We came to a wide place, a natural crossing. The ground was covered by hoof prints and cow pies.

"Look, someone is coming."

In the distance we could see a rider on a black horse running full our way. We descended the creek bank, and as we came up on the other side, he was nearly to us. I had never seen such a fine horse, big, black, and shiny, and so well muscled. I can't explain, but the man sitting on the horse was not sitting but *setting* with a prowess I had never seen. They raced up full speed and stopped in one motion, and the man in the saddle never even shook as the horse stopped dead.

"You must be Able and Emil?"

We shook our heads.

"Tom Ryan. You just crossed Cow Creek. That big one is Omaha Creek. This is Cow Creek Ranch, boys. I've been keeping an eye out for you. Did you get caught in the storm yesterday?"

"Ya, we did, but we took shelter with some settlers on the big road."

"Ya, that was a tough one."

Mr. Ryan pulled the reins and spun his black to the north and started walking. We walked alongside.

"Got some boys coming in from Pender this afternoon, and tomorrow, we can start roundup."

We came around a bend in the creek, and off in the distance were a set of white buildings, the first set of buildings we had seen since yesterday.

"Ole John should have some dinner when we get back to the ranch." At that he put his heel into the black's side, and we started to trot toward the ranch buildings.

Able and I were fair skinned, but tanned from the sun, and our hair was more blond than brown in the summer, just like all the people in Oakland. Mr. Ryan had reddish-brown hair from what was showing beneath his sweat-stained yellow straw cowboy hat. His skin was burnt brown with a speckling of red freckles and a couple days' growth of beard, and the way he sat on that fine black horse, no one had to tell you that he was the boss.

We trotted into the ranch yard and up to a hitching rail.

"Ya guys wait here. I'll get Ernie. He'll show you around."

We got down off the horses and tied them up. Mr. Ryan rode over to a big barn and yelled, "Ernie!" a couple of times. He pulled and turned the reins, and the big black reared to his hind feet, turned, and shot through the yard faster than any of the racehorses at the county fair. Yet even with the speed in change of direction, and the suddenness of full speed, Mr. Ryan sat on the horse like he was part of it. They raced through the yard, around a building, and stopped on a dime in front of a corral.

"Ernie." He waved his arm in a come-hither motion.

A fellow came over and talked to him. We could see Mr. Ryan pointing at us. He spun the black and raced back to the barn, where a man was waiting. He slid off the black before it hardly stopped, the man took the horse, and Mr. Ryan walked into the house.

Across the yard an old cowboy was walking toward us. He was a skinny old bowlegged man with a straggly beard and black sweat-stained cowboy hat. As he got closer, he showed us a friendly smile.

"Hi, guys, did ya git your riding lesson?" He laughed as he pointed to the house. "He does that for every newcomer. He has to show he's the best. I guess I've never seen any better. I'm Ernie. I'm the lead man out here."

He held out a hand to shake ours. We shook hands and introduced ourselves. Just as I was shaking his hand, I could hear a ringing noise.

"Dinner, guys. Leave them nags tied there till after dinner. This way to the grub shack. Damn, I'm hungry. I could eat the ass out of a skunk."

We laughed. We had never heard that before.

We walked to the grub shack, and as we did, we saw a man ride out with a pack on the back of his horse.

"Lunch for the guys riding the herd," Ernie said, pointing at the horseman.

The grub shack was near the ranch house. The ranch house was a big two-story building, at least twice the size of ours, and it had three chimneys. There was a big front porch with a stained-wood front door with a stained-glass transom window above it. In the stained glass, blue letters were set in: CCR. The ranch had a side door with a roof awning going to an outside kitchen. The outside kitchen was connected to the grub shack by an enclosed hallway with screened windows. We went into the grub shack by way of a screen door. The room was square with hinged sashes folded in and screens on the windows. Lots of windows, and there was good breeze coming through. There were two long tables with benches on both sides of each. There was a table on the end of the room where the hallway from the summer kitchen entered in. There stood a man like I had never seen dishing food from big pots.

There was one man in front of us, and when it was our turn, Ernie announced, "John, this is Able and Emil. They're here to work for the summer."

John smiled. "I'll feed um good, boss."

He slapped a big piece of roast beef on a plate, a spoon of potatoes, a spoon of gravy, and a biscuit. We sat at the table as other men straggled in.

I looked at Ernie. "Is John a Negro?"

Ernie grinned. "You boys ain't never seen a nigger, have ya? Ya, John's a breed nigger. His pappy was probably his mama's owner. Real niggers are black as axle grease. You can tell John had a white papa. He's light colored with freckles and brown hair. Ya kin tell he's still a nigger 'cause his hair is nappy and his nose is big. John is a good fellow, though. He was a buffalo soldier out west at Fort Robinson. When he mustered out, he decided to stay out west. He drifted through the Sand Hills till he come across Tom Ryan's place and has been here ever since. Damn, that nigger can cook."

"You and John talk alike, not like people from around here," I said.

"Na, John's from Mississippi, and I'm from Georgia."

Able asked Ernie, "How'd you end up in Nebraska?"

Ernie scooted back from the table, pulled a sack of tobacco and tablet of papers from his pocket, rolled a cigarette, lit it, and leaned forward on his elbows.

"After the Civil War, I didn't have anything left. So I decided to head west, west into Texas. I found ranch work here and there. After a few years of that, I heard of a man named Robert Ryan putting together a herd to trail north to Nebraska. I thought I'd like to see more of the country, so I signed on. Tom was barely more than a boy then. We drove them cattle all the way to Nebraska, and Robert Ryan staked out a place in the Loup Valley. Damn, that was a pretty place. So pretty I never wanted to go back to Texas or Georgia. We were there for six, seven years. Then this deal came up, and we pulled up stakes and drove the herd over here. Too many homesteaders moving up in the Loup Valley. Now it's going to start happening here. Bob Ryan died, and Tom took over. Tom has a lawyer in Lincoln, and he hooked up this deal on this place.

The government let the hunters in, and they killed the last of the buffalo. The next year Tom comes up with a lease on this land and a beef contract for the Indian agencies. When the right lawyer is involved, sweet deals can happen. The grass is a lot better here than the Loup Valley. It's not quite as pretty, but it's all right. And the squaws are better here."

Able said, "If you were in the Civil War, did you kill anyone?"

Ernie smashed out his cigarette on the floor and looked up. "It was war, boys, kill or get killed. Let's tend to them nags and get you boys settled in."

We left the grub shack and put the horses in the corral. The corral had a big hay feeder and stock tank that was filled by a wind-powered pump. The windmill also pumped water to a big tank on tall legs.

Ernie pointed at the tank. "Pressure water, boys, it's great."

We put our saddles in a big tack room with nail kegs hooked to the wall. We laid our saddles over the nail kegs, and Ernie marked *A* on one and *E* on the other with a piece of chalk. We grabbed our saddle-bags and headed for the bunkhouse.

Ernie looked down at our saddlebags. "Them's interesting."

Able grinned. "Our ma made them." Ernie grinned back.

The bunkhouse was a little bigger than the grub shack but had the same kind of screen windows. Beds lined the walls. Each bed had a table with two drawers next to it. Ernie took us over and showed us two beds.

"Those are yours, and the table to the left. If ya don't want yer ass kicked, ya keep out of other people's tables, and if ya don't want them in yours, ya best be prepared to kick their ass. Pillow, sheets, and blankets washed on your day off in the wash shack. You guys, come here. This is my desk. No one touches it—ever. You guys' last name Nelson, right?"

We nodded our heads, and he wrote our names on a list with a bunch of squares ruled on it. He went over several squares and put check marks by our names.

"You guys have the rest of the day off. I'll get you scheduled for crew work. There ain't no crew work during roundups. Roundup takes three or four days. After that, your day off is the day after you have night watch on the herd."

Ernie could change from friendly to bossy real easy. I guessed he would be a good boss. Looking around the bunkhouse closer, beside the beds and the tables were a bunch of chairs and a heat stove in the middle of the room. On the right of the screen door was Ernie's desk, and next to that was a rack with rifles standing side by side.

"Do we need those?" I asked, pointing at the rifles.

"Oh ya, those buffalo hunters took the buffalo but left the wolves. And on occasion we get a thievin' Injun. I got things to do. You boys look the place over and check on them nags so they're ready for a hard day's work tomorrow."

Ernie got up from his desk chair and went out the screen door, leaving us to ourselves. We went over by our beds, unpacked our saddlebags, and put our belongings in the drawers.

"Look, Emil, some of these guys have pictures of naked women hung above their beds." Able walked over to get a closer look, and I followed.

"Able, don't get too close. If someone would come in, they might mistake us for thieves, and we don't want to fight."

We looked around some more and went outside. Looking to the south, we could see a lot of the ranch, the long and sometimes wide creek valley surrounded by hills, and dark green grass dotted with cows, for as far as we could see. We both thought it was a beautiful sight. How could such a place be just a long day's ride from nearly flat Oakland, with its town and farms and people? We walked by the four outhouses and looked into the wash shack.

Able shook his head. "I was afraid we'd have to do laundry."

We walked by the corral, and Pete and Ida seemed to be doing fine. We went up to the big barn to see about getting some oats for their feed bags. There was an old man in the barn.

"Hi, I'm Emil. This is my brother Able. Do you know where we can get some oats for our horses?"

He pointed at a big bin. "Ya, good to meet ya, boys. I'm Billie. I got busted up two years ago, so all I do now is look after the boss's horses."

Able went back to the tack shed to get the feed bags, and I looked through the barn. Billie limped over and got an armload of hay and put it in a feeder in the

stall of the big black. I followed him and looked in the
other stalls, two roans and two matching dapple-grays.
Across from the grays was the tack room. A beautiful
black harness was hung perfectly. Saddle racks held a
lady's sidesaddle and three small English-type saddles,
a brown western saddle, and the boss's black western
saddle with silver studs mounted on it. Beside the tack
room sat the finest buggy I had ever seen. The box
stalls were so clean, not a dropping to be seen. And
the alleyway was raked clean with only my footprints
showing. I felt guilty leaving my tracks.

Able came back with the feed bags, and I told him
to look at the barn. I followed behind, raking out our
footprints.

As we left, Billie yelled, "Thank you!"

"Have you ever seen such fine stock in all your
life?" I asked.

Able answered, "And that beautiful black harness
must look fine on that dapple-gray team and that
buggy."

Pete and Ida looked terribly plain after coming
from that barn.

"Look at these horses. Guess you can tell we're the
hired help," Able laughed.

After the horses were done with their feed bags,
we put their lead ropes on and led them around to
the back side of the corral to let them eat some grass.
Just east from the ranch place, we could see a bridge
across the big creek. We walked up the creek until we
reached the bridge. It was big enough for two buggies
to pass. It had the heaviest timbers and planks I had

ever seen. The side rails were taller than me, and on the west end, a gate closed the bridge so stock wouldn't go over if you didn't want them to. On the other side was a trail heading east. We walked the horses back through the ranch yard on the way back to the corral. Billie was sitting on a nail keg in front of the barn.

"Billie, where does that bridge lead to?"

"Oh, that bridge crosses the big creek so we can get to Winnebago Agency. The banks on that creek are too steep to push cattle through, and we got a section of ground to cut hay on over on the other side."

Able looked at me. "I thought we were going to be cowboys, but I bet we got to stack hay and do our own laundry."

"A dollar a day for a day's work is what the letter said, and maybe if we're good cowboys, we won't get put on the hay crew."

We put the horses away and went back to the bunkhouse. We made up our beds and flopped down. This bed was not as comfortable as my bed at home, but it was sure better than the hard ground under that Conestoga wagon. I had almost dozed off when I could hear voices coming closer. The screen door opened, and in walked Ernie and two young men. One was about my size. One was over six feet tall. Ernie gave them the same introduction, word for word, that he had given us.

When he was done, he turned to the big guy. "I can't believe Ryan hired you back this year. I ain't gonna take your shit this year. You do what I say, or I'll kick your ass clean back to Pender."

The big kid snapped back, "I'll do what I'm told this year, and Ernie, you ever try kickin' my ass, you better bring help."

Ernie stood there shaking his head. Finally he said, "Able and Emil, this is Mike, and this big sack of shit is Murphy."

Ernie turned and walked out the door, and Murphy looked at us. "Well, it looks like another summer of digging postholes and pitching hay. That little asshole won't ever give me a break. If I could find a better job, I sure the hell wouldn't be here."

Slowly men started coming from their day's work. They all introduced themselves, but they came by so fast I couldn't keep them straight. Soon the bunkhouse was near full. We could hear the supper bell, and the room emptied before we got our shoes on. As we were about to go out the door, I noticed a sign above it, and I pointed it out to Able.

NO LIQUOR TILL AFTER SUPPER —T. RYAN

By then we were by ourselves some distance behind the others.

Able spoke quietly. "Do you suppose they drink alcohol in the evenings? And have you ever heard so much cussin'?"

I never answered. I was thinking the same thing.

We were at the end of the line, and when we got up to get our plates, John gave us a big grin. "Able and Emil, right?"

Supper was just the same as dinner except we got a scoop of apple cobbler.

John yelled out in a voice you could hear back to Oakland, "Got sum chow left if'n y'all want more."

Able looked at me. "They must eat beef at every meal, like we eat pork at home, and there ain't enough hens in the yard for any more than eggs."

John bellowed out, "Quiet!"

There was Mr. Ryan standing there. "Except for the night crew, you're all here now. Tomorrow we start roundup, and I think it's going to be a good year. Don't drink too much whiskey tonight. Be ready to go at first light and go till dark."

He turned and walked down the hall toward the house. I was feeling so disappointed when I saw Mr. Ryan standing there. I thought he was going to ask the Lord's blessing on our supper.

No one seems to pray here. Can't they see how they are blessed? And Pa and Ma must have known. They warned us of smokin' and drinkin'.

The grub shack was emptying out so we followed the men back to the bunkhouse. We stopped at the corral and checked on Pete and Ida.

When we opened the screen door, the tobacco smoke was so thick we could hardly see across the room. Most of the men had bottles of whiskey and were taking drinks. Able and I went back out and sat on a bench that was on the front of the bunkhouse. We sat there as the evening cooled and looked at the shadows starting to fall on hillsides.

Ernie came out with another fellow. "Able, Emil, this is Ben. He's my leadman, and I want you boys to work with him tomorrow. He'll show you boys how to herd cattle."

Ben shook our hands and said, "You boys get a good night's sleep. You'll have saddle butts tomorrow."

We assured him we already had saddle butt. They went back in, and we sat there until the mosquitoes forced us in. The drink was making the voices in the bunkhouse louder and louder. Murphy was standing talking to another man, drinking and cussing. His friend Mike came over and talked. I could smell liquor and tobacco on his breath, but he did not seem drunk like Murphy. He told us that he had worked here for the last two summers and he was going to start farming a piece of ground north of Pender and maybe get married. He said he needed this job to get a little money ahead. He said that he came with Murphy because he had to, but he thought Murphy was a bully, and everyone around Pender felt the same way.

"That's why he can't get a job anywhere else."

"Where are the Indians? I thought we'd see Indians all over up here."

Mike laughed when I asked that question. He yelled, "Hey, guys, these dumb Swedes are wondering where the Indians are."

The room filled with laughter.

Mike finally caught his breath from laughing. "Don't you know those lazy bastards never leave the agency? The government has to buy the beef to feed um. You'll get in on a drive to the agency. You'll see them lazy bastards. They should have killed them all. The only good thing about 'em is the squaws."

Mike walked away and visited with some other guys. Able and I looked at each other, not knowing what to say. It was starting to get dark outside, and the men lit lanterns and hung them from the rafters and kept on drinking and smoking and cussing. Occasionally one or another would come by and tell us how we'd enjoy the agency squaws.

"Ten minutes, boys, roundup in the morning," Ernie yelled as he put out all but one lantern.

Murphy came by. "Old bastard gonna tell us when to go to bed like he's our pa."

I think Ernie overheard him 'cause he looked at Murphy and scowled. Able and I watched as the men got ready for bed. They all seemed to sleep in their underwear, so we did the same and didn't put on our pajamas. I lay there waiting for sleep, thinking of our day.

We woke under a Conestoga wagon, saw our first Indians and our first Negro, but I don't think that we met another Baptist. Tomorrow we start a cattle roundup. What an adventure that will be!

A breeze was gently blowing from the west, and the smoke was clearing from the room. The snoring was terrible, broken only by an occasional fart. It is hard to fall asleep in a strange place. The rigors of the day must have caught up to me. I drifted off.

FOUR

"Rise and shine!" woke me from a sound sleep.

The lanterns were lit, and I hadn't heard a thing.

"John has breakfast on."

Once we were dressed and outside, it was still dark with just the slightest bit of glow in the east. After we came out from breakfast, the dawn was starting to lighten up.

We went down to the corral and got the horses out, and as we finished pulling our cinches, Ben rode up. "You boys ready? Ernie gave us the southeast. You boys grab you a couple slap straps off that hook over there."

We tied those straps on and trotted south along the big creek. In the twilight, I could make out groups of three men heading out in all directions. As we slowed to cross Cow Creek, Ben pointed to the west.

"We got to bring 'em back up that way a mile or so."

We followed the big creek as it turned southeast. We never saw a cow. We followed till there was no more chewed grass or cow pies. Then we turned south, following the line in the grass, but still no cows. We topped a hill. Near a small creek were three or four hundred cattle. We pulled up the horses.

Ben pointed down the hill. "These hills are good for cattle. There's a creek at the bottom of nearly every hill so the stock can water, and when the grass grows, it really grows. But it does dry up sometimes, and you ride for miles to find the end of the graze. Now these cows get moved several times a year, and they get used to it. We'll walk the horses down. Able, you stay on the west side, Emil on the east. I'll get behind them and start 'em moving. Slap a few of them with that strap, and they'll start moving. Emil, you stay on the east side, keep 'em moving north and west. Once we get them moving, Able and I will pull off and look for more."

As we walked down the hill, the cows started to beller. Soon we had the rear of the herd surrounded. A few slaps and they closed together and started moving, just like Ben said they would.

Ben and Able stayed for half a mile or so. Then they slipped back, and I was by myself moving more cows than I had ever seen in one place in my life. The herd slowly moved north. At one point, I noticed a carcass of a calf with the bones picked clean. *There must be wolves out here.* Later, a few head started spreading out to the east to stop and eat. I booted Ida into a trot, got around them, gave one a slap with the strap, and the whole herd closed together and kept moving. I slowed to get to the back corner of the herd.

"Good job, Emil."

I about jumped out of my saddle. With all the hoof noise of the herd, I had not heard Tom Ryan ride up.

"I didn't mean to spook you," he said half laughing. "Where's Ben and Able?"

"They got me started, and they headed south and west to find more."

Mr. Ryan told me to keep 'em moving, swung his big black, and took off on a run heading south. Maybe a half hour later, the herd rounded a hill, and there was another creek with maybe a hundred more cows hanging there. I didn't know what to do, so I let them all mingle together. I got Ida a drink and just sat there.

I could hear a rumbling noise. Then, over a ridge on the west, cattle came pouring over like from an overfilled coffee cup. I could make out three riders, one on a big black. I could see them pulling up, and the cows slowed, then mingled in with the others. The three riders were coming my way.

"I came up on these other cows, and I didn't know what to do. So I remembered what my pa says. 'Sometimes doing nothing saves more time than doing something wrong.'"

Mr. Ryan laughed. "Your pa ain't no dummy. You did the right thing, Emil. Able, you stay here. Emil, you go east. I'll go west. Ben, check between us. Let's make sure we get all the stragglers."

I went just over the first hill, and there were two cows with calves and a yearling. I got around in front of them and turned them to the west. "Yeehaw."

They started running back over the hill. I stopped on the hill and watched them run down and join the herd below. Oh boy, I was feeling like a cowboy now. I rode from hilltop to hilltop and could not see any more. I headed back to where the herd was. As I came over the last hill, I looked into the little valley. What a sight! The herd must have been over five hundred head. What a sight. As I came down the hill, I could see Mr. Ryan coming from the southwest pushing seven or eight head. Ben was already back with Able.

We all joined up, and Mr. Ryan told us to get down and stretch our legs. When I got down, my legs felt like rubber. Mr. Ryan got some cookies from his saddlebag and shared them with us.

I started a question. "Mr. Ryan?"

"No!" he fired back. "When I'm the boss, you call me Mr. Ryan. When we work side by side, man for man, you call me Tom."

"Well, Tom, I see a few of the calves have a big red mark on them. What is that for?"

Tom went over to his saddlebag and pulled out a big fat paint pencil. Then he went to his rifle scabbard, took out a stick with a funny end on it. The paint pencil fit in the end of the stick.

As he was taking it apart, he told me, "The last two weeks, Ernie and I have been going through the herd culling. Each year I go through and pick two hundred heifer calves from the best cows, and then when we brand, they get an extra bar brand so they stay in the herd. At the same time, I mark any cows with no calves. They'll be Injun food."

Able looked up. "Pa has us do that. We only plant corn from the biggest ears."

"Able and Emil, I'm starting to see you boys have a smart pa. Well, guys, I think we're a mile and a half south of Cow Creek. We'll get the herd moving. Then, Emil, you pull off and check the area northeast. I'll check northwest, and if it looks like you guys are doing OK moving them, I'll move over and help the guys in the next sector. That's where most of the stock is. When you get these in, come and help. John will know where to send you."

We all mounted up and started the herd moving. I pulled off like Tom said and looked for stragglers from the hilltop. I could see the big creek, all the area we had covered, and the herd off to the west. No stragglers, so I joined Able and Ben. Tom came down a hill from the west pushing two cows with calves. He stopped as they joined the herd, waved, and headed west. Able and I took position at the rear corners of the herd, and Ben moved toward the front. As we approached Cow Creek, we could see Ben turn the cows west after they crossed the creek. We drove them west, and in the distance, we could see corrals. We kept the herd close to the creek. We approached a corral fence and two more men on horseback. The cows turned in to a fenced area. The other two guys shut the gate, and we all got down.

"First ones in, hey?" Ben yelled.

The men said that we were.

"Let's move the corral fence. The rest will all be coming from the west."

We moved the corral fence to the east side of the gate and went for dinner. We rode to the corral area where John had a chuck wagon, but it was a long way. The fenced area must have been more than half a section with heavy post and four stands of barbwire, and two windmills with stock tanks overflowing. When we got to the chuck wagon, there was another man there packing tin saddlebags with food. Ben went over and talked to him. They talked awhile, and then the man mounted up.

As he rode by, he shouted, "Boss says you Swedes are good cowboys."

Able and I looked at each other and grinned.

"Ya, and I bet y'all eat your pay's worth," John quipped as he started to fill plates.

Baked beans with chunks of beef and bread. I was so excited, I forgot I was hungry till I started eating. Able must have been the same way 'cause he beat me for seconds.

Ben laughed. "John's beans will be raisin' ya off your saddles this afternoon if you eat too many of 'em."

John fired back, "Dem beans won't hurt dese boys. Der guts ain't rotted out from whiskey yet."

We all laughed and talked while we let our lunch settle. Ben rolled and smoked a cigarette. He told us that Jerry had told him that they got stock all over the southwest sector and Tom said we should head down that way and help. So we mounted up and headed south across Cow Creek and into more hills.

We went maybe two or three miles, and we could see Tom on his big black pushing maybe twenty head down a hill. He saw us and motioned for us to come his way. We got over to him, and he told us that they had cattle scattered everywhere and this big bunch was getting restless. He wanted us to take them back to the corral. This bunch looked to be bigger than the bunch we took in already. Tom and another man helped us get them moving. Then they pulled off, and Ben, Able, and I kept them moving north.

As we spilled over the last hill coming down to Cow Creek, we could see a big herd nearly all in the holding pen. Just as before, Ben started for the front, but other riders came back from the holding pen and waved him back. The cows crossed Cow Creek and were turned east a short distance and into the big fenced holding area. One of the men was Ernie.

As I passed, he heckled, "How's that Swede cowboy doing?" I looked over, grinned from ear to ear, and gave him a thumbs-up. After the gate was closed, we all got down and stretched our legs. Most of the guys rolled cigarettes, and a couple of them put big, stringy gobs of tobacco in their mouths. One of the men offered some of that tobacco to Able and me, but we gave him a "no thank you." In a couple minutes, those guys were spitting big brown slobbers though their ugly brown teeth.

Able and I stood near Ben and Ernie so we could hear what they had to say. Ernie told Ben that they had the northwest sector clear, and since we had the southeast clear, we'd all go help Tom finish the southwest. Maybe we could be done by dark.

We all mounted up and crossed Cow Creek. Ernie and his men headed west, and us south. We moved south, found twenty or thirty in bunches, and shooed them west. A couple miles in, we could see other riders doing the same. We pushed them west to where we had run the first herd from this area. We could see Ernie and his men pushing cattle from the west. Tom and some other riders were bringing a big herd from the south, and our stragglers were joining in.

Tom came running full-out to Ben. "East flank clear?"

Ben yelled back that it was.

The big black wheeled around, and he was across the valley in a heartbeat. I could see Tom pull up to Ernie and say something. He wheeled his mount around and waved with his cowboy hat in his hand.

Ben said, "This is all of 'em. Let's get 'em in."

Now we had ten riders, and the cows had the trail from the first herd to follow. We pushed them to a trot. Ernie pulled ahead and was there to turn them east as they crossed Cow Creek. The herd went into the fenced area. I couldn't believe it. Over half a section fenced and it was full. There was some for them to eat, but the waist-high grass in the pen would probably be gone by tomorrow or the next day.

We rode over to the chuck wagon. John was dishing plates as fast as he could, and Tom sat right with us. He didn't go back to the ranch house but ate as he walked from man to man, talking with each of us.

Even Murphy seemed to have respect for Tom. After we ate, Tom yelled to give a hand, and we all helped John load the chuck wagon and hook up the team. John got in the seat and headed for the ranch place. We all mounted up and followed the wagon, leaving Tom in the twilight, sitting high in his saddle looking over his herd.

Tom caught up to us but didn't race by. He walked alongside and visited with all of us. "Able, Emil, what do you think of ranch work?"

We grinned.

"Well, the next two days are going to be a lot of work. But you earned your pay today."

Ernie pulled up with us. "Tom talks good of you boys. He's a good boss. Men want to work for him."

It was getting dark by the time we got the horses grained and put away. By the time we got into the bunkhouse, the lanterns were already lit. A few guys were smoking and drinking, but some were turning in, and Able and I joined them. I never heard Ernie call lights-out, but in my dreams, I saw the back ends of cows crossing Cow Creek.

***

This morning started as early as yesterday. All the men were in their saddles and heading out to the corral by dawn. Ben was over by the calf chute tending to the branding fire. He came over and talked to Ernie and Tom. They came over to where all of us men were standing and told us what we were to do and whom we were to go with. That guy named Jerry was to go with Ernie, Able and I to the center sort.

The way the corrals were set up was like this: First was the big fenced area that we put the herd into yesterday. The center sort was a good-sized corral with high white painted sides. In the west side of the corral was a gate opening into a large fenced area maybe thirty acres. On the north end of the center corral was a small gate just big enough for a calf to fit through, and they had an orphaned calf tied inside so the calves could see him and feel safe to come through the gate. On the east side of the corral was a big gate to let the cows out. The calves would go through a chute, get branded, castrated if needed, and back out to join their mothers and be shooed back toward the hills. On the northeast corner of the corral was a ladder climbing up to an oversight box. There was a well-dressed man up there with a ledger.

All was set. Able and I were to operate the gates. Jerry and Ernie were to work the stock. There were men in the big fenced holding area crowding the herd our way. We opened the gate and let about thirty cows with their calves in and closed it. Then, we went to the west side gate. If Jerry and Ernie found an old cow in the bunch with a paint mark on its back, they'd cut it from the herd, and as it headed our way, we opened the gate for it to go to the small fenced pasture. Then we went and opened the small calf gate. Ernie and Jerry worked the small herd back and forth, squeezing them, and soon the calves were going through the gate. When the last calf went in, we closed the gate, went to the east gate and threw it open, and Jerry and Ernie herded the cows out.

We pulled the gate closed and rode over to talk to Ernie, but Ernie just shouted, "Get over and get some more in here, or we won't be done by tomorrow night!"

Pete and Ida were a bit uneasy at first with the cattle so close. But they were workhorses and soon realized this was just another job. Ernie and Jerry's horses were bigger quarter horses. They called them cutting horses, and they moved and separated cattle like a herding dog. On the second batch, they cut out a bull and a cull cow.

We moved over to open the calf gate, and the man in the oversight box yelled, "Say, young man, pull out a little so I can see the calves as they go through, and don't open the east gate so far. Just let them out one or two at a time."

I think I looked puzzled.

Ernie yelled, "That's the guy that counts the boss's money," and laughed.

Cattle in, calves and cattle out. The noise was deafening, calves screaming at the branding iron, cows calling for their calves. This work was so different in some ways. Instead of seed by seed, as corn planting, it was cow by cow. Thousands of them. Tom rode from position to position all morning, and for a while, he sat in the oversight box with that man and Mrs. Ryan, who rode out to watch. I watched John, with Billie helping, bring out the chuck wagon, and I knew dinner was close. The dust in the corral was terrible. I felt like I had swallowed a pound's worth. I couldn't wait for dinner to chase the dust down.

Dinnertime was welcomed, a time to refresh us and our horses. We had the same thing today as yesterday. Ernie said it was roundup food, and we'd be tired of it at the end of roundup, but we wouldn't have it again for a while. Before dinner, a well-dressed man in a suit drove out in a buggy. The Ryan's and the well-dressed man sat over away from us but ate the same food. I thought I might see Tom say prayers with his family, but he didn't. We took a long dinner break, and everyone seemed happy to have roundup under way.

Ben came and sat with Able and I for a while. He told us that we shouldn't mind the dust. "Dust is bad, but once we start, we don't stop. Come hell or high water. And believe me, dust is better than high water."

We laughed and visited for a while. Then Tom mounted his black, and everyone did the same.

The afternoon started out as more of the same. Then it happened, and it happened so fast that I could see it in one picture of my mind. The last calf from that pen went through the gate. Able pulled on the gate, and it bound. He gave the rope a hard pull, and it came undone.

He jumped off Pete, and in that instant, Ernie yelled, "No!", and a big roan cow drove Able into the corral wall. She flipped him up, and he came down in the dirt, lifeless. Ernie and Jerry raced in and cut the cows away from Able.

From nowhere Tom was there. "Get these cows out of here. John—John!"

94

I was off the saddle and at Able's side. Tom had pulled his head up from the dirt and manure. Able was all white, with his mouth open and tears running from his eyes, but he wasn't crying. Just as John got there, Able breathed in a little bit of breath. They sat him upright, and he started taking little tiny breaths. Able looked so bad. His eyes were watering mud lines down his face, and his mouth was open, trying to get air. Blood was coming through his shirt.

Tom looked at me. "Didn't Ernie tell you guys not to get off those horses?"

"Yes, sir, he did. Able must have forgot."

John had hold of Able. "Don't move, son. You got da wind knocked out cha. I hopes dat's all dat's wrong witch ya."

Slowly Able started to breathe. John was wiping his face. It took nearly ten minutes before Able was breathing right. John opened Able's shirt, and a big scuff from the cow had taken a couple of layers of skin off in an area on his right side. The wound was oozing blood.

"Move your legs, son."

Able moved them.

"Move your arms, son."

Able started to move his arms, and he grimaced in pain and grabbed his right shoulder. John felt around his shoulder, then started pushing on his ribs. Able winced again.

John turned to Tom. "Broke collarbone an' busted ribs, boss."

Tom went and talked to the man with the buggy, and he brought the buggy into the corral. We all helped Able to his feet and helped him into the buggy.

Tom looked at me. "Son, don't worry. He's in good hands. John was a medical helper in the army, and he keeps us all patched up around here. The doctor won't be back to Winnebago Agency for five more days. John can do it fine. You guys see what happens when you aren't careful? Let's get back to work."

I tied Pete outside the corral, and Mike came in to take Able's place. Ernie fixed the gate, and cows started coming in to be sorted. I kept seeing Able crumpling to the ground in my mind. About an hour later, Tom took off, heading for the ranch. He was back shortly and let me know Able was doing fine. The afternoon crawled by.

At suppertime, Tom came and got me. "You go ahead and eat first, then head in and see your brother. He's in the main ranch house."

Mrs. Ryan was helping Billie dish supper. She seemed nice and gave me condolences for Able's troubles. I grabbed Pete's reins and led him back to the ranch. I put the horses in the corral and walked over to the main house. John was standing outside having a smoke. He took me into a bedroom where Able was. Able seemed glad to see me.

John said, "I think that Able is all right. He ain't spittin' any blood, so I don't think he punctured anything inside. You boys gonna have to decide what y'all gonna do."

John left the room. I couldn't get my eyes off Able. He had no shirt on, and he was wrapped with tape all around his ribs. His right arm was all taped up, clear over his shoulder, and tied to his body.

"You look like a mummy."

Able started to laugh, then grabbed his side in pain. He looked up. "John says I won't be able to work for at least eight weeks. I just wasn't thinking. I guess those range cows get mad when you take their calves away."

We talked about the accident, and he told me how good John was at doctoring. We looked around the room. It looked like Dr. Engdahl's office back at Oakland. John had told Able he could sew stitches in people and everything. Neither of us said to each other what we were really thinking: *What are we going to do?*

At dusk, Tom came in. He asked Able how he was feeling. He said that as the evening wore on, the pain was increasing.

Able said, "I'm sorry, Mr. Ryan. I just forgot what Ernie said about not getting down off the horse. I guess he knew how unpredictable those cows are."

Tom replied, "I know you're sorry, son. Accidents happen. This cuts me shorthanded for roundup. John told me that if everything goes well, you will be eight or nine weeks mending. The other thing he told me was you won't be able to ride horseback. If I were to send Able home, will you stay on, Emil?"

"Yes, sir, our family needs the money that we were expected to earn."

"I'll make arrangements for John to take Able to the road at Winnebago Agency tomorrow. We'll have to get by shorthanded until my son, Tim, gets back from the university in Lincoln. You stay and visit with your brother. I'll stop in later."

Tom left the room, and Able, who had been so brave all day, started crying. "Pa will be so disappointed. He was looking forward to the money we'd earn, and…and I wanted to be a cowboy."

I carefully put an arm around him and said nothing. After a while, Able regained his composure, and we started to make plans. We decided he should take Ida home, and Grandpa's saddle, and I'd keep Pete at the ranch. Able told me of his pain and how it felt getting hit by a cow. We talked of roundup and branding and all that Able would miss out on.

Tom came back in and told us that he had talked to John. "In the morning, Emil, you help John clean up from breakfast and get the stuff in the chuck wagon. Then you help John get Able loaded. After that, come out and help on the sort. Let's call it a night."

I told Tom and Able good night and headed for the bunkhouse.

As I walked through the yard, I had a strange numb feeling, like so much was going on, and I wasn't part of it, but rather an onlooker. When I got back to the bunkhouse, about half the guys had already turned in. I think everyone asked how Able was doing, even most of the guys that were in bed already. Murphy was drinking yet, and he asked of Able. I told him that

Able had broken his ribs and collarbone and that Mr. Ryan was sending him home.

Murphy grunted back, "One less dumb Swede."

This comment rose a feeling of anger in me like I had never felt before.

"Dumb Irish, you'll be working harder to make up fer him," Ernie's familiar voice rose above the noise.

My eyes glanced around the room to find Ernie. When I found him, and he saw that he had my attention, he gave me a wink and a nod.

I got ready and went to bed. As I lay there waiting for sleep, I kept seeing Able being pitched like a rag doll by that big roan cow. Twice during the night I shot up in bed. I could hear the bang of the corral boards, and see Able flying in the air and the big roan cow. Each time I would lie in bed almost shaking, and the only thing that could get my mind off of it was to think of Murphy and what I could do to get back at him.

I got the "Rise and shine!" call as though it was coming from miles away. I must have fallen asleep hard. After breakfast, John fixed a plate for me to take for Able and told me to get back and help him.

As I was going to the ranch house, Mr. Ryan came by and nodded at me. "John, you get that boy on a wagon and get back here. Don't be takin' any time with those damned squaws."

Able was glad to see me. He ate slowly and complained of his pain and how hard it was to get comfortable to sleep.

Able said, "Mr. Ryan set an envelope on the little table. What's in it?"

I looked on the table, and there was one of those blue envelopes with the printed Cow Creek Ranch return address propped there. I looked at it. It said "Able Nelson," and it wasn't sealed. I opened it, and there was six dollars in it. Able told me to take it and pack it in his saddlebags. Able finished eating, and I went down to help John. I washed all the tin plates and silverware and put them in a tin box in the chuck wagon. John was putting all the ingredients for more roundup bean stew in a big pot and telling Billie, who had joined us, how to cook it and keep it warm for the evening meal. John and Billie joked and laughed. Billie complained he didn't get to go for mail run since John was going to town.

John just laughed. "Well, I guess dat's 'bout it. Let's go harness some teams, an' boy, you get your brother's things together."

I went back to the bunkhouse and packed Able's clothes in his saddlebags. The new slicker was still in the one side, never used. I put the envelope with Able's pay in with his clothes and headed for the corral. Ida seemed somewhat reluctant to leave Pete, but these were workhorses and obedient to their tasks. I just set the saddle and bags over her back and hooked the lead rope to her halter. I led her back through the yard, where I saw John pulling a buckboard up to the house. He got off and helped Billie hook up the chuck wagon and start them off for the corral. I tied

Ida to the back of the buckboard and put the gear in the wagon.

John came over, and we fashioned a bed with the saddle blanket and some flour sacks that he had stuffed with hay.

"Der, dat'll keep dat boy at ease on da trip home."

We went in the house to get Able. We put his shoes on, but John warned not to tie them.

"Don't tie dem shoes, boy. Sometimes folks with broke bones swell. Dey got a doc in Oakland? A'll have da driver leave him dere, and yer folks can fetch him dere."

"Ya, we've got a doctor in Oakland. Doc Engdahl, he's right on the main road next to the hotel."

We got Able on his feet. He was a bit shaky, but after a couple of steps, he seemed fine. He climbed up on the buckboard with our help, and he grimaced as we laid him back. He gently twisted and moved, sometimes giving little shouts of pain, till he found a position of some comfort.

I told him, "We hadn't written to Ma and Pa yet. Tell them I'll write soon." I grabbed his left hand and ran my other hand through his hair and told him good-bye.

Able started crying a little. I wiped his tears so John wouldn't see, and hopped down from the wagon. John was already in the seat, and he started the team heading for the bridge across the big creek.

"Emil, have fun being a cowboy," sounded from the back of the wagon as they pulled from the yard.

I stood there watching as the buckboard crossed the bridge and climbed the hill on the east and disappeared over the top. As I headed for the corral to get Pete, I had a strange feeling come over me. The melancholy of the loss of my brother's companionship was quickly replaced by a feeling of almost joy, but I guess almost selfishness.

This will be my story, my adventure, not Able's and mine. And when the family gathers, I'll tell my story, of my adventure, on Cow Creek Ranch.

FIVE

I saddled Pete and galloped toward the corral. Billie, in the chuck wagon, was almost there, and I flew right past him. Tom was riding from workstation to workstation, and I rode up to him. He told me that he already had other men working the sort and I would do the driving today.

"Don't try pushing any cows that haven't met up with their calves yet, or you'll end up like Able," Tom said as he spun the black around to check on the chuck wagon.

No one had done any driving yet, and there must have been over two hundred cows with their calves loitering around. A few slaps with the strap and I started turning them around and heading them around to the south across Cow Creek, where they would slow and start to graze, then slowly move in all directions up over the hills, looking for greener pastures. Once the first large bunch were across the creek, the others moved easily. They could see the others on the other side of the creek and were tired of confinement.

I could see now that this was a pretty easy job, as jobs go, on this roundup. The cows would come out from the sort corral and wait for their calves to come from the branding pen. It seemed amazing to me that, out of the hundreds of cow calves, when a calf screamed from the branding iron, its mother would be the one to beller back, and when the little one would be released, how they could go right to each other and nuzzle.

I noticed a cow waiting by the branding pen. She looked so much better than most of the others. She was a bit shorter of horn and squarer of build. Her calf came out of the pen and nuzzled, and the calf nursed. As they turned to head out, I noticed the calf had a bar preceding the "CC" brand, and a paint mark on it. I looked ahead, and its mother also had a bar brand. These were the select females for the herd.

As morning passed, I started really looking at the cows to see if I could pick the select ones. I soon was able to pick them out. This was something to do to help pass time. I noticed as the morning passed, the big holding area was starting to empty, and by dinnertime, I figured only about a fourth of the herd was left in there.

We all stopped for dinner, and Tom walked from man to man, giving encouragement.

When he got to me, he said, "Well, you did a good job moving them across the creek this morning. Looks like we're gonna make it today. All day, but we'll make it. John and Able made it out all right?"

I nodded my head and told him how I was able to pick the select cows from the herd. He had a proud, satisfied look on his face.

"When I first started doing this selecting process, I had trouble finding two hundred to mark. Now it's easy, and more and more the herd looks like Herefords rather than longhorns. You can't give away a longhorn anymore. The buyers all want corn-fat beefs. Hell, the Indian agents don't even want longhorns." He gave me a slap on the back and kept moving to visit with other men.

In midafternoon, I was sitting waiting for a pen of cows to link up with their calves so I could push them across the creek. There was a loud bang as a cow crashed into the side of the corral, and suddenly I could see Able flying in the air and falling limp to the ground. It took me so by surprise to have this dream-like vision while I was wide-awake. I had stayed so busy all day I guess I had forgotten about Able. I felt kind of guilty. I wonder if they had trouble finding a wagon to get Able on. What if John couldn't get him on a wagon and had to bring him back? John should have been back by dinner or shortly thereafter, and he wasn't back yet.

Later in the afternoon, I noticed the buckboard coming from the yard. John pulled over and talked to Tom. I could see Tom pointing to me, and John started to drive around the branding pen. I cut through the cows and met John on the north side of the corral. I pulled up alongside him.

"Well, I got Able on a wagon heading south. Da mule skinner said he'd be in Oakland tomorrow afternoon." John grinned and winked. "I had to wait a spell for a wagon. I had time to see a squaw." He laughed as he pulled away. "Emil, you don't need to tell Boss dat."

Why are these men so excited to see Indian women? The one I saw on the trail was not too attractive. Nothing like Gilbert's girlfriend, Anna Olson. Maybe the ones at the agency are pretty. Must be.

I shooed more cows across the creek, and the holding pen continued to empty. Late in the afternoon, I could see the buggy with the well-dressed man and Mrs. Ryan coming out to the corral. Tom joined them, and they climbed to the oversight box and talked to the man counting. The supper bell rang, and everything stopped. At supper, everyone was looking in the holding area. Two or three more sorts? Four or five? Not more than we could get done before dark. I heard Tom tell the two guys that were squeezing the cows in the holding area to go in and try to get some shut-eye till we got back in. They finished their supper and headed back to the bunkhouse. We all went back to work knowing the end was near.

Tom was in the holding area all by himself, the big black moving back and forth, pushing the cows toward the gate so smoothly and gently so as not to spook a one. I think the cows in the holding area wanted to get out of there, because they seemed fairly patient to have their turn to move to the sort pen and their freedom back in the hills.

At the end of the fourth sort, there were only about fifteen cows and calves left in the holding area, and in short order the last were in the sort pen. As soon as the last calves were sorted out and the cows ran out, Tom opened the gate to the holding area, and the other gate where the cull cows and herd bulls were, so they could go back to where they could get water. Tom's big black danced under the oversight box.

"How'd the count come out?"

The man that drove the buggy yelled back to Tom, "Well, it looks like you got more cattle than you got borrowed against them."

Tom waved, his hat in hand. "I'll drink to that!"

I had the last job, and by the time I had the last cows across the creek, the shadows were growing long, and the men and buggies were strung out on the way back to the ranch yard. Ernie waited for me and was checking out that everything was in order around the corral. We started back, and he pointed to the east. There was stacked a huge pile of new black creosoted fence post and rolls of barbwire and nail kegs of staples.

Ernie grinned. "Well, Emil, cowboy work is over 'cept for night watch. Now it's just postholes and pitchforks." As we rode in, he told me that we had to build a new hay lot fence. "If'n we don't keep them cows out, they'll eat or ruin the hay. An' they don't get no hay till they're 'bout starved."

Tom came racing back, pulled up by Ernie, and handed him a piece of paper. "Hang 'er up in the bunkhouse. Time to get the banker drunk and agreeable."

Tom put his heel into the black's side and sprung away from us.

When I got Pete put away and came into the bunkhouse, the men were all standing looking at the piece of paper.

Breeding cows	1,736
Cull cows	213
Yearlings	1,583
Calves	1,720
Herd bulls	22

The two guys who rode in earlier were putting rifles into scabbards to go out for night watch. The rest of the men were sitting around drinking and smoking. There was a different feeling tonight, one of relief. Just like when we finished planting corn. It wasn't long past dark when guys started turning in, and I was among the first. It seemed strange not to have Able to talk to. I still had that selfish feeling that this would be my adventure and tried many ways in my mind to justify this feeling. It had been nice to have Able to talk to. It seemed if you didn't drink, you didn't fit in, and they all seemed to ignore me. The day's activities caught up to me, and I soon fell asleep before the lanterns were turned off, only to wake suddenly in the middle of the night. That bang, as Able hit the corral boards, and him falling to the ground. I was wide-awake. I tried thinking of ways to get even with Murphy, but I wasn't so mad at him tonight. In the far distance, I could hear a wolf howl, and I lay trying to see if I could hear more

***

I must have fallen asleep because when I was woken by the sound of the bell for breakfast, the sun was up. The men were rolling out of bed and getting dressed.

I heard one man say to that Jerry, "Oh, this is better. None of that roundup up-before-dawn shit."

So this must be the regular time they get up around here.

Everyone headed for the grub shack, and while I was eating breakfast, I could see Tom and Ernie working on a piece of paper on the end of the other table. Tom left, and Ernie started around the tables, telling everyone what to do.

Ernie came by to me. "You're a farm boy? You know how to run a mower?"

"Ya, my pa taught me last year."

"OK, when the dew comes off, I'll come and get you. Until then, you go down to the hay lot. Just ride out on the buckboard."

Ernie moved on to the next man, and I finished eating. Some of the men started to leave, so I did too. I was nearly right behind Murphy.

Ernie said, "You're s'posed to ride herd, you son of a bitch. You went over my head."

Murphy cracked back, "I told you I wasn't going to spend my summer diggin' postholes and pitching hay. I had enough of your shit last summer."

Ernie's eyes grew red, and he fired back, "Well, you ain't gonna ride herd all summer. You're gonna put time in fencing and haying."

Murphy stopped in front of me and turned and looked right at Ernie. "I'll take my time on the other crews. I just want fair time, and that's all."

Ernie was fuming, and he put his face right as close to Murphy's as he could. "You'll screw this up, and then your ass is mine. Then you'll be sorry, you bastard."

Ernie stomped off, and Murphy let out a big belly laugh. When Ernie heard the laugh, he clenched his fists and walked even faster. Murphy laughed even harder.

Billie was helping Ben hook up the buckboard. As I approached, Ben nodded his head toward Murphy and said quietly, "There's a storm brewing there."

Ben waited till we were all there we and piled in, then went off to the new hay yard. I asked Ben why the hay yard was so far from the place.

He answered, "In the winter, the boss wants the cattle close, not too close."

There were six of us in the wagon, and we talked some on the way out.

One guy said, "All the stiffness in my ass from the last three days will be in my back by tonight."

We all laughed. The pressure of roundup had been lifted, and other than Ernie and Murphy, the whole crew seemed so much more lighthearted. As we pulled up to the new hay yard area, Tom appeared, racing in on his black.

Tom looked at one of the men and put a heel mark in the ground. "Put a corner post here."

Tom motioned for another fellow and me to come with him. Ben and Tom got some steel rods and balls of twine from the wagon. Tom went over just west of where he told the guys to put the corner post in and kicked at the ground. He uncovered a round cement stone with a hole in the middle that had a steel rod down it. Tom put a steel rod in the ground and tied a roll of twine to it. He told Ben to pace a hundred yards, and us to unroll the twine. Tom stood behind the rod he hammered in the ground and watched as we went east. As we were unrolling the twine, I noticed on a far hill on the other side of the big creek a pole with a flag tied to it.

The fellow I was with already knew that the pole was there. "That's the boss. Anything we build has to be square with the world. Those cement things are survey section markers."

Ben got to the hundred yards and looked back at Tom. Tom motioned him to the south a little and yelled for him to drive it in. We tied the twine. By then Tom was there and told us to unroll about another hundred yards to the south. He had a big ruling tape, and he measured back from the rod and tied a little string, then did the same on the piece we were unroll-ing. He went back and tied the end of the ruling tape to the first string and pulled it diagonal across our string.

"Emil, pull it tight."

We pulled it tight. Then he motioned us east, then back west a little.

"Drive it, Ben." Tom unhooked and rolled up his tape, then walked our way. "There's a straight corner to start with if you want to make things square. Emil, you gotta know geometry. It's digging time, boys." He slapped us on the back and laughed as we walked back to the buckboard.

Ben took shovels and post diggers out of the wagon. They took another guy and went to the post pile to fill the wagon with posts.

The fellow I was working with said, "You're Emil, right? My name's Tom. Tom Tailor. But, so as not to confuse me with the boss Tom, they all call me T.T."

T.T. told me how to pace between posts and how deep to dig the holes, and so, to work we went. When Tom left us, he went over to the sort corral. There were men working there. After he talked to them, he galloped back to the ranch. After a couple of postholes, Tom came back. I saw him give one of the men at the corral an envelope. They opened the gate, and thirty or forty cull cows came out with four men driving them. The herd came our way and edged to the south.

As they neared, all the other men stopped what they were doing and started yelling.

"You lucky bastards!"

"Have fun in town!"

"Don't drink the town dry. I get to go next month!"

"Save a squaw for me!"

112

The guys on horseback were laughing and waving their arms. The herd turned south and crossed Cow Creek, then followed the big creek on the south side.

T.T. looked over. "That's this month's order from the Omaha Agency. Them guys will be gone for three days, four if they have a good excuse. They'll be drunk, lying up with squaws, and come back with enough whiskey and tobacco to last them a month, and no money."

We went back to work, and I started thinking. I thought they went to town just to see Indian women. They weren't just looking at them. They were sinning with them. How could that be? How could a woman sin like that? I remembered Johnny told me and Able about a sinner woman, "a floozy," at the hotel in Oakland. The people in town pulled her out of her hotel room and put her on the stage to Fremont. Johnny said she was kicking and cussing all the way to the stage. This floozy called Mr. Ulmquist to help her, and Mrs. Ulmquist started hitting her with her umbrella, then turned the umbrella on Mr. Ulmquist. Sometimes, living on the farm, you miss a lot. This started me thinking about Oakland. *Able should get home this afternoon. I bet Pa and Gilbert are doing the same thing that I am, digging postholes.* I wouldn't think that the Catholic priest would let those Indian women sin like that. It must just be a story that they tell, for to fool the new guys.

The morning wore on, and soon Ernie came riding up with those big tin saddlebags on the back of his horse. "Come and get it!" I didn't think it was dinner

113

yet, but when Ernie opened the tin container, my nose got the smell of something I had never smelled before. My mouth watered.

"John's barbecue!" someone yelled.

Shovels dropped, and men ran. T.T. told me John made this only a few times a year. "An' wait till tonight. The big chunks that take all day to cook are the best."

Stringy beef with a sweet red sauce on slices of bread. This was something I had never tasted. It was so good I couldn't stop eating it.

Ernie came over and sat next to me and T.T. "I told you that nigger can cook! The dew's off. After dinner I'll get you started mowing."

Ernie finished his dinner and smoke, and we went to his horse. He mounted up, then lent me a hand and stirrup. I was surprised by two things: how strong skinny little Ernie was and how much broader his cutting horse was than Pete and Ida. Ain't no wonder he was bowlegged. We trotted back to the ranch yard and up to the barn.

"Billie, fix Emil here up with a team and mower. Emil, take the mower across the bridge. Tom will get you started," Ernie said as I slipped off the horse.

Ernie turned and was gone. Billie took me around to the back side of the barn. There was a lean-to for the teams to get out of the weather, and a corral just for the teams. Billie pointed out that each team had a color-matched halter, and one would have an *R* on the halter.

"You harness them that way, and they'll work much better."

114

I pulled two with blue halters out of the corral, and Billie helped me harness them. We led them around to the north side of the barn and hitched them to a fairly new-looking mower.

As I got up in the seat, Billie said, "See the way that mower's greased and oiled? That's the way it's put away every day."

I went through the north side of the yard and turned east to cross the bridge. The big gate was open, and the team's hooves clomped as they struck the bridge planks. Just as I got off on the far side of the bridge, I could hear clomping again, and Tom appeared at my side and motioned for me to follow him. I followed him up over the hill to the east and down the other side to a post alongside the trail.

Tom got down and motioned me to join him. "This is the east boundary. We cut everything on this side of Omaha Creek. All totaled, about a section and a half. Just cut squares that are five or six acres, about what you can do in a half a day. That's enough work for the team. If it's dry in the morning, just change teams at dinner. If it stays dry, we'll put this in the barn for the horses. This is the best time to cut choice hay for the horses. As the summer goes on, the hay is poorer. That's winter hay for the herd. I remember when we never fed 'em. If they couldn't scratch down for grass, they died. Selective breeding. Only the smart ones lived. Now I've got too much money in 'em to have 'em die off. Well, Emil, get her started."

"Yes, sir," I answered as Tom mounted up.

I dropped the sickle bar and engaged the gear and started the team south, then west, then north, then back along the trail east. I thought I had about five acres in a square, and so I went round and round the square. The mower made kind of a *chich chich* sound as it cut, and the waist-high grass fell right over. After about five or six rounds, I was going parallel to the trail Out of the corner of my eye I saw Mr. and Mrs. Ryan, dressed in finery in their beautiful buggy. What a scene as that fine dapple-gray team, sped by. That was the finest rig I had ever seen. I kept watching as they went over a far hill, and nearly forgot to turn my team at the end of the square.

I kept mowing all afternoon, and for a while, I got to thinking how tedious life is: corn, seed by seed; thousands of cows, a pen of thirty at a time; a section and a half of hay, five acres at a time. The ranch had six teams of horses, and I saw two other mowers. I supposed on some days there would be more than just me out there. The square kept getting smaller, and my stomach began to groan. I had nearly forgotten about how good dinner was and the promise of an even better supper. But I couldn't remember what it was called.

It seemed like all I was doing was turning now. *The last few passes, I'll just go on two sides.* As the standing grass narrowed, a flock of prairie chickens flew up, and I about jumped out of my seat. I knocked down the last of the grass, got the oilcan, poured some oil on the bar, moved ahead a little to work in the oil, raised up the bar, and turned the team for home.

This team was used to the routine, and they knew when they were going back to the barn. I had to hold them in, or they would have been at a full run, and they would have bounced me right off the seat of the mower. It must have taken longer than I thought. As I was putting away the team, men were coming from the grub shack. I quickly headed there as soon as I washed.

John was waiting there with a big piece of meat and a big carving knife. "Lord, son, I was 'bout to send Billie to fetch ya. Don't cha know dat nobody's late when John has barbecue brisket?"

"I was trying to remember all afternoon what that was called."

John answered back, "You ain't never heard of barbecue before? You damn Swedes don't know how to eat. Dems was tips for dinner. Dis is brisket. Dis is da good stuff. We won't have dis again till Fourth of July."

John cut me off some slices and put sauce on them, some beans, and bread. Oh what a smell, oh what a meal.

There were a few men left in the grub shack.

As I looked to find a place to sit, I heard, "Emil."

It was T.T. He offered a seat next to him, and we talked of the day's work. He told me that one of the guys hit Ben with a dirt clod. It surprised Ben, and he jumped, stepped on a post, it rolled, and he fell on his ass. He said they all laughed, and Ben did too. I didn't have much to say. My only excitement was seeing Ryan's buggy and team and a flock of prairie chickens.

John came over. "Ya, Mr. Ryan, he'll be eating wid a banker at Decatur by now. We won't be seeing dem for a few days. Mrs. Ryan insists on da company of woman folk from time to time."

It was plain to see John was trying to get stuff cleaned up, so we finished up eating and headed for the bunkhouse.

T.T. joined the others back at the bunkhouse. He offered a pull off his jug. I offered a "thanks but no thanks." I noticed Ernie putting a piece of paper on the wall, and I walked over to read it.

NIGHT WATCH

I looked down the list to see if my name was on it, and sure enough it was.

Ernie said, "Yup, you made the list, boy, day after tomorrow."

I thought to myself, *Oh good, a change of scenery. Mowing can get real boring.*

Then it hit me. "Ernie, I've never shot a gun before. What if I see wolves?"

Ernie grinned. "Well, there's plenty of daylight left. There ain't nothing to it."

Ernie went over to the rifle rack and grabbed a rifle and box of cartridges. He told me to dig through the trash and find some empty whiskey bottles. We went over to the big creek, and he showed me how to lie down to hold the rifle. A few of the other fellows followed, and they gathered around to watch. Ernie showed me how to load the gun. He took one of the whiskey bottles and threw it over to the far bank of the creek.

"OK, Emil, lay down. Pull that lever down and back up. That'll put a cartridge in the chamber and cock the hammer. Careful of the trigger, it'll go off now. Aim at the bottle. Blade of the front sight, right on in the center of the *V* of the rear sight. Top of the front sight level with the top of the rear sight right on that target. Then, pull the trigger."

I followed his directions, and when the gun barrel steadied, I touched the trigger. *Bam!* The bottle exploded, and a violent shake and pain shot through my shoulder. I jumped to my feet and grabbed my shoulder. Now I figured out why the other fellows had followed out. They were all laughing.

Ernie cackled. "Winchester .45-70 kicks like a mule but sure does the job. Least ya hit what you were shootin' at."

I had no idea that these guns kicked like that, but I was proud I hit the target.

Ernie threw another bottle across the creek. "Now, lay down, and try it again. This time pull the gun back tight to your shoulder. Pull the lever aim, and shoot."

Bam! The bottle exploded, and the recoil just rocked me slightly.

Ernie said with a laugh, "Bet you'll remember to pull that gun tight to your shoulder. Makes a lot of difference, don't it?"

I shot three more bottles before I missed. Ernie was watching closely and told me the rifle barrel was

119

moving when I missed, and told me how to correct it. He gave good advice, and I broke four more straight.

Ernie was nodding his head with approval. "I think that's enough. You'll be able to hit what you're shootin' at."

Ernie showed me how to unload the gun. Then we headed back to the bunkhouse.

As we walked in, I heard someone yell, "Deadeye Emil," and laughter erupted.

I put the rifle back in the rack, and Ernie motioned me over. "See this chart with everyone's night watch schedule?"

"Ya." I nodded.

"Well, I'm the boss, and I make the schedule. This here calendar has the moon signs on it. And over here, when the moon is full, I'll be out there with you, and maybe we can get a shot at some wolves."

I answered, "What about the other times? Do you think I'd get a crack at any?"

He shook his head no. "Well, maybe at morning twilight, but probably not."

Ernie got a bottle of whiskey out of his desk and headed across the room after he offered some to me. I turned him down and went out to sit on the bench in front of the bunkhouse. I sat there and watched the shadows fall over the hills, and the cows blend into the shadows and disappear. The lanterns were lit in the bunkhouse, and the voices grew louder as the evening wore on. Men were always coming out to pee, and most of them stopped and visited on their way back in.

Ernie came by. "This breeze keeps up all night, there won't be any dew in the morning. We'll be able to start mowing hay for serious."

It had been dark for some time when a fellow—I think his name was George—burst through the screen door, stumbled by me, and fell down by the corner of the bunkhouse. He got up on his hands and knees and started to vomit. He crawled over to the bunkhouse and pulled himself up to his feet, then turned and bent over and vomited some more.

He stumbled by me on his way back in. "So much for John's barbecue."

The stench of vomit made its way to my nose, and it didn't smell like barbecue. It sickened me, and I felt like I was going to puke. I was off the bench and out in the yard gasping for fresh air. When I felt better, I went back and turned in.

Some of the men had turned in already, but some men were still up, and the room was full of smoke. I must have been getting used to bunkhouse noise, because I fell asleep in short order. The bang of something hitting hard on the boards, and I sat up in bed, seeing Able's lifeless body hitting the ground. I felt an instant sweat break just above my ears, and I was breathing hard. I began to realize my surroundings. Only one lantern was dimly lit, and four men were sitting in chairs in the middle of the room. That George was trying to get himself off the floor. Murphy went over and grabbed him by his belt and shirt collar and pushed him through the screen door and out into the yard.

I could hear Murphy yelling, "You drunken bastard, you lay out here. I don't want you puking in the bunkhouse."

I lay back in bed thinking. *Able, I hope Able is safe at home. Why do I keep seeing the accident? Does whiskey make you vomit if you drink too much? Why would anyone do that? My God, Murphy is strong; he picked George up and all but threw him out the door. George is at least my size.*

I lay there trying to go back to sleep. Then it hit me.

Tomorrow is Sunday! I should have asked Ernie what we do on Sunday. Do we go to Winnebago Agency, to Catholic church? Do we just stay around here or what? Ernie said if there is no dew, we'd mow. Maybe he forgot tomorrow is Sunday. I'll bet that's it. He forgot tomorrow is Sunday.

***

Something woke me. It was the breakfast bell. I sat up in bed, and all the men were putting on their work clothes, so I did the same and headed for the grub shack. Out in the yard, Ernie was pushing George with his foot. George had slept in the yard with his head near a half-dried puddle of vomit. When I saw it, I held my breath so as not to get a whiff of it and ruin my appetite. There was a place at the table next to Mike, and I sat down to eat my breakfast.

I asked Mike, "Isn't today Sunday?"

Mike got a funny look on his face, then got up and went to the other table and said something to Murphy.

Before Mike got back to sit down, Murphy stood up. "This stupid Swede wants to know if this is Sunday. Like we're gonna go to church or something. Stupid shit."

The grub shack erupted with laughter. I did feel stupid. Then I felt mad. Why did Murphy have to do that? I thought I could talk to Mike. Why did he go tell Murphy what I said? I was mad. I felt stupid. I felt like getting up and running out. I sure didn't feel like eating anything else. I sat there not saying anything, dabbing at my food, just waiting for someone else to head for the door so I could escape. The screen door opened, and George walked in. He looked all nasty, kind of a gray color to his skin. He grabbed a cup of coffee, sat down, and sipped at it as he held it in both hands.

Ernie came by. "No dew. Start mowing after breakfast. You'll have help. I'm sorry, Emil. I thought I told you your day off is after night watch, and then you'll get a couple days a month in town. Don't let these guys get you down, son."

Then Ernie yelled, "These assholes all asked the same questions when they came to work here, 'cept the ones that's goin' to hell anyway."

Laughter broke out again, and I did start to feel better. I was mad at Mike, but he had kind of a sheepish look on his face after Ernie talked, so maybe he was a little sorry for his part in making fun of me. Then, to make matters worse, I had to work with him that day.

After breakfast we went out to the corral to get the teams ready. There was another fellow named Chuck with us. Mike made small talk, and I made small talk back. I'd never say anything to Mike again that I didn't want shouted around the bunkhouse. I wasn't that stupid.

The mowing crew crossed the bridge. We each made a square of about five acres and started mowing. While we were harnessing up the teams, this Chuck told me that, by the time the men that drove cattle to the Omaha Agency got back, we'd have enough hay down for the men to start stacking. After they started stacking, there would be no more fence work except for rainy days. This hayfield would be my summer work. As I worked the team around and around, I noticed how much faster Chuck could turn his corners. So I practiced turning my team like he did, and it worked better. I was really disappointed. I thought that I was going to be a cowboy. Now I was going to be a hay farm worker. To think how selfish I was about Able getting hurt.

My adventure! Mowing hay in the Indian territories! I can see that my big adventure will be riding night watch once a week. I don't know why I had to have my horse. I should have my own team. I guess I'll have lots of time to think riding around a hayfield.

The morning turned to noon, the afternoon to evening and suppertime. Then it was back to the bunkhouse and a replay of the night before. My entire day was totally depressing. Then it hit me this was Sunday. Just a week ago, I came out of church ready to take on the world, and in the whole week, I hadn't picked up my Bible or even taken time to pray. I spent all day feeling sorry for myself and only briefly thought of poor Able.

I must turn my life back to God for strength. I got up and went into the bunkhouse, over to my bed table, and got out my Bible. I thought I would take it down by the creek and read till dark. I made a mistake.

Murphy saw me. "Hey look! Swede has his Bible. I used one of those once, to convince the judge I didn't do it."

The men all laughed, and that egged Murphy on.

"Hey, Swede! I bet you think we're a bunch of sinners. You come near me preaching that damn Bible, I'll kick your ass back to Oakland."

The men didn't laugh so much on his second comment. But as I looked at their faces, I could see they were in agreement with Murphy.

That was twice today that Murphy had made fun of me. This time I felt something that I had never felt before. The muscles in my back and shoulders tightened, and the hair on the back of my neck felt like it was sticking out. I felt a rage come over me like I had never felt. I was going to tear into Murphy. My look must have shown. Ernie was immediately at my side.

He put his arm over my shoulder. "Emil, why don't you forget what he says, and you go outside and read your Bible."

As we walked out the door, I heard Murphy beller, "Ernie, you asshole! Why don't you let the Swede try me? It's plain to see he'd like to. You're just helping him to be a chicken shit, just like you."

I looked over at Ernie, and he looked just like I'm sure I looked. He was boiling. He never said a word. He just turned and walked through the yard.

I went over by the creek to read. I sat there the longest time. I had never been this mad before. After a while I settled down. *I'll read the scripture from last Sunday.* I couldn't think of it. I thumbed through and couldn't find it. The more I thumbed, the madder I got.

Why can't I find that text? I should know it. I need to read it. I have to carry this damned Bible back into the bunkhouse. If Murphy says anything, I'll try him. I'll try him.

I sat there dwelling on Murphy. My hands started shaking and pulling at the pages. *I'm not going to be humiliated again. If I need God, God is everywhere.* I stood up and threw the Bible in the swift water of the creek.

As soon as I threw the Bible in the creek, I felt guilty. Ma and Pa got that for me for my baptism. I'd have to think of something to tell them. This would never have happened if it weren't for that goddamned Murphy. I couldn't go back in the bunkhouse, so I walked out to the fence job for the new hay lot. All the way out there, my mind was racing. I had never met anyone like Murphy. Pa told me there were some mean people in the world. Murphy had to be one of the worst. I walked around the fencing area and watched the shadows come over the hills. This time of day gives me a peace of mind, and slowly the fury in my mind softened. I walked back to the bunkhouse but couldn't go in. I walked through the yard up near the grub shack. I could see, by the light of a lantern,

Ernie and John talking and passing a bottle between them. It seemed like having a friend to talk to had lightened Ernie's spirits. I thought that Mike would be a friend, but I found I couldn't trust him. A little sliver of moon showed in the southwest sky, and lots of stars were twinkling. *The world goes on, and I'm afraid to go in and go to bed.*

I watched the lanterns go out and the last one dim. I knew some of the men were going to bed, and I could probably slip in. I walked in and quietly closed the door, went straight to my bed, and never looked at anyone. I got my clothes off, got in bed, turned my back away from those who were still up, and pretended to sleep. In Oakland it seemed like everyone liked me, but here, I was not sure. I was sure of one thing: this summer couldn't get over soon enough.

SIX

The next day passed without incidence, and this day the same. After dinner, I could see the fine dapple-gray team bringing the Ryan's back home. And within the hour, Tom, on his big black, was out in the hay-field looking over progress. He did not stop to visit but raced off to check on the rest of the progress that had taken place in his absence. I was looking forward to tonight: my first night watch.

Chuck finished his section and came to where I was working. "Ernie said to send you in early if I could. Night watch tonight, hey?"

I oiled and put up my mower and headed in. After I put up the team, I headed for the grub shack. I was to work with Jerry tonight, and he was already at a table eating. John dished me a plate, and as we were eating, he put two sacks on the table.

"A little sompin' for you boys to eat during da night."

Jerry explained how we should section off the range and get a feel for the lay of the herd if we could before dark, then just sit out the night. "Summer is the best. Nights are short. If everything is OK, we can have them checked before dark, and we ain't got to ride around in the dark. Winter is a bitch. Always dark and too damned cold to catch forty winks."

We finished eating, told John thanks, and headed for the corral to get the horses. Pete seemed happy to get out of the corral, but he couldn't feel as happy as me. Time to be a cowboy. We saddled up and led the horses to the bunkhouse and tied them to the hitching rail.

Jerry pointed to the west sky. "You got a slicker?"

I answered that I did as I looked at the sky. A cloud bank was gathering in the southwest. While it didn't look too threatening, I was excited to think I could wear my new slicker. I put my lunch in my saddlebags and tied them on behind the saddle. I went back in and took a rifle from the rack and got a scabbard from the wall. Jerry showed me how to hook it to the saddle.

Jerry asked me, "On roundup, you worked the southeast sector, didn't ya?"

I shook my head.

"Then you check that sector. Then, do you remember seeing three cedar trees on the side of a hill in the southwest sector? Meet me there."

I shook my head again. We mounted up and went our separate ways. Of course I remembered the three cedar trees. Other than a few scraggly cottonwoods on Cow Creek, those were the only other trees out there. The other men were starting to come in from their day's work.

Both Tom and Ernie came by and wished me well on my night watch. I crossed Cow Creek and turned southeast, following the big creek till I found the graze line in the grass and headed south. As I climbed the first hill, I noticed to the east four riders. *This must be the men who drive cattle to the Omaha Agency.*

I climbed hill after hill, spotting cattle in every nameless creek bottom cooling themselves. I had sat on that mower for three or four days, which felt like a lifetime. *Chich chich* was all I heard. Now, the squeaking sound of well-oiled saddle leather sounded like music to my ears. Soon the thoughts of my bunkhouse troubles were far behind me, and I had the feelings I'd had on our journey here and roundup. I stopped on the top of a hill, got the rifle out of the scabbard, and practiced pointing it. I pointed it at imaginary wolves concealed in clumps of grass.

I hope I can shoot a wolf. I would like to see one. Around Oakland, all the wolves have been shot or poisoned. I got back on Pete and kept riding.

I saw six yearlings out away from the group by a nearby creek. What would it hurt? I put my heel in Pete's side and raced down the hill. I cut three out. I tried to copy the moves of Ernie's cutting horse. Pete wasn't a cutting horse, and I wasn't Ernie, but in a few minutes, I had them separated and three put back with the others. I went back to the three I had separated and drove them west around a hill just to see if I could. *Ya! I can do cowboy work.* I turned them back over the hill and down the other side to the group they were with. *Ya! I can do cowboy work.*

I went back to riding the hills, checking on cattle. They all seemed very content. The grass was tall, and all the creeks had water. The dark clouds had moved northeast. The sun was shining through holes in the clouds, showing patches of glimmering bright green grass every so often over hill and vale for as far as I could see. I kept traveling south and west, seeing cattle here and there. The setting sun was nearing the horizon as I topped a hill. I looked over the terrain. I spotted the hill with the three cedars about a mile northwest and headed that way. As I came around the hill from the south side, I found Jerry was already there.

He was just unsaddling his horse. "Emil, you may as well unsaddle. I think this is going to be a slow night."

I unsaddled and staked Pete out for some fresh grass. Jerry was setting up a bed with his saddle for a pillow like Able and I did under the Conestoga wagon. He told me I should do the same. After we got all set up, we sat and watched as darkness set in.

"Not much going on. The grass is tall. The cows are content. The wolves would rather get a jackrabbit than fight a cow for a calf," Jerry said, yawning.

We talked of our tasks around the ranch. Jerry looked at me hard.

"Emil, don't you let that goddamned Murphy goad you into a fight. He's at least four years older than you and a hell of a lot bigger than you. He's always been a troublemaker and has lots of fighting experience. Hell, I don't think I'd try him. I heard he broke a guy's jaw in Pender. He keeps that crap up, someday

131

they'll find him along the road, bushwhacked. The bastard will have it coming. 'Bout midnight, that sliver of moon will set, you wake me up. If you hear cows bellering, wake me. Gud night."

Jerry went and turned in. I had had such a good evening. I had forgotten about Murphy for a brief time.

This is such a good place to work. I know I'm just a boy trying to learn men's work, and the men will make fun of my inexperience of the world and work. But they all are just having fun at my expense, and just fun. Murphy, on the other hand, is mean, and it's plain to see the other men don't want to cross him so they go along with him. And I'm the one that is stuck.

Why did Jerry bring him up? I was feeling so good about being a cowboy all evening.

The twilight turned to darkness, and the sliver of moon cast no light. The only sound that I heard was an occasional gentle moo of a cow calling her calf, a bug buzzing, or a snore from Jerry. I got up and walked around. I didn't know that we would take turns sleeping. I thought that we had to stay awake all night. I was glad we didn't. I was so sleepy right then. The sliver of moon slowly moved to the west, chasing the sun and the stars. It was breathtaking. Off in the northwest, I could see just an occasional lightning flare from the storm that passed. I had nothing to do but think. I had to do laundry tomorrow. I needed to write Ma and Pa a letter.

Then it hit me. *I've got to tell them I lost my Bible. What am I going to tell them? That goddamned Murphy! Why does he have to ruin my summer? What if wolves are watching me?*

That thought sent a chill through me, then, kind of a terror. The same kind of terror I remembered feeling as a little one when Gilbert told me of the outhouse ghost. I wished I had not left my rifle by my saddle. I couldn't believe how scared I was making myself. The wolves would rather take a jackrabbit than a man with a gun. When I mowed, I would see lots of jackrabbits. I bet I saw at least twenty this evening checking the herd. I spent the rest of the night listening for every sound and convincing myself that the wolves would eat jackrabbits. As the sliver of moon set, I woke Jerry and turned in. I felt safe and secure under my blanket knowing Jerry was watching, and sleep came fast.

***

I felt something hit my leg. My eyes popped open to see Jerry grabbing his saddle in the dawn of morning. We saddled up and headed for the ranch. As we topped a hill, I could see four wolves running up the hill to our east. I started for my rifle.

Jerry said, "Don't waste any cartridges. It's all but impossible to hit a wolf running at that distance."

Well, at least I seen some, and when they saw us, they ran even faster. Maybe they were afraid of people.

Jerry looked over. "Damn, I was hungry overnight. I ate my lunch. I checked, and you hadn't eaten yours, so I did."

I guess eating wasn't on my mind overnight, but by now I was starving. By the time we got back to the ranch and put up the horses, some of the men were coming out of the grub shack. Jerry and I sat and ate and watched all the others go to their jobs.

Jerry looked over. "No work today for us. What are you going to do today, Emil?"

I answered, "Well, I'm gonna do laundry and write my ma and pa."

Jerry grinned. "I'm gonna go to Winnebago Agency for a squaw-and-whiskey run."

I got back to the bunkhouse and felt sleepy. That was a short night's sleep. There was a bathtub in the wash shack, and Jerry was heading that way, so I lay down and fell fast asleep. I couldn't have slept too long, because I woke when Jerry came back in. I felt so refreshed even though it was a short nap.

"There's fire in the stove. Sure you don't wanna come with?" Jerry said as he put on his good straw hat and walked out the door.

I gave him a "no thanks" and gathered my laundry.

I filled and put the big kettle on the stove and threw a couple pieces of wood in. In no time, I had hot water and went about the task of doing laundry. As I hung the things out to dry, I figured it would only take an hour or so for them to dry. *Ya, these will be dry by the time I get done with my letter.*

It seemed so strange to be the only one in the bunkhouse. It seemed so quiet. I got out the paper and pencil and stared at the blank piece of paper, thinking what to write.

Dear Ma and Pa,

I hope Able is feeling better. Able may have told you we saw our first Indian and Negro all in the first day. The Negro's name is John. He is very nice, and he cooked beef in a way that I have never tasted. It is so good. He calls it barbecue. I rode a night watch last night and saw wolves this morning. They seemed to be afraid of people. Other than that, all I do is fence and mow hay. I will write again soon.

With love,
Your son Emil

PS: The other night, while walking along the big creek reading my Bible, I stepped into a badger hole. I fell down and nearly slid into the creek. I lost grip of my Bible, and it fell in, and I could not find it.

That sounds good to me. I bet they'll believe that. I folded the paper, put it in the envelope that already had a stamp and address on it. I took the sealing candle from Ernie's desk, lit it, and sealed the envelope.

Up in the grub shack was a place to put mail. As I walked there, I checked my laundry. It was nearly dry. The grub shack seemed so different empty and all. The box for the mail was empty. As I dropped my letter in, John looked down the hall from the kitchen.

"Say, boy, yuz too late. Jerry took da mail to town. But dat's all right. I gots to go to town tomorrow. Yes, sir! I got to meet da stagecoach. Mr. Tim is comin' to home. Ya! Tim, he'd rather ride horseback, 'cept for his ma. His ma says gentlemen ride in coaches."

I went down the hall to the summer kitchen. John was stirring a big pot with beans and meat. He could fix beans a hundred different ways, all good, some better than others. He had loaves of bread cooling by the window, and the smell was making me hungry.

"What's ya doing today, boy?"

I answered, "Laundry and letter writing. But I think I'll be done before dinner."

"Well, Mrs. Ryan has been wantin' fish for supper for some time. I think the creek water is warm enough for da catfish to bite. I could sure use some help catchin' her a mess o' fish. I been brewin' up some my famous bait for several days now."

I grinned from ear to ear. "Ya! I'll help after dinner."

John and I talked fishing awhile, and I went to check on my laundry. I thought I'd stop by the corral and check on Pete. From the corral, I could see across the big creek to the hayfield. Someone, I think Chuck, had the hay rake out and was putting up windrows. Long lines of lime-green cured grass were running from the east side of the creek up over the hill. As was usual, Pete was glad to see me, even more so now that Ida had gone home. Pete loved to be scratched behind his ears, and he especially loved the carrot I'd snitched from the kitchen. When I turned to leave to take down my laundry, Pete whinnied and stomped his feet. I guess I maybe should have been taking

Pete for a ride at night rather than sitting outside the bunkhouse.

I got my laundry down from the line. I used the big basket from the wash shack to carry it back to the bunkhouse. I folded Able's bed linen and placed it on his bed, made my bed, and put away my clothes. It was getting hot in the bunkhouse, but there was still a nice breeze coming through. I lay on my bed. How could I have seen that big creek and not thought of fishing? I liked to fish. This time of year, when we went to church, Ma and the little ones would stay and visit some church ladies, and Pa would take us down to Logan Creek to fish. I lay there thinking about fishing and must have fallen asleep again, because the next thing I knew, the dinner bell was ringing. As I lay there blinking my eyes, I began to remember the smell of John's bean pot and fresh bread.

Most of the men were in the grub shack by the time I got there. Ernie went over to the other table and told the fence crew that they would be pitching hay in the afternoon. Since the men had gotten back from driving cattle, Murphy had to go back to the work crews.

When Ernie told them they had to pitch hay, Murphy piped up, "Same old shit! Postholes and pitchforks."

Ernie fired back, "If you don't like it, there's the door."

Murphy said, "I told you I'd do my turn. As long as I get my share of herd work." Ernie and Murphy glared at each other. Then Ernie walked away.

As he did, I could hear Murphy say in a low voice, "That skinny old shit has to keep pushing. One day. One day!"

The men finished eating and headed back to work.

John shouted, "Emil, if'n you help me, we'll have more time to try to fool dem fish."

I helped John do dishes and wipe tables. We joked and laughed. John was such a good man. It seemed like he was going out of his way to be friendly to me. That was more than I could say for the other men.

"I got my favorite spot down near the bunkhouse," John said as we headed out of the kitchen with cane poles in hand. He cradled a can he said was his special bait. "Dis here bait has caught fish from Missusip' to Montana, always works."

We found his spot. The bank of the creek had washed by a slight bend, and there was a small flat area where we could sit near the water. It was still kind of hard to get down the bank, but we managed. John opened his bait can, and the smell almost made me puke. These baits were a round, doughy substance wrapped around a hook. They were wrapped in a tiny piece of cheesecloth that was tied in place with a thread.

"I only ever used a worm or a night crawler."

John answered, "Shit, boy, ole Mr. Catfish can't smell dat worm ten feet away. Why, once dis bait's in de water, dey'll be comin' from a mile an' a half." He tied a bait on my pole string, and I put it in the water.

He tied one on his pole and put it in the water. "Jus' gotta sit her till dey come lookin' for what smells so good."

John got close to the water's edge and washed his hands. "A little more smell for Mr. Catfish." He came back from the water's edge and sat down. "How'd ya like it here by now, Emil?"

I looked over at John and smiled. "Today is great. Sometimes the men pick on me. They make fun of me, and that damned Murphy is mean. And this is the Indian Nations, and I thought I'd see some Indians."

John looked over. "How old are you, Emil?"

"Fifteen."

"Well, dat's da problem. All dose men dat was picked on when dey was kids got to pass it on to you. And dat Murphy, he's a hard case. He's got Ernie rattled. Ernie, he don't know what to do with him.

"Dis ain't da Indian Nations no more. Poor damned Injuns got da smallpox, and hell, half of 'em died off. Now we're on da Winnebago Reservation, and south of here is da Omaha Reservation. Since so many of 'em died off, da government sold da west part of da nation to da state. Dis side of da creek is state owned. Da line on da far side, da hayfields, is reservation. Boss lost his lease, but somehow he cooked up a way to buy a big chunk of land. Now dey gonna start letting dem sodbusters in on dis west part of the nation. Boss is worried. Sodbusters ran us out da Sand Hills. Boss says da days of free or near-free grass is over. An dem Injuns, dey don't get far from de agency, poor devils."

I felt a violent shake on my pole. It shook clear up my arm and took me so by surprise. My cork bobber was completely underwater, and the line was going hither and throw.

"Pull dat fish out da water, boy," John laughed. "Dem fish got da whiff of my bait now."

Before I could get the hook out of my fish's mouth, John pulled one in.

"Squish dat bait back around da hook an' get it back in da water."

I did what John said, and almost instantly, another fish was on the line. I had never seen anyone catch fish like this before. John knew how to make bait. In short order, we had ten fish. Each one must have weighed at least two pounds.

John looked over at the fish in the basket. "Dat's enough for today, Emil. See, dat bait ball is so big dat de little ones can't get it in dere mouth. Ryan's got fish for supper, and so do we."

We got up from the creek bank and walked back to the kitchen. Men were putting hay in the barn, and they hooted at us as we walked by. John told me to come back before supper bell, and we'd have southern-fried catfish. That sounded like an offer I couldn't pass up. I told John I would surely be back and went out to watch the men put hay in the mow.

I thought of going back to the bunkhouse, but it was too hot. The breeze had died down. The days were turning from very warm spring to summer hot.

The trees in the ranch yard were not as big as home, but they did offer some shade. *Boy! Wouldn't some of Ma's lemonade go good right now?*

It seemed so strange to be sitting in the shade watching the men work. I guess no different than me sitting up all night while they slept. I nodded off and ended up sleeping for some time. Tom came through the yard. He asked me how I liked the night watch and the day off afterward. I told him I liked it. I liked doing cowboy work better than farm work.

"Well, I'll see you get on the sort crew. We have an order for two hundred yearlings to sort out in a few days. Cattle business is changing, Emil. Corn-fat cattle bring the most money. There's a man in West Point that buys yearlings from me. He feeds them corn and then ships them to Omaha for top prices. All we have to do is sort them out. He and his men come and drive them back to West Point. All the yearlings will be gone before winter. I hear I've got southern-fried catfish for supper. I'll go for that." He gave me a pat on the back and headed for the house.

A moment later, a very slight breeze carried a smell from the kitchen that was new to me. *If this is southern-fried catfish, it sure smells good.*

A screen-door slam caught my attention. I looked to the covered walk that went from the outside kitchen to the house. John was carrying a silver platter with a big silver cover.

John yelled over, "Emil, let me serve da Ryan's. Den we can eat ours."

141

A couple minutes later, John came out and motioned me to join him. The kitchen was blazing hot, so we retreated to a table in the grub shack. With a fork, I pulled back the golden crispy crust to see the flaky white flesh of the fish. It had a delicious flavor like I had never had.

"You like dat?"

I shook my head.

John went on, "Yes, sir, dat's my mammy's recipe. My mammy was a house nigger. She did all da cookin', an' I helped. I caught da fish, killed da chickens, and what all. I learned to read and write some, living in the house. My mammy never said, but I tink da massa was my pappy. The missus was always after Massa to sell me. Den da war come. After da war, we was freed. My mammy stayed wit da family, but Missus come out an' give me twenty dollars an' told me to be gone by morning. I found da Union army and joined dem. I was a cavalry soldier. Dey called us buffalo soldiers. Dey sent us out west to fight Indians. It wasn't much of a fight. We had carbines, cannons, and Gatlin' guns. Dey had old muzzle-loaders and bow and arrows. We'd go out in late fall and early winter and kill 'em and burn 'em out. Ya, dey'd lose dere winter food, an soon dey'd turn up at Fort Robinson starving and cold. I hated da killin', but I did like da army life. Since I could read, dey taught me some doctoring so da white doctors didn't have to work on da black soldiers. When I had enough of da army, I mustered out. I liked da west, so I found dis job wit da Ryans. Dey was in da Sand Hills den. Now we's here. I been patching da men and fixing da food ever since."

I was eating the whole time John was talking, so then I told him about our farm. He seemed so interested. I don't see how he could have been, after living such an exciting life.

"Well, looks like da men are coming in. I best set up for supper. Y'all come back. I gots a good peach cobbler for supper. Dat'll top off dem fish."

John grabbed our empty plates and headed back for the kitchen. I decided to walk down to the corral and see Pete. Before I got there, I heard the supper bell, and men passed me going the other way. I killed some time with Pete, then headed back to the grub shack for dessert.

As I held out my plate for a scoop of cobbler, John grinned. "I knew you'd be back."

There was an empty place next to Ernie, so I sat down.

"You must not have worked up an appetite today. You're just eatin' dessert," Ernie said.

I told him I'd gone fishing with John and he fixed catfish for us.

"Well, you had a good day off, then," Ernie answered.

From down the table, a guy named Jack spoke out. "Looks like the Swede is a nigger lover. Don't you know, boy, that niggers are best as tree decorations."

A look around the table, and I could see that all the men's faces looked to be in agreement with Jack.

The room quieted for a few minutes. Soon, individual conversations started back up, and I felt safe to turn and look at John. The happy, smiling John that I had been with all afternoon now had a strange broken look on his face. How could anyone say such a thing right in front of him like that? John was a big, stout man. I'm sure he could have whipped that Jack. But instead, John just stood there looking down with that broken look on his face. I took a look back at Ernie, and he appeared to have the same stern look on his face as the other men. I didn't know what to do, let alone say. So I went back to eating dessert.

Most of the men had left when Ernie turned to me with that stern look. "Emil, ya can't be too friendly with John, or they'll be all over you." Then his stern look turned to a smile. "I told you, that nigger can cook, and them assholes are always ready to eat his vittles."

I left the grub shack. I walked out to the barn to see how much hay was in the mow. I walked by the creek. I walked by the corral. I walked till dusk, avoiding the bunkhouse, hoping to steal away and talk to John. Jerry came back from town, got off his horse, and took a mailbag into the grub shack. Jerry's footing was poor. He must have been drunk. He led his horse down to the corral, unsaddled, and headed for the bunkhouse. His saddlebags made a clunking noise like they had whiskey bottles in them, and I'm sure they did. As I approached the grub shack, I could see John sitting at a table with a bottle of whiskey and a smoke. As I entered he turned and smiled.

144

I felt like crying. "Oh, John, I am sorry for what was said at supper. I didn't know those men felt that way."

John took a puff off his smoke. He held it in a while and blew it out his nose. "Oh Emil! You are a breath of fresh air. You ain't learned who to hate yet. You are always welcome to visit me. And if you don't come back, I'll understand."

John took another puff off his smoke, then turned and grinned. "Dere's two tings dem damned dummies never thought of. Dere ain't a tree for miles around dat's big enough to hang dis big ole nigger from. An' da other ting is dat Mr. Tom would shoot anyone dat tried."

I held out my hand to shake his. He put out his. Our hands grasped. It looked so different to see a brown hand and fingers grasping my hand. It felt warm and safe, like a kiss from Ma. I felt a heaviness lift from my heart.

I saw a twinkle come back to John's eye. "Well, Emil, it's getting near dark. Best turn in so I kin have breakfast for y'all in da morning."

We said our good nights, and I headed for the bunkhouse.

The bunkhouse voices were loud, and the smoke hung around the lanterns. I did my usual evening thing and sat on the bench outside the bunkhouse. I wondered why these men drank whiskey every night. Pa said a drink on an occasion won't hurt you, but a man must be careful, or he can be a slave to alcohol. Pastor Nielson said the same. Pastor Nielson said never drink it, or you could be a slave to alcohol. How could these men, who were willingly slaves to alcohol, hate a man that was a forced slave by another man? I sat there thinking of all the things that had happened in the grub shack. I could not find anything wrong with John.

He's nicer to me than any of the men here. Maybe John is right. I'm as big as a man, and still I'm a boy. Not that long ago I played hide-and-seek with the little ones, and it was fun. I guess if being hard is part of being a man, maybe I'd rather be a boy longer. I know Ernie and John are friends, but Ernie doesn't let the men see them together. That doesn't seem right.

I saw Ernie come out of the bunkhouse and walk out in the yard to relieve himself. He came back and sat down beside me. I was so disappointed in Ernie. He would not stand up and defend his friend in front of the others. I didn't know what to say. We sat there silent. Ernie sat there puffing on a short cigarette. I felt like I should say something, but I couldn't think of anything to say. I finally looked at the sky. The sliver of moon was now more of a crescent moon.

"Ernie, look, the sliver moon is a cow moon now."

Ernie looked at me. "What the hell's a cow moon?"

I answered, "You know, 'Hey Diddle Diddle.'"

Ernie got a puzzled look on his face. "What the hell you talking about, 'Hey Diddle Diddle'?"

I laughed. "You don't know 'Hey Diddle Diddle,' do you?"

Ernie fired back, "I ain't got a clue what you're talking about."

"It's a nursery rhyme. I thought all children learned them."

Ernie still had a puzzled look on his face. "We didn't learn that in Georgia. Tell it to me."

I laughed and thought it through to be sure I remembered it all.

> Hey diddle diddle,
> The cat and the fiddle,
> The cow jumped over the moon.
> The little dog laughed,
> To see such sport,
> And the dish ran away with the spoon.

Ernie laughed. "I ain't never heard that before. Tell me again so I can remember it."

I went through it four or five more times. Ernie spoke it with me and soon had it committed to memory. I asked him if he had any nursery rhymes he learned as a boy.

"I got one, but we didn't call it no nursery rhyme."

> The boy stood on the burning deck,
> Eating peanuts by the peck.
> His mother called him,
> He would not go,
> Because he loved the peanuts so.

I laughed. I had never heard this. I urged Ernie, and he went back over it, over and over, until I committed it to memory.

I told him, "This is kind of what I imagined we'd do in the evenings. I thought we would sing and play guitars at night."

Ernie laughed so hard he nearly fell off the bench. He laughed so hard he couldn't catch his breath.

When he caught his breath, he stood up and went to the screen door and yelled, "Hey, guys!" He stood there a moment thinking, then turned and smiled at me. "Turn off some of those lights."

He came back over to me, put his arm on my shoulder, and said softly, "Boy, you read too many dime novels." He laughed softly as he went back out to the yard. When he passed me on his way back in, he grinned and said, "Hey diddle diddle."

As the lights dimmed and the voices quieted, I slipped into bed. As I lay there trying to fall asleep, the lines of "The Boy Stood on the Burning Deck" kept running through my head.

SEVEN

The mowing continued, cutting little squares in a sea of grass. The day off had been refreshing. The square I was cutting had a view of the trail to Winnebago Agency. Shortly after I started, I saw four riders pushing thirty to forty cows up the trail. I figured that this must be the monthly contract for the reservation. After dinner, I saw the Ryan's fine buggy and team heading for town. John was driving it, and he was dressed in good clothes. I had nearly forgotten that he said he had to meet the stage and Tim Ryan.

It seems so different that the Ryan's seem so regular around the ranch, so easy to talk to. But it seems like they really live in a different world. They got their catfish on a silver platter. The way Tom sits on that black. The way Mrs. Ryan walks. She doesn't walk—she just glides. I guess if you're the boss of this big operation, you have to be special, and your family also.

The hayfield was full of activity. Mike and I were mowing. Chuck raked in the morning, and was now driving a hay wagon. There were men pitching big balls of hay stuck on the end of a pitchfork up into the wagon. Another wagon was waiting to be filled. All of this activity was taking place back up the field where we had mowed three days ago. All I had for excitement was an occasional jackrabbit or prairie chicken, and the constant *chich chich* of the mower.

Shortly before quitting time, I saw John driving the fine buggy home. In the grub shack at suppertime, Tim Ryan walked around the room renewing acquaintances. I was sitting next to T.T. when he came over.

"Little Tom! I see you haven't given up on us yet."

T.T. answered, "Hell, Timmy, ain't like there's another cow outfit down the road to work for. You know I'll always be here. This here is Emil. He's new this summer."

Tim put out his hand to shake T.T.'s hand, and then he turned to shake mine. He had a firm handshake but not the kind that tries to squeeze you. Tim looked me right in the eye with a fair and honest look, just like his father.

"So you're Emil. Old John was telling me about you. Your brother got hurt and had to go home. I'm sorry about that."

T.T. fired back, "You'll be sorry for real, Tim, when you start putting calluses on those soft schoolboy hands."

Fellows sitting near overheard T.T.'s comments and began laughing, and Tim laughed too as he moved to visit with some of the other men. Tim was a handsome young man. His complexion was not freckly like his father's, but smooth and lightly tanned. His hair was a darker shade of brown, more like his mother's. If you looked at him, you knew he was Tom's son. They looked that much alike. I guessed he was maybe an inch taller than me, but as he walked through the room, he looked much taller. Just the way his mother walked, and his father sat on that black, he had that presence that he was special, that he knew he was in line to be the boss, and he would be a good boss just like his father.

As the day cooled to the evening, I was sitting in the shade of the yard. The Ryan family came out of the house and went to the barn. Even Mrs. Ryan had on black riding pants and long black boots. Billie had the black and the two roans saddled with English saddles. They mounted up and headed south through the yard at a graceful gait. I had been right in my thoughts. Tim sat on a horse like his father. They rode out— the masters. The masters out to survey their domain. I watched them disappear, then reappear on the far side of Cow Creek, three specks racing up over the hill.

***

The next morning, Tim was in work clothes eating breakfast in the grub shack. The windrows of hay were too damp to stack, so he went with the men to dig post-holes. The grass was not too wet to mow, so us mowers headed over to the hayfield. A strong southeast wind blew, and by midmorning, the men returned to stack hay. I noticed Tim from time to time. He worked the way he walked. As the days in the hayfield had worn on, I saw less and less of Ernie and Tom. It appeared Chuck was the lead man out here. As Mike and I finished our morning squares, Chuck came over and told us that he felt a storm would be coming. We wouldn't cut anymore, but help stack in the afternoon.

"With this wind, the hay is drying fast. This is choice hay. The more we get in today the better. I'll bet what we're knocking down today will be cow roughage. I'd bet six bits it'll rain before dark," Chuck said as he wheeled his hay rake away.

Pitching hay is about as bad as it gets. As we were leaving the grub shack from dinner, Mike whispered in my ear, "Emil! When we're out there pitching hay, you keep telling everyone how easy this is. We don't want them to think that we got the best job on the crew, mowing."

I laughed to myself. Those other guys couldn't be that dumb. Pitching hay wasn't that bad at home. You pitched for a while, then took the wagon to the barn and pitched some more. But here, it was different. We filled a wagon, and the driver took it to the barn. This barn had a big grapple hook on a pulley. The pulley was on wheels that went down a track hooked to the top beam of the barn. One big scoop, and the whole wagon was unloaded and back to the hay field, waiting. You never got caught up. The sharp-cut stems punctured your skin. As you slid your pitchfork down the windrows, sometimes you gathered mice or snakes that jumped out on you as you picked up the hay ball to pitch it into the wagon. I saw T.T. grab a bull snake by the tail and crack it like a bullwhip. It killed the snake. Crows and hawks patrolled the bare field for easy pickings.

All through the afternoon, Tim worked alongside, keeping a good pace. Chuck was turning hay rows for the second time, trying to get them to dry in the heat and wind, and we all kept pitching. Chuck had it figured right. As we were loading the last of the dry hay into the last wagon, the thunder was getting close.

We made it in before the rain started, and I did what the other men did. I took off my shirt and let the rain wash it and myself—a refreshing shower. Tim ate supper with his family. After supper, I sat in the barn with Billie, and he told me of driving cattle up from Texas. It seemed so strange to me that there was a breed of man that liked this work so much that he would do it his whole life. They had nothing, no family, no land of their own—just work and whiskey at night.

Billie told me, "Ya, I tried settling down once. It didn't work. I tried homesteading. I had a wife. She died givin' birth, and the little boy died the next day. I went back to cowboyin'. This is the best job I ever had. Boss don't say nothing 'bout drinking as long as you're up to work the next day. And there's squaws just a little over an hour away."

I went back to the bunkhouse. It was pretty quiet inside, and I snuck into bed and fell to sleep with the patter of rain on the roof.

***

At breakfast, Tom and Ernie were talking and writing on a sheet of paper. Ernie stood up and read four names followed by "two days in town." A whoop went up by those four. Ernie then read eight names followed by "cut out two hundred forty yearlings." My name was on the list. A cowboy day.

The rain had stopped, but from time to time, a light sprinkle would pass. The men had their slickers on as they were saddling up. So did I. We all headed south, with Tom on his black and Tim on his roan leading the way. We got to Cow Creek, and the others splashed through. Pete seemed a bit hesitant. Cow Creek is usually ankle-deep and three feet wide. This morning it was belly-deep and at least ten or twelve foot wide.

Tom yelled over "Emil, put a heel in him."

I kicked Pete in the side, and he obeyed and crossed the creek. We went south past the three cedars and found cattle everywhere. They were not bunched as they did in the heat, but they were scattered all over the hills.

We all stopped at the top of the hill, and Tom spoke. "Let's gather 'em in that draw over there. Check to make sure we don't get any select heifers. Let's get 'em, boys."

This was like I had dreamed, horsemen racing off in all directions. I swung back around to my left and raced down a hill.

Pete remembered his short lesson on cutting. I found a group of them. There were six yearlings in the bunch. I cut out two and pushed them off a ways.

154

As I turned to go back for more, the first two ran right back with the group. The rain had refreshed the cattle also. They were spunky. Every time I would cut two or three out and turn my back, they would run back with the others. On the fifth try, I got three out and decided to keep them moving back to the draw that Tom had pointed out. I hope I don't look foolish just pushing three. As I came around the hill, I could see two men in the draw with about thirty cattle. I pushed my three hard, and they joined the others in the draw.

One of the men watching the herd was George. He yelled over to me, "They ain't cutting worth a damn this morning!"

In the distance I could see a man with just two in front of him, so I didn't feel too bad. I trotted back to my bunch and worked them till I got the other three yearlings off to one side. Then Pete raced through and cut them off. This was fun. I put them in the draw with the others and went to find another bunch.

This went on most of the morning, and the herd in the draw grew to over a hundred. I brought two head around the hill, and all the men were gathered around the draw. I joined in with them. Tom told us that we would move northwest a mile or so and find some more. He then told us that we'd take this bunch to the holding pen.

"Emil, Ben, Jerry, take 'em in. Emil, you go see John and bring out dinner."

Everyone worked the herd. Once they closed ranks and started moving, the other men fell back and left me, Ben, and Jerry to move them in.

Ben came close by as we were moving. "When we come down the last hill to Cow Creek, push 'em hard so they'll cross the high waters."

We pushed them along. The sprinkles had stopped about an hour ago, and I was able to take off my slicker before we started this drive. The slicker kept me dry till the day warmed. Then I was sweating in it. The clouds were moving back to the west. It was not done raining. Hopefully it would hold off till after we got the rest of the order in. The cool breeze felt good on my sweaty clothes, and riding herd made me feel even better. I loved this cowboy work. Maybe that's why some of these men did it their whole lives.

We topped the last hill, and Jerry and Ben started yelling and whooping. The cattle started to run. I stayed in the back. Jerry and Ben moved up along the side to keep them tight as they crossed the creek. The lead cattle ran down the bank, splashed through, and up the other side. The rest of the herd followed. The creek was not half full now as it was when we crossed earlier. Pete balked at the bank, but a gentle nudge and he went right down and through. We worked the herd around the big holding pen to the sort corral. Ernie and another man were waiting to help turn them in.

Ben rode near me. "Emil, we got 'em. Go get dinner. We'll wait for you."

I carefully moved off from the side of the herd so as not to spook them and galloped toward the grub shack.

John must have known to have dinner ready, 'cause it was. He asked how the day was going as he carried out the big tin saddlebags. I took off my saddlebags and helped John lift these over Pete.

"John, I don't care what those guys say. I value your friendship."

John just grinned. He never said anything as we tightened the straps on the dinner bags. I didn't know what to say. I felt really awkward, so I just mounted up. I pulled the reins to head back to the corral.

"Emil, I'd play checkers in da evening if'n I had someone to play with."

I grinned and nodded, put my heel in Pete's side, and galloped through the yard. Oh, I was so glad I'd said something to John.

Jerry and Ben were waiting by the corral, and they started off before I caught up to them. Pete must have felt safe crossing the creek this time. He never missed a step. As we galloped up and down the hills, those big tin saddlebags slapped on Pete's sides. He didn't seem to mind. And I was getting hungry.

Ben must have known which draw they would be in because he led us right to the rest of the men. We stopped the horses on a knoll overlooking the draw, and I started taking the dinner bags down. The other men started drifting up our way. The one bag had a tightly sealed coffee jug, forks, plates, and bread. The other had one of John's bean dinners. As soon as the tight-fitting latches popped open, the smell of dinner filled the heavy air. Everyone grabbed plates and dug in. I filled mine and sat down. Tom sat over by Ben, and I could overhear them talking cattle numbers.

Tim filled his plate and sat next to me. He never said a word. He grabbed his fork and started shoveling food into his mouth.

After a couple of minutes, he looked over at me and said, "All the good places to eat in Lincoln, and there isn't a one that compares to John's ranch food."

I nodded in agreement. This was the first time I had a chance to visit with Tim. I didn't want to sound like a dumb farm boy. What to say! What to say!

"Are studies hard at the university?"

Tim answered, "It was difficult for me last year. This year I think I have it figured out. It's much easier."

"What are you studying?" I asked.

"People."

"People," I said with a quizzical look on my face.

"Ya," Tim laughed. "You see, Emil, you go to the university to meet people that will be helpful through your life. You go to class so you can communicate on their level."

I didn't know what to say. I'm sure I looked stupid sitting there.

I think Tim picked up on it. "Ya, Emil, it's not what you know, but who you know, if you want to get ahead in this world. Ya, Emil, if you aren't ahead in this world, you're behind, behind a mule's ass, steering a plow."

I must have had my mouth open. I didn't know what to think. My dream was to be a farmer.

Tim looked over and must have seen the look on my face. "I'm sorry. I suppose you want to be a farmer?"

I still didn't know what to say, so I just nodded yes.

"There's really nothing wrong with being a farmer if that's the life you like, Emil. But this is the life our family loves, and with the changing times, we need all the friends in Lincoln we can get."

"Tim, come here!" Tom shouted.

"We'll talk later," Tim said as he got up to join his father and Ben.

I could see that I didn't know how to think like that. *All Pa ever talks about is hard work and gifts from God. I'm out here working so we don't have to mortgage our corn crop. Ryans work hard, but I don't know how they got so rich. What do people in Lincoln have to do with us out here?*

I finished a second plate and still didn't know what to think of my conversation with Tim. I didn't think he was making fun of me. I thought you went to the university to be a teacher or a doctor or a lawyer. I never heard of anyone studying people. Maybe I'd learn of this, year after next, when I graduated high school.

Tom stood up. "Let's get 'em, boys! Emil, just leave the dinner tins here till we head in. Get out there and cut some critters out."

I was on Pete and over a hill in no time. We were moving back and forth with little bunches of yearlings most of the afternoon.

Tom came racing over to me. "Get the dinner tins. We should have the order filled. Let's get 'em in."

I went over and put the tin saddlebags on Pete and joined the men. They already had the herd moving. With all of us, we moved them quickly. Cow Creek was back to its regular size by the time we crossed this time.

I took the tins back to the grub shack. It wasn't suppertime yet, and John was cooking. I told him of my day. I didn't tell him about my conversation with Tim. I hadn't figured out what he was talking about yet, so I kept it to myself.

Rain came up again before supper, and after supper, the bunkhouse seemed more crowded than ever. No one noticed me slip out to the grub shack for a few games of checkers with John. Days go by fast when you stay busy.

***

One morning after breakfast, Ernie said, "You're on night watch tonight. The moon is near full. I'll join you for a wolf shoot."

He winked and slapped me on the back. I guess I had forgotten about night watch. I sure hadn't noticed the moon getting full. The day riding the mower went fast. I could see myself shooting a wolf in my mind all day.

After early supper and lunch snacks, Ernie and I saddled up. We put on saddlebags and rifle scabbards. The plan was the same as before: ride and check the herd and meet up at the three cedars. I didn't waste any time practicing cattle cutting with Pete this time. Every time a jackrabbit flushed out, I was pointing a rifle at him.

The moon rose in the east nearly full. The excitement had refreshed me. Even though I had mowed hay all day, I was wide awake. The sun was setting by the time I got to the three cedars. No Ernie. Darkness set in, and though the moon was near full, it was dark. After a while, my eyes adjusted to the dark as the moon moved overhead. I could see quite a distance. The white on the Herefords shone surprisingly bright in the night. From a distance I could hear a wolf howl at the moon. Then a wolf howled close by. It sent shivers down my back and a fear into my mind. I went over to where I had my saddle bed set up and got my rifle. This made me feel safer.

I was surprised how easily I could make out a rider coming over a hill at least half a mile northwest of where I was sitting.

In a few minutes, Ernie rode in. "Did you give up on me, Emil? I found a few head that were wandering kind of far off, so I took the time to push 'em back. If the rains stop and the grass gets thin, they'll move a long way."

I felt glad to see Ernie. I felt safe to see Ernie. "I've been hearing a few wolves. Did you hear any wolves over in the northwest?" I asked him.

Ernie unsaddled his horse and slapped him on the rump, and his stout cutter moseyed off to find fresh grass. His horse would return at a whistle. Pete came when you called his name, when he felt like it. But to be safe, I had him staked out.

Ernie pulled his rifle out and came and sat next to me. "Ya, it don't matter much if the cattle roam now.

'Nuther year or two, the state's gonna start selling ground for sodbusters. That rascal Tom figured a way to have the university scrib cover the ranch, and he bought it cheap. What pisses Tom off is that you can't make money in the cattle business without free grass. Tom, he cusses the government. Every day a boatload of sodbusters come from Europe. The government lets them come. Now there ain't nothing left for them that started out here."

A wolf howled in the distant west, and my close wolf answered back, this time with another joining in harmony. Ernie's head perked up, and he pushed his ear in the direction of the howling beast.

Ernie now whispered, "Them goddamned wolves got ears like you can't believe. I think they're within a mile of us."

He cocked the lever of his rifle and set the hammer in the safe position. He looked at me and nodded. I did the same. We sat there straining our eyes to see any movement come over the hill just to the east of us. I poked Ernie and pointed. He turned and looked, grinned, and nodded. Three wolves moved steadily our way. They moved in a way that looked like they were half crouched down, and they moved slowly. We lay down and shinnied to where we had a better view of them. They kept coming closer. My heart was beating out of my chest. What if the wolves heard it? Ernie nudged me as he pulled back the hammer on his rifle. I did the same. They were still coming. They were within a hundred yards of us. If they stayed on the same track that they were on, they would pass right in front of us about thirty yards out. Here they came, closer and closer, not even making a sound as they skulked through the grass. I was sure they could hear my heart or smell my sweat. Three wolves this close, and if I wouldn't have seen them, I wouldn't have known they were there. I guess I had reason to fear. If I weren't the hunter, I could be the hunted. In the distance off to the east, a wolf howled. Now our wolves were only about forty yards away. They stopped.

Ernie touched my foot with his, and we took aim. One wolf sat back on his haunches and started to howl. Before that one even started to howl, a second one did the same. The second one started to howl, and I put my sights on him. Ernie touched my foot again. The silence of the night with the howl of the wolves ended with the explosive sound of two big Winchesters going off at the same time. I had my sights put right on the chest of the second wolf, and he ripped off to the side at the same time I heard the concussion. I heard the familiar sound of the lever cocking and another shot from Ernie. I could see the two wolves that were howling kicking in the throes of death, and now I could hear a whimpering.

Ernie was on his feet and running down the hill. I could make out this wolf trying to escape down the hill, pulling for all it was worth on its forelegs, dragging its hind legs. Ernie ran down the hill. When he got close, another shot rang out. This shot echoed through the hills. I suppose our first shots echoed. I had too much excitement to hear that. Without even knowing it, I was running down the hill to see my wolf. He was lying in a big pool of blood and not moving anymore. Right at the spot I had been aiming was a hole the size of a dime. I looked at Ernie's, and it appeared to be in the same condition. What a thrill. My heart was not beating so hard now. I don't think I could have lasted much longer the way my heart was beating before we pulled the triggers. I got one. I got one.

Ernie came walking up the hill.

"We got 'em, Ernie."

Ernie answered, "Ya, we got the two we should have got. And I got a lucky shot at the other one. I told you, Emil. It can be fun out here on a moonlit night."

Ernie had the ears off the one he had shot down the hill. He came over and cut the ears off the one he shot next to mine. "You got a pocketknife, Emil?"

"Ya, I do."

"Cut the ears off that wolf. We give 'em to Tom. When the guys from West Point come for yearlings, Tom gives the ears to them. They get bounty in Cumming County. Three bucks a pair. The guys get a night in the bar on us."

I pulled the wolf's head up to cut his ears off. His head was heavy. He was big boned and long but looked kind of thin. He looked to be twice the size of Willie. Willie wasn't fat but solid from all the table scraps of a family of eight. I felt so proud giving those ears to Ernie.

We went back to our saddle beds. Ernie got a sandwich out of his lunch sack, put the ears back in the sack, and put them in his saddlebags. The sandwich looked good, so I got mine out too.

As we sat there eating, Ernie said, "After those gunshots, there won't be a wolf within two miles of us the rest of the night. I'm gonna catch forty winks."

Ernie pointed at a distant hill and told me that when the moon was over it, to wake him. Ernie turned in and in short order was snoring. I was too excited to sleep. I think Ernie must have been right. I could hear wolves howling at the moon all over in the distance, but none near us. In my mind, I kept seeing that wolf spinning down as the bullet hit him. What a thrill.

The day's activities caught up to me, and I became so tired I had to get up and walk around lest I would have fallen asleep sitting. The moon was not yet over the hill. It needed to be so I could wake Ernie. I walked down to the wolves. The moon had moved farther west, and they were in the shadows. I could hardly find them. I moved Pete's stake out. I didn't think I could keep on my feet any longer. Finally, the moon hovered over the distant hill. I woke Ernie, threw my blanket over me, and was out.

When I felt Ernie's boot on my side, it was twilight. We saddled up and started in. I had to ride down the hill to get one more look at the wolves. In the morning light, it was not so pretty. On the far side of the wolves, the grass was splattered with blood and hair. The blood splatter was in a three- or four-yard circle behind each wolf. I must have had a sickened look on my face.

Ernie looked over and said, "I told you that Winchester .45-70 gets the job done."

We rode down the hill and looked at the death site of the other wolf and headed in.

As we started in, Ernie said, "Well, what's better, huntin' or fishin'?"

I grinned. "I'll have to think about that."

Ben covered Ernie's work that day. Ernie and I had a nice day off. We did laundry, took naps, I told him about my family, he told me about growing up in Georgia, and we fit in a few games of checkers.

***

The work went on at the ranch. The hay lot started to get wired, and haystacks were starting to go in there. The men put up a temporary bridge over Omaha Creek so the hay wagons could cross from the hayfield to the hay lot. The center supports had to be put in and out every day, for fear the big creek would come up and wash the whole thing downstream.

I worked with Tim one rainy day cleaning horse stalls. I didn't bring up the university. We did talk about baseball. He liked to play too. We played catch during dinner hour. He told me about city life. He told me about dates with many girls and his conquests. My life seemed so boring next to his, I didn't say much. That didn't seem to bother him. He had stories enough to last all day. Tim told me that they would go to Sioux City and stay in a fine hotel and visit other businessmen and their families. I liked Tim. He could go to fine hotels, yet still come back here and muck out horse stalls.

Mr. Ryan had wheat straw brought in just for stall bedding for his horses. As we cleaned a stall, Billie would tie that stall's occupant in the alleyway. We cleaned and rebedded the black's stall. Billie led him in and closed the gate. The big black pranced into his clean bedding. He kicked up his heels and struck the side of the stall. The sound of the hooves on the boards made a bang, and suddenly in my mind, I saw Able fall lifeless to the ground. I jerked back. It seemed like I was there again. A shudder of fear overtook me, and I fell back against the stall I was in. I was breathing hard, and a sweat broke out above my ears.

"Are you all right?" Tim yelled out.

I was. I was fine. Why did that happen? I was fine. I must have looked fine, because Tim went on telling me about this grain dealer's daughter in Sioux City that would let him touch her breast. Working with Tim was fun.

A couple of days later, I got a letter from home. It was written by Gilbert.

Dear Emil,

Able is doing fine. He can't write for Ma and Pa, so I am. The corn is all about eight inches tall now. The best-looking field around Oakland. Pa is cultivating. We have hay in. We are all well. Doc Engdahl says that whoever patched up Able at the ranch did a good job. I like having Ida home to ride to town at night. Oly Olson says I can help at the post office after wheat harvest. It won't pay big ranch money like you make, but Pa says we may make it to harvest without a loan. This will be a good year for our family. Ma and Pa send their love.

Your brother Gilbert

Corn seems so distant. It is so wonderful to see it grow. All we have here is tallgrass, grass that I cut off and the cows eat. Where we've cut hay, the land sits just brown. Where the cows eat, the grass loses its bright green color, and it's splattered with cow pies. On the farm, things stay green all summer. Here, everything starts to die off. Home sounds so good.

That night at supper, Tom came out to the grub shack. He walked from man to man and gave each one a blue envelope, the same envelope with the printed return address that our letter had come in. *It must be payday*, I thought to myself.

When Tom came to me, I said, "Mr. Ryan, can you keep that for me? Sometimes in the bunkhouse, someone loses their tobacco or their drink. I would not want to lose my pay. My family needs my pay."

Tom smiled. "Sure, Emil, I can keep it. I think you're due to go to town soon. You'll need some spending money."

"Well, sir, Ernie told me that the ranch pays board and room in town. If that's the case, I don't need any money."

"Don't you need some money for liquor? They do have cold beer in town. That may be more your liking."

"No, sir," I answered, "I don't drink or take tobacco. Pa says you can be a slave to them. Look at these men.

After they buy smokes and liquor, they don't have anything left. My family needs the money."

"You're right, Emil," He sat on the bench next to me and talked low. "You might need to buy a bottle of liquor to pay a squaw. Or you might want a root beer or candy. You've worked hard, son. You need a good time in town."

I felt Tom's hand pushing into mine. "Here, you take your bounty money. You have a good time in town." He gave me a pat on the back and moved over to the other table. I looked in my hand. He had given me three silver dollars.

The next day I saw four men heading for town. One of them was Murphy. I was glad he wasn't going to town the same time I was. I would get to go next time.

I had to ride night watch one night, and nothing happened. Nothing happened except rain. I learned how to sleep leaned against a tree with a slicker on. I also learned how dark it can be out there. On my day off, I thought I should write my folks a letter. All I had to tell them about was shooting a wolf. If I waited till next week, I could tell them about Winnebago Agency.

I didn't think I would be that excited about going to town, but I was. Ernie put the list up. "Town this week—Bob, Jerry, Emil, Jack."

I liked Jerry. Bob I didn't know well. Jack was the one who called me a nigger lover. He hadn't said any more about it. One day I worked with him, and he even seemed friendly.

On Friday night I played checkers with John. Ernie came by, and he and John teased me about spending all my money on one squaw. I never told them I didn't take any pay. I didn't tell anyone that Tom gave me three dollars. He kind of did it on the sly, so I kept it to myself. If he had wanted anyone to know about the three dollars, he would not have pushed them into my palm.

I went to bed that night and lay there thinking. *I'm finally going to see Indians. I wonder how friendly they will be. You know, if I take my good clothes along, I can go to church. I can go to Catholic church with the Indians. I bet, if the Indians see me at church with them, they will be friendly. They may invite me to stay for lunch in the churchyard. That would be nice. I could put one of my dollars in the collection plate.*

Somehow church sounded so good. I had not thought much of God lately, only a few times since I threw my Bible into the creek.

Whoa! Ma and Pa didn't even mention the Bible in their letter. They must have believed my story.

I laughed to myself. Then sorrow set in.

I lied. I lied to my parents. Of course they believe my story. They raised me in God's ways. I wouldn't lie to them.

I had a hollow feeling, and I couldn't sleep. The poker game broke up. The room darkened and quieted. I still couldn't sleep. I even cried a little in silence.

EIGHT

The ringing of the breakfast bell woke me. The sun was already shining bright. The sorrows of the night before had vanished. This was going to be a big day. I had never been to another town other than Oakland.

I think Oakland is bigger than Winnebago. No, that can't be. Winnebago must be way bigger—they have hundreds of Indians living there.

I must have been lost in my thoughts.

"Emil, you gonna eat?" Jerry yelled as he walked by.

I about jumped out of my untied boots. I had put on clean overalls and a clean shirt. I quickly tied my boots and ran to catch up to Jerry.

While we were eating, Jerry said, "I can't wait to get to town. I must be getting old. John's a good cook, but I'm ready for bacon and ham. Beef is good, but not every day. Anymore, I almost look as forward to pork as squaws."

I guess I never noticed. Ma always had pork. We sold our cattle. We only had two a year, one from

Hanna and one from Sara. If we would fatten the year-lings on corn, Pa would sell them at the fair. I guess, since I always had pork, the beef always tasted good.

At any rate, shredded beef in gravy over biscuits was really good for me, two plates good. Jerry and I never said anything walking back to the bunkhouse. We just grinned at each other as others passed on their way to their days' work. I put my good clothes in my saddlebags, checked my pockets for the twen-tieth time for my three dollars. In moments, we were saddled up and clomping over the bridge. The older three guys rode side by side. I kind of followed behind with dreams of dime novel cowboys riding into town for a gunfight. We didn't have any guns, though. We waved at the men in the hayfield. Once we passed the hayfield, the grass was all new again. No signs of life, just grass.

After we traveled about five miles, down in a creek bottom there was a cornfield. I think this was an Indian farm. There was a mule tied out near the creek. A single walking plow lay rusting at the edge of the field. The whole field was no more than two acres. There was a small garden patch at the far end of the cornfield. The cornfield was about the size of our garden at home. There was no house on the farm, just a little hog house. By the time we went another mile, I could see these little farm plots every so often. One of the plots came very near the trail. There, dug into the hill, was one of these that I thought was a hog house. In front of this little shack was an Indian family, a man and woman with little ones.

"Jerry, do people live in there?" I shouted.

He looked back at me. "Shit, Emil, that's a nice house compared to some."

All those sheds I thought were hog houses were Indian houses. As we neared town, we passed Indians walking. They were all in tattered old white man's clothes. They all seemed to have a sad look in their eyes. As we passed, they looked away from us, just like the ones on the trail that Able and I saw.

The trail came over a hill. Down below was Winnebago Agency. We had to cross another bridge just outside of town. This creek was much bigger than Omaha Creek. Maybe this was a river. The bridge was built with heavy timbers and looked very strong. Off to the north was a big brick building. There was a cattle corral behind it. This brick building had smaller frame buildings built to the north and south. On the back of the frame building on the south side was a lean-to. The brick building had "Winnebago Agency" painted on the side of it. Off to the south was a large frame building. It was three stories tall. We pulled in behind this big building, to a livery stable. An old man with a white beard greeted us.

"Ranch horses in the corral."

We unsaddled and put the horses in the corral. I followed the other men carrying saddles to the livery. The old man gave us each a paper tag to sign and put on our saddles. This old man smelled of sweat and whiskey. His white beard was stained from chew spit. He didn't seem any too friendly. I followed the lead of the others, threw my saddlebags over my shoulders like they did, and headed for Main Street.

The main roads, Sioux City to Omaha and Sioux City to Lincoln, ran through Main Street. On the south end of town, the main road veered to the east, and the high trail kept going south. Across from the Indian agency was a jail. There was also a small brick-built bank building that was boarded over. There were only a few small wooden houses on the east side of the street. A large hill ascended to the rear of Main Street. This hill was covered with little shacks and huts. We turned the corner. The hotel was big. Right on the corner on the main floor was the bar, then the hotel lobby, the café, and finally the general store. The hotel rooms were on the second and third floors. Standing along the board sidewalk was about fifteen or twenty Indian women smiling at us as we walked by. We went into the hotel and each signed a book and were assigned a room. We climbed the stairs.

Bob turned to me. "Free rooms are clear on the top floor."

I had never been in such a tall building. The men opened the doors to their rooms and threw their saddlebags in. They just turned and headed right back down the stairs.

"I'll be down later," I said.

My room was very small. The door had a transom window, which was nice. I opened the transom window, then went over and opened the front window. The window had a screen that was ripped, and someone had tried to fix it with thread. At least it would keep a

bird out. The room was hot and smelly. I hoped the
fresh air might help the problem. All that was in the
room was a bed and a wash table. There was a wash-
bowl and pitcher on top of the table. I looked to see if
there was water in the pitcher. There was. There were
two dead flies floating in the pitcher. On the bottom
shelf of the table was the chamber pot. I was afraid to
look and see if it was clean. I pulled the blanket back.
The sheets seemed to be clean. I turned back to the
window and looked out. What a view! This was taller
than Grandpa's windmill. I could see over the tops of
the small houses and buildings on the east side of the
road. I could plainly see now all the huts on the hill
behind Main Street.

I expected to see Indians living in houses. I really
hoped to see Indians living in tepees, like in the dime
novels. Our hogs lived better. The shacks were helter-
skelter going up the hill, with paths worn down to the
yellow-brown clay between them. From my viewpoint,
I could see at least a hundred shacks. Most of the
shacks had people sitting in front of them. There were
small groups of children playing throughout the community. There was trash everywhere, with skinny dogs
digging through it. On the south edge of the shanty
town was a handful of skinny horses in a rope corral.

The street below was busy. Two freight wagons
passed in just the time I was looking out the window.
A white woman with two little ones came out of one of
the small houses and came across the street and disappeared beneath me. I was so high up I couldn't see
the sidewalk below. I could stick my head through the

repair in the screen. Actually, the hole in the screen looked to be the size of someone's head. Most of the activity on the street was Indians walking around with tattered white people's clothes on.

My curiosity was getting the better of me. *I think I'll get a root beer.* I left my room and started down the hall.

Jerry, with an Indian woman, entered the hall from the top of the stairs. He almost sounded drunk already as he said, "Emil, get out there and find you one. If'n you don't see one you like, come back in an hour. They change every hour, 'cept the real ugly ones."

As they passed, the Indian woman slapped me on my rear and smiled at me. That was strange.

The stairs had landings, and the final flight of stairs was much wider. The final flight came back to the hotel lobby. There was a big counter with the old lady that had us sign in. On the left was a big open doorway. "SALOON" was painted above the door. A smaller sign hung from tiny chains from the top of the door, "NO INDIANS SERVED." On the right was another big open doorway. "DINING ROOM" was painted above it. This doorway had the "NO INDIANS SERVED" sign hanging in it too. I looked in the dining room. It wasn't dinnertime yet, and all the tables were empty. It looked clean and bright, with big windows facing the street. It was so big. I counted eight tables that each sat four people. You could sit at three different tables and look right out the window. This was a very nice place, and Jerry had said the food was good.

I'm gonna have a root beer. I walked into the saloon. This was maybe bigger than the dining room. The room was well lit. It was not bright, though. It was smoky. The windows had a yellow cast to them from the smoke, and so did the walls and ceilings. There were ten tables in this room, but some of them held only two people. Three tables had people at them. Five men were sitting at the bar. That's where Bob and Jack were. There was a place next to Bob, so I sat down. The wood on the bar was polished like a pitchfork handle from people's elbows. The big counter behind the bar had stacks of big glass mugs. The stacks looked twice as big because there was a mirror on the back of it. The big mirror had a crack across the whole length of it. In the top left corner was a bullet hole that had cracks going out from it like the rays of the sun. The bartender was a short fat man. He was completely bald on top, with scraggly black-and-gray hair around his ears. He had no shirt on, just a dirty white apron. His arms and back were covered with hair. I had never seen a man with so much hair on him.

"What'll you have?" his gruff voice croaked out.

I answered, "Do you have root beer?"

He never said anything. He just grabbed a big mug. He walked over to the middle of the bar, put the glass under a spout, and pulled a handle. The brown liquid poured out with a white foamy head on top. He set it on the bar.

"You want a pint to go with that?"

I shook my head no.

"Five cents then."

177

I took out one of my silver dollars and put it on the bar.

As the bartender was getting my change, Bob said to me, "Emil, we're going to get some squaws. Do you want to come?"

I shook my head no and took a sip of my root beer. The cold drink made the glass sweat, and I could draw pictures on it with my finger.

Bob and Jack stood up and each ordered two pints of whiskey. The bartender went to the far end of the bar. He opened a door and. I could not believe my eyes. There was case after case of whiskey. That room must have had two freight wagons full of whiskey. Bob and Jack each laid a dollar on the bar. They took their bottles and walked out the door that opened to the front of the building. Since Bob and Jack got up, I had a good view of the sidewalk. I couldn't hear, but the women were talking to them. I saw Jack leave. I looked to the lobby and saw him pass by the big doorway and go up the steps with a woman following. A minute or two later, Bob did the same.

There was a clock in the saloon. It was eleven o'clock my root beer was nearly done, and it was warm enough it didn't sweat the glass anymore. It was too early for dinner. I decided to go to the general store and see what kind of candy they had. As I was taking my last swallow, I heard a loud banging coming from the room at the end of the bar. The bartender turned and went to open the door. The room lightened up as a back door opened. That old white bearded man from the livery was in the doorway. He gave the bartender some money and took a whole case of whiskey. The door closed and latched. I thought to myself, *I'd better check Pete. That man will be too drunk to feed him.*

I walked out the front door and past the hotel lobby and dining room. The general store was built on the end of the dining room and hotel. It was also a wooden building. The wooden boardwalk went all the way to the general store and past to where a half-finished building sat weathering and falling back apart. On the north side of the door going into the lobby, one of the floorboards of the boardwalk was painted red. This must have been the line that the harlots must stand behind. Once I passed that board, they left me alone. I could see that if I would have gone through the lobby door and out, I would not have had to walk by them. These women had better clothes than the other Indians. I never pictured Indians in white people's clothes. Somehow I just couldn't get over the fact of the clothes. One of the women had a dress on that looked like the one Ma wore to church. I will say, Ma looked better in it. This woman was kind of fat. She had a very round face. When she smiled at me, she had a tooth missing. Some of the women were fairly pretty for their race, not so pretty compared to Swedish women.

Most of them just smiled as I walked by. Two of them said, "An hour a pint." Is that what they charged? Fifty cents for a pint. Half a day's pay for me. I'd not do that.

The general store was about the same size as the one in Oakland. It had about the same things. Yard goods, staples, a few ready mades, overalls, shoes, candy, nuts, and whatnot. The store had two other people shopping. I had plenty of time to kill, so I carefully looked at every item in the store. I was trying to figure how much I should spend. This would be a hard decision. They had licorice. Then I spotted them: brand-new dime novels.

I have not read any of these. I have never been the first one to read one. I have never bought a new one. I'm gonna. I'm gonna buy that novel. I can read it this afternoon.

I told the store owner, "I'll take the new Buffalo Bill novel, a quarter pound of licorice, and six of those peppermint sticks."

The man got everything and put it in a sack. He took a pencil from over his ear and added right on the sack. "Twenty-three cents, my good man," he said.

I gave him a two-bit piece, and he gave me back two pennies. I started for the door and stopped. Near the door in a barrel, he had peanuts in little sacks, and a sign: "2 cents." I went back to the counter and gave him back the two cents. Back at the barrel, I searched for the sack that had the most in it. I found the one I wanted, put it in my other sack, and was out the door. I was sure I hadn't killed an hour. I'd go around back and check on Pete.

The horses in the corral seemed fine. There was hay for them, and water. Pete came over. I gave him an ear scratch. *I bet Pete would like a peanut.* As I reached in the sack, I thought of Ernie's rhyme and laughed to myself. Pete seemed to like his peanut. I thought I would go put my sack in my room and wash for dinner. I don't know why, maybe curiosity, but I started around the hotel to the north so I would have to walk by those women again. As I passed the livery, I could see that old man with the white beard trading a bottle of whiskey for money from a skinny old Indian. *I guess he ain't gonna drink it all himself.*

I came around the building and climbed the stairs to the boardwalk. I walked past the women without looking directly at them.

"Hey, you."

I stopped and turned.

"Ya, you." Finally, a real pretty one, and she was talking to me.

I smiled. So did she.

Then she said, "How would you like to see me naked?"

I'd bet my eyes were as big as silver dollars. I didn't know what to say. I don't think I could talk.

"Well, do you want to see me naked?"

I couldn't talk. I think she could see that I was surprised, shocked, embarrassed, and too shy to do anything.

She smiled. "You think about it. I'll be here off and on till dark."

I turned and nearly ran into the hotel. When I hit the stairs, I did run. I ran to the top, down the hall, and into my room. I stepped in, closed the door, and latched it. I stood with my back against the door. I was breathing hard. From the fear? From the run up the steps? What was I afraid of…myself?

I crossed the room and looked out the window. I couldn't see directly below. I pushed my head as hard as I could against the screen. I pushed as hard as I dare lest I break the repair. I couldn't see that girl. There was, however, two freight wagons stopped in front of the hotel. I thought to myself, *It must be dinnertime. If I would go out and pretend to look at the freight wagons, maybe I could steal a look at her.* As I came down the last flight of stairs to the lobby, I could smell that dinner was being served.

As I passed the doorway, I could see that three of the tables were occupied. I tried my best to act calm as I walked through the lobby. I went out the door, not even looking the way of the women. The inspection of the wagons did not take long. Each wagon was loaded with fence post. They had been coated with creosote, and the smell of the freshly treated posts made my eyes water. As I walked around the wagons, I glanced at the women. I thought I could see her, but two others blocked the view. As I returned to the lobby, I snuck one more look. She was there, and our eyes met. She smiled, and I think I did too. I wanted to run back upstairs. But I controlled myself. I walked into the lobby and just looked around. I noticed a bulletin board. There was a notice of livery service behind the hotel. Below that was a small card: "Mission Church, Sunday service 10:00 am." Well, that was some good information.

I thought maybe some of the ranch crew would be in the dining room, but they weren't. I passed one table with two men, and the smell of creosote led me to believe they were the freight drivers. I sat at one of the tables in front of the windows. From where I was sitting, I couldn't see the women. The activity on the street kept my interest. I told the lady that came to the table that I was from the ranch so I wouldn't have to pay.

She pointed to a slate board. "Pork roast, apple-sauce, potatoes, and gravy. Ranch help can only have the special."

That was fine with me. Within a few minutes, I had a plate that tasted as good as it looked. A man that was well dressed came and sat at a table next to mine.

He gave his order, and while he was waiting for his food, he said to me, "Are you just passing through?"

I told him I was working at the ranch for the summer and this was my first trip to town. "Well, what do you think of our fine town?" he asked.

I thought for a second and answered, "This hotel is sure nice. I am disappointed about the way the Indians live."

"Oh yes, the Indians. Are you spending the night?"

"Yes, sir," I answered.

"Well, if you want to see the Indians at their best, tomorrow morning, go look in the lean-to behind the agency building."

His food was delivered, and he began eating as I finished mine. The lady came to my table and had me sign a meal ticket.

I got up to leave and told the man next to me, "Nice talking to you, sir."

I walked out to the lobby, and I knew where I was going. While I was eating dinner, I was thinking. If I went into the saloon and had a root beer, if I sat at a table with a view of the women, but not too close to the window, I could see that girl. I went to the bar and ordered a root beer. I was relieved none of the ranch crew was in the room. I took my root beer and walked to a table that was directly in front of where that girl was standing. I think that, since the windows were in the shade now, they could not see in unless they put their faces to the window. Most of the women were kind of heavy through the middle, but she was fairly slender. Her blue dress was unbuttoned from the top to reveal the upper part of her breast. She did not look to be much older than me. Her shiny black hair drifted in the slight breeze, and her nearly black eyes would sparkle as she looked at each man that passed. Her face was not as round as the other women, nor was her nose quite so broad. She was indeed the prettiest woman out on the boardwalk. Before I had finished half my root beer, a man came up to her. They talked for a second and then came into the hotel. They passed by the lobby doorway, and it seemed like my heart sank in my chest.

I finished my root beer, went to my room, and flopped onto my bed. I lay there thinking.

I've seen the pictures of naked women in the bunkhouse. I bet she would look as good as any of them. If I looked at her naked, I would maybe sin. I would not be pure for my wife when I got one. I could never do that. Or could I? No one in Oakland would know—I would know.

I opened my sack from the general store and took out licorice and the dime novel. The first one to read this book—me. And it was Buffalo Bill. It only took an hour or so to read a dime novel. It was a good one. Buffalo Bill came up on a wagon train that was being attacked by Indians. The people in the wagon train were not faring too well. The Indians had broken the circle of wagons and stolen a woman and a little girl. Buffalo Bill rode in with six guns blazing, dropping Indians off their ponies. The Indians knew they were no match for Buffalo Bill and retreated. One of the Indians was wounded, and he was a chief's son. Buffalo Bill took him to the Indian village and met with his father, a great and noble chief. Bill traded the son for the woman and child. Bill and the chief agreed not to fight anymore. All were happy in the end. A good book indeed, and I was the first to read it.

I lay there in bed thinking of the good story I had read. In time, my thoughts turned back to the Indian girl. *I wonder if she's back?* Ma had packed a needle and thread, but I put that in my drawer in the bunkhouse. Damn. I could have cut the repair on the screen and fixed it later. It would be so much easier to look out the window than to buy more root beer. I thumbed back through my favorite parts of the book. But that girl kept popping back into my mind. I had money. I could buy a needle and thread. As soon as that thought jumped into my mind, I was out the door, down the stairs, and over to the general store. As I walked back to the hotel lobby with my purchase, I glanced down the line of women. She wasn't there. I had my pocketknife out before I got the door latched. I ran to the window and began cutting the repair. I burst my head through the screen. They were right below me. She wasn't there. I flopped back into bed.

Why did I do this? I spent seven cents. I'm not going to do anything with this girl. I'm not. But I just have to look. I don't know why.

I spent the afternoon eating peanuts and sticking my head out the window.

She came back for about a half hour before she left with another man. This window was so high up that no one noticed me. I was enthralled by the young girl. But heck, no one could see me up there. I could look at all of them. They would just stand there. They would not talk to each other. When a man would come by, they would come to attention. They all seemed to do the same thing. They would push a little closer to the center of the boardwalk and kind of turn little pivots on the balls of their feet. Because I was looking straight down at them, it looked like they were dancing. As soon as a man would pick one, the others would fall back to the edge of the boardwalk and just stand there. I was amazed how many people sinned! Men on horseback, freight wagon drivers, hotel patrons, even a small troop of army. The girl would be gone for a while and then be back. She was never there for very long. It was nearly suppertime, and she came out to stand.

I noticed a young Indian man come from the shantytown and cross the street. He had old, torn army pants on. He had no shirt on, and his hair was long and in a single braid down his back. He walked up to the girl, and they said a few words. She reached into her handbag and gave him a pint. He opened it and took a long drink. He never looked back at her. He just walked up the street. He walked just a short distance and stopped. He took the bottle again and took a long drink. He took the bottle down from his mouth and stuck it in his waistband. Then he threw his arms out wide, arched his back, and looked to the heavens. He let out a scream that raised the hair on the back of my neck.

"Hey ya, hey ya" was the sound, but it was so loud and so long.

After that, he stood in the same position, arms outstretched, back arched, and face looking to the heavens. He stood there, and all the sounds of town quieted. It seemed like dead silence. Slowly he lowered his arms and head and continued to walk. At this altitude, I could not see the women's faces. I could see one of the women turn to the girl and say something to her. The girl brought her hand to her face as if to wipe a tear.

I went down to the lobby for supper. Over half the tables were full. The same thing was on the slate board that I had for dinner, so I ate it again. Jerry was right. It did taste good to have pork for a change.

As I left the dining room, Jerry was coming in. "Emil, ain't that pork roast good?"

I laughed and nodded my head.

I thought I might have a root beer to settle my supper. I entered the saloon and looked the room over.

In the back corner was a round table with six men seated playing cards. Two of the men were Bob and Jack. I got my root beer and sat at the same table that I had sat at earlier. From a distance, I watched the men play cards. I still watched the front boardwalk. No girl. My root beer was nearly gone when, out of the corner of my eye, I saw her pass the lobby door. She walked past the windows and down to the street. That was the last I saw of her that day.

I stood and watched the card game for a while, till one of the men said, "Sit down, or get the hell out of here."

I decided to go check on Pete. The shadows were getting long and the air was starting to cool as I walked around behind the hotel to the corral. Pete was glad to have his ears scratched, and I'd saved him a peanut. All seemed in order in the corral. As I headed back around the hotel, I looked to the north. The lean-to at the back of the agency building had four or five Indians standing near it. One of them appeared to be the younger man I had seen that afternoon. Maybe it was another Indian without a shirt. I walked past the women on my way to the lobby. There were only eight or ten of them there now, and they weren't the best-looking ones. Darkness was starting to set in on my room. I lit my light and checked out the window again. There were only seven women on the walk now. A moth flew in the hole in the screen, attracted to my light. I repaired the hole and reread Buffalo Bill.

***

There was a golden glow in the east sky. I rolled over. When I woke, the sun was shining brightly. The dreams of my overnight had my willpower nearly depleted.

I want to ask that girl to my room. If I still feel this way after church, I'm gonna do it. I can't get her off my mind.

I must have slept fairly late, as a few people were stirring on the street below. I put my good clothes on and went downstairs for breakfast. I had slept late. The clock in the lobby showed 8:40. I thought to myself, *I'll eat, check on Pete, walk overt to that lean-to and see the Indians at their best, then walk up to the Mission Church. I wonder what "Indians at their best" is? Maybe they put on their native clothes. Oh well, I'll find out.*

Bacon for breakfast was something I had been missing, and it sure tasted good. There were no women in front of the saloon this morning. The air was staying fairy cool, and it felt good to be up and about. Pete seemed fine and once again glad to have his ears scratched.

It only took a few minutes to walk from the corral to the lean-to. As I approached, I didn't see any activity. I walked over to the west end, where the opening was. A tattered old tarp covered the opening. It was pulled back partway, so I walked over and looked in. I froze in fear and shock. I stood there with my mouth hanging open in disbelief. My eyes surveyed the awfullest sight they had ever seen. Right inside the opening lay an old Indian. He was lying on his back.

He still had a whiskey bottle in his hand. His old hat lay smashed under his head. He had slobber running from his mouth, and his pants were wet. An old Indian woman had her foot over his shoulder. Her other leg was cocked up under her as she lay on her side. Her skirt was up far enough to reveal her soiled underwear. A large puddle of half-dried vomit covered with flies was near her face. Two people down from her was an old man laying buck naked. There must have been twenty people in there, some lying on the right side, some on the left, with a path of sorts in the middle. My eyes followed up the right side. I think one of the women that had been in front of the hotel was lying on the ground. She was wearing a native dress. The plaid dress she wore in front of the saloon hung from a nail above her. The right side of her face rested on a damp spot that probably was from the man lying next to her with wet pants. My eyes followed up the right side of twisted bodies, then over to the left. The same disaster of humanity continued down the left. Then suddenly my heart dropped. I took two steps in to make sure my eyes were seeing right.

It must be right. There is that blue dress hanging on a nail. My girl—my girl!

She lay next to the young man I saw her with yesterday. He had his arm draped over her with a whiskey bottle leaned against his hand, as though he had lost grip of it in his stupor. Her beautiful shining black hair was partially immersed in a puddle of vomit from his mouth. She lay there with her mouth partly open and snot running out her nostrils. A fly came out of her mouth and joined the several others dining on the snot coming out of her nose. I was frozen there. I couldn't move. Dead silence except for the constant buzz of flies. The stench of urine and vomit got to me. I ran outside and lost my breakfast. I kept vomiting even though nothing was coming out.

I suddenly felt obvious. I looked back at the lean-to, and no one was stirring. I got to my feet and headed back to the corral. I tried to walk, but I wanted to run. I never saw the old man in the livery, so I snuck back to the corral and washed my one shoe and face with water from the horse trough. I don't think anyone saw me back there. I didn't want to tell anyone what I saw. I wanted to go back to my room and hide. I thought as I walked. *If I go hide in my room, it will not help. Maybe I should go to church.*

I walked past the agency building on my way to the hill on the north end of town where the Mission Church was. I figured I was a little early, but there were no buggies or people visiting in the churchyard. I felt kind of out of place standing on the church steps. An old Indian couple walked from the east. They came right by me and went into the church. They didn't even look at me as they passed. I felt I may as well go in.

As I started to go in, I stopped. From a big building off to the right, I noticed a door open. A single-file line of about twenty-five children were headed my way. They were led and followed by two women dressed in black and white. *These must be nuns. I've never seen one of them before.*

I felt I might be in the way, so I went in and sat in the last pew. The church was even smaller than ours in Oakland. The windows let a nice filtered light in. The Catholics had an altar in the front. Above the altar was a cross with a likeness of a bleeding Jesus. The church lightened as the doors opened. I had a good view as the parade of nuns and children came by. They went slowly because each one went to one knee as they entered the pew. The children seemed to be washed clean. Their hair was all cut short like white people's. The little boys' hair seemed to bush out like it wasn't meant to be cut like that. The little ones' clothes were a mismatch of donations, and some of them wore shoes that didn't match. The doors opened two more times. Two old Indian women came in, and the man I talked to in the dining room yesterday, and his wife with a little boy and girl. They walked in and sat in the front pew on the left, opposite of the mission children. The church was dead silent. All those little children, and it was still silent. I sat there thinking. *That no-good bastard sitting in the front seat, telling me to see the Indians at their best, to look in that lean-to.* Thoughts jumped through my head, as they had ever since I looked in there.

The silence was broken by the ringing of high-pitched bells. Two bigger boys dressed in red-and-white gowns followed the priest in from a side room. The service was so different from ours. Some of it was in a foreign language, I thought Italian 'cause that Pope lives in Italy. The priest spoke a short sermon in English. He told us how Jesus died for our sins. The priest was very young. He was a good speaker. He seemed so genuine. He seemed like a man of God. I guessed Pa was right.

"Same God, yust anudder vay of vorshippin' him."

The old Indian man from the couple that came in passed a basket on a long pole, and I put in a silver dollar. He put the contents in another basket and took it to the front.

After the service, the priest led the children out, and us few others followed. The priest was very nice. He greeted us all with the same graciousness that he did the wealthy white family that followed right behind the children. I was the last one out the door.

The priest put out his hand for a handshake, and I obliged. "Welcome to our mission, son, and thank you for your generosity. I'm Father Michael Kelly. They all call me Father Mike. And you are?"

"I'm Emil Nelson from Oakland. I'm working for the summer at Cow Creek Ranch."

"I'm so glad you came to worship with us. You didn't come up for Sacraments, so you must not be Catholic?"

"No, sir," I answered.

He said that he would be glad to have me back. I started down the steps, but I couldn't take it anymore. I needed answers.

"Father, can we talk a minute?"

Father Mike got a very soft look on his face and led the way to a cement bench under a shade tree. We sat. He didn't say anything for a while, just looked at the children playing in the yard.

"What would you like to talk about?"

"My pa said that you priests were making Christians out of the Indians and they would soon be good citizens. There was hardly any Indians in church."

Once I started, I couldn't stop to even let him have a word in. Everything on my mind flew out.

"Look around. These people live worse than our hogs. All of them I see are drunk. The women are whores. Are these people worth saving? They aren't Christians. They are sinners. The only white man in church told me to look in the agency lean-to to see the Indians at their best. That was the worst thing I have ever seen. It made me vomit. Can't you do any better than this?"

Father Mike's face looked liked Able's face did when he got the wind knocked out of him. He just sat there with his head hanging. He raised his head and looked off at the children playing. He turned to me. His face looked so sad.

"I try, Emil. I really try. I pray for God's help every day." A tear came to his eye. "Father Patrick at the Omaha mission and I have talked, and we agree on the problem. His people, the Omaha tribe, always lived along the Missouri in peace. Now they're pushed up here. These Winnebago people always lived in peace over near the Great Lakes. They were free people. They fished and hunted. The women had gardens. They lived off the land and prospered. They gave thanks to their god, the Great Spirit. They were a people that were at peace with their god and man. The white people moved into their lands, and they had to move. Then more white people, and they had to move

194

again. They were peaceful people. They would not fight. They did what they were told. The government moved them to South Dakota to a reservation. They were not fighters, and the Sioux stole their horses and killed some of them. They moved down here on their own. The Omahas let them stay. The government wasn't happy with them, but they were peaceful, and the Omahas agreed to share this land with them. This was good land. The treaty gave them a good amount of land. They could not wander wherever their whims took them, but there was a good herd of buffalo here. They could have their life back. They could hunt and fish. They could thank their god for a successful kill and the food it brought.

"Their happiness was short-lived. The white men passing through brought many diseases that they couldn't handle. Over half of them died. The government let hunters in to kill the buffalo. They were stuck. No hunting. Just the beef from the white man. They lost their freedom. They lost their god. They lost many family members, with no god to welcome them to the New World promised land. They lost the independence to feed themselves. They found alcohol to make them feel better for a while. These poor people, their resistance to the white man's alcohol is as weak as their resistance to the white man's disease. But the white man won't sell it to them. So their women sell their bodies for alcohol. It beaks their hearts. It breaks their spirits. Emil, look at their eyes. There is no sparkle. There is no sparkle, just a hollow, blank look. Look at these children. We work so hard.

But without a mother and father's love, the sparkle soon leaves their eyes. Hopefully some will remain as Christians. So many leave here and are treated badly by so-called Christians. They give up and end up with a broken spirit down at the agency. There are a handful that live away from the agency and try to live their old ways. It is sad. The army and the agent are always after them. The government knows that they must kill these peoples' god, or they will have to kill these people. Without their god, they are easy to control. I have been here for two years. I am due to leave for another parish. Two years, and I don't think I've saved a soul. I've tried. I've prayed. I sometimes think I'm losing my own faith."

The priest got up and stood in front of me and put a hand on each of my shoulders. "You can't fix a broken man. Oh my God, I've tried. You can't fix a broken man."

He leaned forward and rested his forehead on the top of my head and sobbed. He turned from me and never said a word. He walked back into the church, leaving me sitting there feeling empty.

Empty.

Empty. I had never felt so sad, for these people, for Father Mike, for myself.

I trudged back down Main Street. I was in a daze. I couldn't stay here. There were three prostitutes in front of the saloon. I'm sure they didn't know what to think.

As I passed, I grasped each one's hand and told them, "I'm so sorry."

I went up to my room. I slowly changed my clothes and packed my bags. I looked at my Buffalo Bill novel lying on the washstand. The first dime novel I had ever bought. I didn't want it anymore. There was no noble red man. Men like Buffalo Bill and the men that wrote those stupid stories stole the red man's nobility! I let the book lie there. When I left the room, I passed Jerry in the hall and told him I was going back to the ranch. He told me I was nuts. I told the lady at the desk I was leaving. I walked through the saloon and out the front door, so as not to look at the women again. I collected my saddle and Pete. As I mounted up, I had a strange urge. When I got out to the trail, instead of turning west, I walked Pete back to Main Street and stopped. I looked up past the agency to the Mission Church. I followed the hill across from the church all the way to the south end of town. Why I needed to see these poor people's dwellings again, I don't know. Finally my eyes rested on the road going south out of town. The main road veered to the east. The high trail and home went straight south.

Home.

I wanted to go home.

I sat there on Pete crying. I wanted to go home. I was crying like a boy. I wanted to be a man. I wanted to be a man. I pulled the reins and walked Pete out of town to the west—to Cow Creek Ranch.

NINE

Pete plodded down the trail and crossed the bridge at the edge of town. I couldn't bring myself to even look back at the lean-to. I had been ready to sin with that girl. She was so pretty. Her young man friend, maybe her husband, I could see him standing in the street with his arms outreached. That yell. That yell. He was dying. His god was dying. His spirit was dying. His self-respect was dying. He had the prettiest wife in the village, and she was sinning for alcohol so they could have some good time together. It was already killing him, and soon she would have no sparkle in her eyes. If I would have sinned with her, I would have helped to kill her spirit.

How blind are all these men? Can't they see that they are just helping to kill these people in a slow, miserable death? Or don't they care? Do they really see them as lazy bastards that hang around the agency for handouts? Are they that blind? Are they this mean? These tribes never hurt anyone. The tribes that did kill white people did so to save their way of life. Are these men mean, or do they need someone to look

198

down on? Do they need someone to have power over just to make their shitty lives feel important? I'll bet that well-dressed man at the dining room and church was the Indian agent, "Indians at their best." I hope that bastard burns in hell.

I had never felt so empty.

Pete plodded past the last of the Indian farms and back toward the tall grass. It was hot and calm, not a soul in sight. Off in the distance, a riff of wind would roll the tops of the grass then die. What a big, beautiful land. Wasn't there room for all of us?

The men were going into the hayfield as I topped the hill to the east of the ranch. I had missed dinner. I had no appetite. I rode through the yard, put Pete away, and went to the bunkhouse. I lay on my bed. It was so hot, and I didn't feel like talking to anyone. I went out to the big creek, at the spot where John and I had fished. I climbed down the bank and sat on the ground near the water. The work in the hayfield across the creek had moved farther south, and I was alone and out of sight. I lay back and spent the afternoon rethinking the events at Winnebago.

My heart can't take it. I'll never go back.

I must have dozed 'cause I was woken by the supper bell. I started to jump up. I was really hungry now. I had lost my breakfast and never ate dinner. My hollow feeling came back over me. I'd wait awhile so I could pick who I sat next to. When I entered the grub shack, everyone was seated. As John dished my plate and looked into my face, his smile turned to a look of concern.

"I seen you ride in after dinner." Then John leaned forward and said quietly, "Eat slowly."

I didn't eat slow. Once I started to eat, I felt ravenous. By the time I finished my second plate, the room was empty.

John came over and sat across from me. "Ya come back early. Did ya see enough of town?"

I didn't want to tell John how I felt for fear I would cry. I think he could tell by the look on my face. I could tell by the look on his face that he knew what I was thinking.

"Dat town. If'n I were a boy like you, dat town would leave me brokenhearted. Emil, dat town leaves me brokenhearted. I feel guilty wit dem squaws. Hell, dey won't let me in da hotel. I have to rent a box stall in da livery. Dem poor damned people can't handle liquor. A while back, dere was an old buck dat used to beg from people dat would get off da stagecoach to stretch their legs. I saw dis whole ting. He came up to dis gent to beg, and da man pulled a derringer from his pocket and shot dat poor old Injun right between da eyes. Dat man said da Indian threatened him. Every white person around him agreed. Da agent heard da shot and come over. Dey told da agent dere story, and da agent told dem dey were free to go. Dat stage pulled out wit dat Injun lying in da street. By now a crowd of Indians gathered. Da agent spoke out: 'He threatened dat man. I'm glad he's dead. I don't like you people begging.' I heard it, Emil. Dat Indian just asked da man for a penny or maybe a five-cent piece. I heard it. If I'd of said something, I'd a been lying in da street next to dat Injun.

"My people have it tough too. Dat's why I don't never go back down south. Mr. Tom watches out for me. If sompin' would happen to me, dey'd have to answer to Mr. Tom. Your mama and pappy raised you too good, son. But dis here world ain't always so good."

I looked at John and told him, "I don't ever want to go back to that town. I don't know what I'll do on my days off, but I ain't never goin' back to that town."

John looked so concerned. "Boy, I don't know what you seen in town. Probably sompin' a young man shouldn't see. But it's life. It's a hard damned life, but it's life, and you ain't gonna change it, so's you gotta live wit it."

John sat silent with a grim look on his face. I sat there with that same empty, hollow feeling.

After a moment, John started to grin. "Dis here is da West. It's damn near gone. Next month, staid of goin' to town, go for a ride and see it. Ernie went to a place up north. He says dese damned old grass-covered clay hills turn to rock and timber and overlook dat old Missouri River. I bet dat would be sompin' to see. Whole hell of a lot better den dat nasty ole town."

TEN

The day of work that followed helped to ease the pain of my trip to town. The day after my next night watch, I sat to write Ma and Pa a letter. I told them of killing a wolf and cowboy work, cutting yearlings from the herd, and my plans to see the Ponca country to the north. I didn't mention my trip to town. I could never tell Ma of all that I saw. Maybe I could tell Pa. Maybe.

All the work continued at the ranch, the same old things, day after day. The hay lot was getting bigger. The hayfield was getting smaller. Not much smaller. Things were gearing up at the ranch. I didn't know. I didn't know that the Fourth of July was the big social event of the ranch. John was so happy. He'd say this is the best time of the year and this was going to be a big year. Tom came up to me after dinner one day and asked if I had any good clothes with me. I told him I did.

"Emil, will you help John on the Fourth of July? We are going to have a lot of guests."

I told Tom that I would be glad to help John.

Late morning of July 3, the first buggy pulled in.
By now all work was done. The big front yard was
mowed, and tables were set out. A game called croquet was laid out in the yard. Horseshoe pits were put
in on the far side of the yard. Billie had gone to town
and brought back four barrels of beer and two bushels of lemons for lemonade. I had been helping John
since yesterday getting things set up. Ernie butchered
a yearling and helped John put it on a big iron rod to
turn it over an open fire. John said it would have to
cook for near a day.

By suppertime, there were four more buggies in
the yard. John told me that by tomorrow there would
be a lot more people here. He served regular ranch
supper to the ranch hands. Then I helped him serve
a fine supper to the guests at one of the tables in
the yard. The lady from town that came from time
to time to help clean was there to help us serve. This
lady had an Indian girl with her for help. This girl
must have been from the mission. She wore a nice
dress, and she had her hair cut like a white woman.
They took care of the house dishes and silverware
and filled the guests' glasses. All John and I had to
do was fill platters and look like "house monkeys," as
John called it.

The guests varied. Some were just older couples.
Some were younger with children. One surrey pulled
in with two young men and three young ladies. These
must have been Tim's friends, as they had been
together since they pulled in. The next morning,
while I was helping John in the kitchen, I saw Tim and

one of those girls take the roans for a ride across the ranch.

Surreys and buggies pulled in all morning. John and I worked at a fever pitch.

"Dis is gonna be a fine party," John kept repeating.

None of the men worked this day. By late morning, beer barrels were opened in the grub shack for the men, and under a shade tree for the guests. The male guests pitched horseshoes right alongside the ranch hands. The ladies sat around the yard, some of them playing croquet with the children. The younger crowd seemed to stay close to the beer barrel. John had pots of corn on the cob, pans of rolls, and was slicing platters of beef and covering it with his barbecue sauce. I never saw anyone cut with a knife like John.

The whole time he kept saying, "Done to a T."

Tom came in and asked John how it was going. John told him, "Real soon."

"Ring the bell when you're ready," Tom said, and John just looked back and grinned.

A few minutes later, John announced we were ready. He rang the bell, and then we carried the last platters out to the guests' serving table. Everyone gathered in the yard, ranch hands and guests. Tom stepped forward and thanked everyone for coming. Mrs. Ryan stepped forward and stood beside Tom and led us all in "My Country Tis of Thee." At the end of the song, everyone clapped their hands.

The ranch hands let out a whoop or two and headed for the grub shack. John gave me a pat on my back. "You feed these folks good." He went to the grub shack to feed the men, and I was to stay here and help the ladies from town serve the buffet line of guests.

I had been nibbling on food all morning, and I wasn't hungry. Everyone had gone through the line, and some for seconds. It seemed as though John had enough food figured. I was just standing there trying to look dignified.

Tim walked up to me. "Emil, do you remember me telling you about the grain dealer from Sioux City's daughter? Well, she's here. I guess I'm kind of tied up with Mary today. Well, she asked who you were. I told her you were here for the summer to learn the cattle business. I told her that your family is big in grain farming and is thinking of going into the cattle business. That's why you are here. Her name is Helen."

Tim gave me a wink. I looked up and through the yard. Over by a shade tree, I noticed a pretty girl with curly strawberry-blond hair looking at me and Tim. When Tim left, she smiled at me. She was really pretty.

Tom came over and tried to be discreet. "John and the house help can finish up now. All the other men have had the whole day off. You may as well get the rest off. Since you're so well dressed, and Tim said one of the guests asked about you, you may as well stay up in the yard. Those guys in the bunkhouse will razz the shit out of you, so just hang up here so they don't see you."

I grinned. "Thank you, Mr. Ryan, you sure have a lovely party."

It was. I had never seen such an event.

I walked over to the end of the serving table and ladled out a glass of lemonade.

"Well thanks, is that for me?"

I turned around. There she was.

"I'm Helen, Helen Deshler. And you are?"

She caught me by surprise, but I didn't feel shocked or shy. I handed her the glass of lemonade. I felt comfortable with her.

"I'm Emil, Emil Nelson."

"Yes, Tim told me about you. You have to spend the summer here to learn the cattle business. Don't you get tired of doing what your parents want all the time?"

I just smiled and ladled myself a lemonade. Helen was easy to talk to. We spent the afternoon and evening walking and talking. We walked up to the bridge over the big creek. We were by ourselves. We kissed. Now, I had kissed two of the Lutheran girls back in Oakland, but Helen kissed better. At dusk, people started to gather back in the yard. We sat on a blanket near her parents and waited for the fireworks. The fountains sprayed showers of sparks and lit the night with a white glow. We held hands.

Shortly after the fireworks, the guests began to retire. Helen's parents called after her, and we said our good-byes. What a fine party. What a fun day. What decent people the Ryans were.

ELEVEN

Every day seemed about the same. The night watches were not so exciting anymore. I did look forward to night watch on a moonlit night. Ernie joined me, but we had no luck with getting a wolf. The guys that had night watch the night before gotten one, so Ernie told me the night we went out that we probably wouldn't have any luck. I really enjoyed the nights and the next days with Ernie. He told me stories of the Civil War and catching wild cattle in Texas. My stories didn't amount to much.

Ernie used to say every so often, "Stories are like wine. They get better with age."

In another week or so, I would head for the Ponca country on my days off, and I was starting to get excited for that. Ernie showed me some camping equipment he had that I could borrow for the trip. I was starting to count the days. The days always passed fast—the nights, not always. I spent some evenings going riding or slipping away to play checkers with John. The guys in the bunkhouse usually left me alone. Murphy would find something from time to time to razz me about. As the summer wore on, he had gotten into it with most of the men at one time or another. Murphy played cards with the other men quite a bit. Everyone that played cards with him usually lost. He'd make fun of them, to add insult to injury. He was short on friends.

Some of the men were on their monthly trip to the Omaha Agency. Murphy was on the day watch with a couple other men. My mower had broken down, and I was near the barn leaving it for Billie to repair. I was hooking up the spare mower. Ernie had happened by and was talking to me. We heard the sound of horse hooves and turned. Here came Bob racing through the yard.

Bob pulled up right near us. "Ernie! You asked me to keep my eyes open. Well, I think we got him. Murphy was supposed to cover the southeast sector today. I had the southwest. I had a lot of cattle right by Cow Creek, so I was behind him getting into the hills. When I started up the hill, I looked east, and I saw that asshole Murphy crossing the big creek about a half mile east of the hayfield."

Ernie had a funny look on his face. He looked mad and happy at the same time. "Bob, you cover the southeast sector, and if Murphy comes back and sees you, tell him you must have wandered over there by mistake. Emil, you cover the southwest, and when you come back in, don't let Murphy see you. I told that asshole I'd get him. I knew he would mess up."

While the men were talking, I had finished hooking the team to the mower. Ernie led the team and mower away. I headed for the corral to get Pete. From the corral I could see Ernie lead the team and mower to the hayfield. I could see him talk to Chuck, then trot back to the trail and head east.

I had gotten to ride day watch only once. We were supposed to look at every critter and check them for cuts or sickness. Ernie had told me a while back that, as the summer dries out the grass, the cattle would move farther out. They were starting to spread out now. I kept busy all day. I was really getting hungry, as I had forgotten to get a lunch before I left the ranch. I was laughing to myself off and on all day. Murphy was going to get his due. It took all day to check all the cattle. I found just two that needed cuts treated with clotting powder. I headed in from the northwest so as not to run into Murphy. I must have been fast or had fewer cattle to check. I was the first one in.

In a short time, the other men were coming in from their days' tasks.

"You keep your damned mouth shut about this whole damned thing. Nobody likes a snitch. You're gonna be gone in a month. I have to work with these guys all year round. Do you understand me?" Bob whispered in my ear when he came in.

I just nodded my head yes. I was wondering what was going to happen. Ernie was nowhere in sight. Murphy rode in as if nothing was wrong. He came by me, and he smelled of liquor. That was not too incriminating. A few of the men had a few belts before supper. The supper bell rang, and everyone headed for the grub shack.

I kind of maneuvered my way among the men. I never wanted to sit near Murphy, but I did today. We got our plates and sat. I sat not directly across from Murphy but over one. Still, no Ernie. All the dirty tricks and remarks that he'd made were running through my mind. I remembered from scripture: "Revenge is mine sayeth the Lord."

Well, I might want to play Lord 'cause this asshole has it coming. If this goes down and a fight breaks out, I'm gonna jump all over him.

I think Bob and I were the only men that knew what was going on, 'cause our eyes met when Ernie entered the room and stood at the end of our table.

Ernie spoke loud enough for all to hear. "I was in town today. Up behind the jail I found a big old mare tied. Damn, Murphy, she looked like yours. But I knew that couldn't be Murphy's. He was back at the ranch riding the herd. Ain't that right, Murphy?"

Murphy looked up at Ernie, just as calm as could be, and answered back, "You know goddamned well I was here."

Ernie reached into his shirt pocket and pulled out a blue envelope, the envelope we got our pay in. He spoke real calmly. "Ya, I didn't figure that would be your horse. The agent happened by. I asked him if he knew whose horse it was. He didn't know. So I had him watch me put a red paint stick mark on her belly. I'll be go to hell! There's a mare in the corral with a paint mark on her belly. Today's pay ain't in here. You ain't getting paid for being in town whorin' while you were leaving cattle unwatched."

Ernie kind of dealt the pay envelope like it was a playing card, and it stopped right in front of Murphy. Murphy just sat there. He turned kind of red. He picked up his envelope and put it in his pocket.

He just sat there calmly and said, "Ernie, I told you, one day I'd kick your skinny ass. Well, I guess since I don't work here anymore, today's the day."

Before he finished saying "day," the table exploded. Murphy jumped to his feet and overturned the table, with food flying everywhere. He flew to the end of the table and hit Ernie with his fist. Ernie's nose looked like it exploded, and blood spattered on the wall. He answered back with a punch that didn't seem to bother Murphy. Another fist from Murphy sent Ernie to the floor. I had never seen men fight before. It was so much more violent than I thought. I was going to jump in. I had to help Ernie. I had to help. I couldn't make myself move.

From nowhere, a fist came flying in and struck Murphy on the side of the jaw. Murphy's knees buckled, and he went down to one knee. Tom must have been down the hall, because it was his fist that came from nowhere. Ernie staggered to his knee and gave Murphy a wallop of a punch that splattered blood from his nose. Murphy fell over backward but quickly got to his hands and knees. He was fuming like a wounded bull. He was making a kind of growling noise. Tom yelled at him to stay down. Ernie, now standing in front of him, was yelling for him to get up. Murphy lunged forward. Tom hit him to the side in the head. As he wheeled over, Ernie hit him with all he had in

211

the ribs. You could hear the wind come out of him, and blood splattered as he exhaled. He was lying on the floor trying to catch his wind. Tom stepped forward and put his boot on Murphy's throat.

Tom looked down and said, "You get your ass off my land now! I wrote a letter to Sheriff Michaels in Pender and Sheriff Bond in Cumming County, and if you show up with my cattle over there, I'll be over and lynch you myself."

I had no idea how bloody a fight could be. Although Tom never took a punch, his knuckles were split open and bleeding. Ernie was bleeding out both nostrils, and he had a bump under his eye the size of an egg. His knuckles were bleeding, but not as bad as Tom's. Murphy was in bad shape. His nose was broken and bleeding. He had a big lump over his right eye that was black and blue with a trickle of blood coming from it. Under his left eye was a bruise and a cut right on the cheekbone. His jaw looked puffy, and blood ran out his mouth. To make appearances worse, his head was in a half-finished plate of beans, and the beans and sauce were spattered all over him too.

Slowly Murphy rolled over and got to his knees, then to his feet and out the door. When the screen door slammed, the room exploded with applause. Ernie told Ben to go after him and make sure he didn't steal, or tear up the bunkhouse.

Ernie added, "I already got the rifles out of there."

Everyone pitched in and straightened the tables and benches. T.T. mopped the floor. Jerry wiped the walls and tabletops. John took Ernie in to fix his nose.

Everyone seemed to hang by the grub shack till they saw Murphy ride out. It was probably the quietest it had been all summer in the bunkhouse that night. It felt so good to be able to be in the room with the other men and not have to worry about being made fun of by a bully. I lay in bed that night feeling bad. I was going to help Ernie, but I was a "chicken shit." But I was glad Murphy was gone.

TWELVE

Ernie looked so bad. He had tape over his nose. Sticking above and below the tape were matchsticks. Ernie's left eye was bloodshot, and the flesh all around it was black-and-blue. Ernie had always been friendly to me, but he was always on guard so Murphy would not make a big deal of it. Murphy was always calling me a "kiss ass." It pissed Ernie off, but he took it. I knew now that Ernie knew that Murphy would get what he had coming.

The night before I was to leave for Ponca, Ernie got out his camping gear and showed it to me again.

"I'll help you pack it the morning," he said as he piled all the stuff by his desk. Ernie took a rifle from the rack, put it in a scabbard, and set it and a box of cartridges with the pile of gear.

Ernie and I sat out on the bench in front of the bunkhouse. He seemed so happy for me going to Ponca.

Ernie told me, "Ponca is the prettiest spot on the Missouri. Lewis and Clark said it was, and they camped there." He took his finger and drew the map to get there in the dust. I already had it memorized, as he had shown it to me before. As happy as Ernie was, I still couldn't get my guilt out of my head.

Finally I couldn't take it anymore. "Ernie, I'm so sorry I didn't help with Murphy."

Ernie turned and looked surprised, but never said anything.

"I got myself seated right near him so I could help you, and when the time came, I couldn't do a damned thing. I feel like a chicken shit."

I didn't cry. I wanted to, but I didn't. I must have looked like I was going to cry. Ernie put his arm over my shoulder.

He had the friendliest soft look on his face as he said to me, "I'm sure glad you didn't jump in. That would have looked bad. It would have looked like you and I were plotting against him. Tom Ryan and I took care of it. We are the bosses. We have to show we are the bosses so these men know what we say is the way it is. Don't think you are a chicken shit. You're still a boy. That goddamned big Murphy would make most grown men think twice about jumpin' in. Don't worry. You'll be a brave man when the time comes."

Ernie made me feel better. I felt like I would like to go to bed feeling this good, but it wasn't even dusk. Ernie and I walked up to the grub shack. He said that we needed to make sure John was getting my camp grub together. When we walked into the grub shack, John saw us and grabbed the checkerboard.

"Ernie said we should check that you're getting my camp food ready," I said as we entered.

John just laughed. "I'll have you ready after breakfast. Shit, it's just one boy. Hell, I could have a whole troop of cavalry ready in two hours and not miss a damned thing."

We all laughed and sat and played winner challenge checkers till well after dark.

I must have slept at peace with myself, because I was sound asleep when the breakfast bell rang. I lay there rubbing the sleep from my eyes, not even thinking. Finally it hit me: *Days off, trip to Ponca.* I shot from bed and dressed. I started for the door, then remembered that I would not get outfitted until after breakfast. Most of the men were off to breakfast already, and I killed time slowly packing my saddlebags. With my bags packed, I walked up to the grub shack and got a plate. John winked at me as he filled my plate, and I found a place to sit. As I sat there eating, some of the men were finishing their meals and leaving. I think everyone stopped by me. A few men wished me to have a good time camping. Most of them told me I was nuts not going to Winnebago. Ernie came by and told me he would meet me at the corral in a half hour or so, as soon as he got everyone started for the day.

I helped John clean things up. He told me a few things to do while he went back to the kitchen "to get you outfitted."

In a few minutes, John was back with a flour sack bulging. He went over to the table and laid everything out.

"Now dis—" John started to say as Tom came in.

"So you're goin' to Ponca?" Tom said.

I nodded my head, and before I could answer, he continued, "I scouted that area years ago, before we moved here. It sure is pretty there. The government moved the north border of the Indian Nations to the south. I wanted to be closer to the agencies. So we picked this valley for the home place. I wanted Tim to go with you to see it. I almost had him convinced. Then he found out we had an invitation to visit the Deshlers in Sioux City this weekend, and he wanted to come with us. You have a good time, and you stay up there two nights. Head back first light Monday."

John explained how to clean river water to drink and wash, how to mix water with his powder to make biscuits, and how to rub his special salts on wild game before cooking. As John told me about each thing, he put it in the bag. Finally he gave me a sack lunch for the trip.

"You have yourself a fine time, Emil. And you tell me about it when you git back."

I assured John I'd tell him about it and headed out the door. I got partway through the yard when I heard, "Emil, wait up."

I knew it was Tim's voice before I turned back around. He was running to catch up and was in front of me in a moment. "Hey, I wish I was going with you. I have to go with my parents to Sioux City. Now, if I run into Helen, I'm going to tell her that I invited you, but you wanted to go camping. Is that all right with you? I hope it is. You haven't written her, have you?"

I turned and laughed as I said, "Yes, yes, and no."

Tim smiled. "Great. This will work out great. You have a good time, Emil. I know I'm gonna have a good time."

Tim put out his hand, and we shook on it. He turned and went back toward the house. I grinned to myself all the way to the bunkhouse. Tim lied to me about having to go to Sioux City. Tim was going to lie to Helen about me being invited. Yet, still I had to admire the way he changed the truth for his advantage. I still liked Tim Ryan.

I put my grub bag in the pile next to Ernie's desk and went to the corral. I got Pete out and saddled him and led him to the hitching rail in front of the bunkhouse. I remembered that my saddlebags were on my bed. I went to my bed, got my bags, came out, and started to put them on. Ernie rode up and told me to take my bags back off. He laid out the tent, and we laid the camping gear, saddlebags, and grub sack in the canvas. Ernie pulled my slicker out and rolled my lunch sack in it. He set them off to the side. He carefully rolled the canvas and tied it with the tent rope. There was enough rope left to tie it to the saddle and still tie my rolled-up slicker on top. We hooked the rifle scabbard to the saddle, and I was ready.

"Can you do that again when you break camp?" Ernie asked.

"I'm sure I can," I answered as I climbed into the saddle.

Ernie gave Pete a slap on the rump, and I was off.

Ernie yelled after me, "You get a deer, bring some back!"

I trotted through the yard. John opened the grub shack door and waved. Billie was hooking up the fine dapple-grays, and he waved. It somehow seemed so strange to cross the bridge and turn north in the tall grass, instead of turning south into the hayfield that now had a road worn into it from the countless trips into it.

The ranch work had made Pete a little fleeter of foot and we trotted easily along the east bank of the big creek. As we passed or crossed each feeder creek, the big creek grew smaller. Just like Ernie had said, up in a draw, I found a marshy area with cattails growing, and that would be the last spring on Omaha Creek. The Missouri River flowed eastward to Dakota City on the south and Sioux City on the north. I'd been told there was a ferry there. At Dakota City, the river turned south. Ernie told me to ride straight north from the end of Omaha Creek, and over the ridge, I would find another marshy spot with a creek coming out flowing north. I was to stay on the west side of the creek all the way there. The grass was tall and untouched. It rolled in the wind like the waves of the ocean. I had never seen the ocean, but this was what I imagined it to be. I'd never seen the Missouri River, but that was going to happen today. For a short time, I could see a graze line on the east side of the creek, but I could see no cattle. The guys said there was another ranch up this way. I think they said Ashford was the rancher's name.

Ernie told me it was about twenty-five miles up to Ponca, and if I pushed Pete, I should make it in four or five hours—just to the bluffs, not to the river. If I followed this creek, it would take me right to the river, but I should veer west toward the timber. Ernie told me he hadn't been there since 1884, and it might have changed some, but back then he never saw a soul all the way there. The hills to the east were steep, the west more gently rolling, but this creek just went north in a fairly wide valley. I never saw a soul, just tall grass and the one area that had been grazed. *This is the Wild West*, I thought to myself. In the distance I could see the hills ending and a large valley open up. I rode Pete partway up a hill, and I could see the Missouri River way out in front of me. I could see the hills to the west stretch around the valley, then head north right to the river and become timber covered. It was just like Ernie's map except for a few things. Smoke was rising over near the timber. It was a lumber mill. The valley was squared off into farms. Not all were farmed, but the whole valley had section roads, and there was a main trail disappearing off to the east. To the west, the trail disappeared over some low hills.

I followed along the base of the hills until I reached the main trail. Then I followed the trail west maybe a mile. A sign read "Ponca," with an arrow pointing north. The path had broken the grass. It was not real worn, but it was well defined. As I neared the timber, the hills got so steep the path went sideways along the side of the hills and slowly climbed till finally I reached the top. Looking north I could not see the river because the timber was heavy. Rocks poked up through the grass that was shorter up here but still untouched. I got down off Pete and let him eat some grass. I stood what I thought was facing north, and my shadow showed it to be around noon. I was hungry, so I got my lunch sack off the pack and ate lunch. It was very hot in the sun, but I could feel a cool breeze coming up from the ravine in front of me. The trail went down this ravine and looked to be treacherous. Ernie told me it would take a while to find a way down to the river, but now there was a path. As I looked around, I spotted a bald eagle soaring in the sky. All we had around Oakland was chicken hawks. This eagle was really big.

I mounted back up on Pete and headed down the trail. I had never seen this many trees before. It was like a steep tunnel. Pete stumbled as rocks rolled from under his hooves. This was all new to him, and he soon steadied himself to this new task. After only a quarter mile or less, the path opened out to a large rock shelf. It was so dark in the timber that the opening glowed in front of me. I couldn't believe my eyes when we walked out onto the rock shelf. This made the third-story window of the hotel seem insignificant. I feared for Pete, so I dismounted and led him back to the trail and tied him. I walked back out onto the ledge. I must have been half a mile in the air. The Missouri River was straight down below me. What a scene. The river must have been a half-mile wide. As it turned into a bank below me, and then as it turned east, it looked as though it widened a mile. Oh, I could see as far as the eye could see, until the white haze of the summer's day blended into the sky. There were a few farms well back from the river in South Dakota. I saw another state!

What a beautiful view. I shall take this in and remember it all the days of my life. I would much rather remember this than the lean-to behind Winnebago Agency.

I stood there for a long time. Then I wondered how beautiful the rest of this must be. I untied and mounted Pete and went back into the timber and steep path. Every so often there would be a tiny opening in the trees, and the sun would shine in and light an area like a mantle lantern. I saw two deer up another ravine. Before I could pull the rifle out, they were out of sight. The path kept going down, then finally to the right. It opened into an open area, maybe a hundred feet wide and three hundred feet long, the river on the one side and a solid rock wall climbing straight up the other side. Here I was. I was sitting on a full-sized horse, and I felt so small. *This must be the most beautiful place on Earth.*

The ground was covered with rocks, but most were covered with silt dirt from times when the river was high. The sun was completely blocked by the high rock wall. Over near the rock wall, there was enough grass for Pete. There were several spots where there had been campfires. I found a spot to put up the tent near an old campfire. Pete was glad to have the pack and saddle off. I took his bridle off and put his halter on but then just turned him loose. He went to the river to drink, then over to find some grass. I quickly unpacked and set up the tent. The ground was littered with driftwood, so I needn't cut any firewood to fix my supper. I had to go shoot my supper or eat canned beans. John had packed me some fish bait and a line and cork but only enough lard for two breakfasts of fish. I would shoot a deer.

Pa had showed me deer tracks down by the Logan Creek back home. Every now and then we would even see a deer. The ground here was covered with deer tracks. I wouldn't have any trouble shooting a deer. I walked back up the path a ways and hid behind a bush. I sat there forever. No deer. Two cottontail rabbits played in front of me, but then they disappeared. It was so overgrown down there, I had no idea what time it was. My stomach was telling me it was suppertime, and no deer. I was ready to go heat some beans, and the rabbits reappeared. They were real close—close enough to hit in the head. I aimed the rifle and touched the trigger. The echo roared up the ravine and back and forth. The rabbit did not fare well against the big Winchester. His head was completely gone.

I started a fire and dressed the rabbit. I got out the rack that Ernie sent and put the rabbit on it. I cleaned water from the river and made biscuits in a pan while the rabbit cooked. The shadows were long in the river bottom before supper was done. I don't know what it was that John had me rub on the rabbit, but it was the best rabbit I had ever eaten.

As luck would have it, as I was sitting there eating rabbit, ten deer walked down to the river to drink. I sat still and watched them. When I tried to get over to the tent to get my rifle, they fled back to the timber. I got all my stuff cleaned before dark. What a night. There was no moon, the stars were so visible, the sounds of running water made me sleep, and aside from a few mosquitoes, it was a perfect night.

Except for a dream about Winnebago that woke me, I slept all night. I don't know why I had those dreams. I didn't every night, but sometimes. I slipped my boots on and crawled out of the tent. The sun was already shining. Early in the morning of a summer day must have been the only time the sun hit the rock wall. In the shade, the moss was not noticeable. With the sun hitting it, the rock wall looked nearly as green as grass. I looked over to Pete. It looked like he had plenty of grass. I stretched the lumps from sleeping on the ground out of me and started for the woods to cut a fishing pole.

John's bait was stored in a tobacco can. It was well sealed so as not to stink up everything near it. I'd have to tell John that his bait worked in the Missouri River just as well as it did in the Omaha Creek. After about ten minutes of waiting, I had a big catfish on the line. As soon as I threw it back in, I had another. This one I left on a stringer line in the water for dinner. I cleaned and rolled the fish in the cornmeal that John sent. It fried to a T, as John would say. I left the grease in the pan to fix the other for dinner. I threw a few rocks in the river and walked the shore for a while. I had all day here. What would I do? After some pondering, I decided to explore more of the area on foot. I staked out Pete, grabbed the rifle, and took to a ravine that angled off to the southwest. I found numerous clearings. Each one had a beauty of its own. This really was a beautiful place. I walked around all morning. I never saw a deer. The rabbit seemed to be everywhere, and one came back to camp with me.

As I was cleaning up from dinner, Pete let out a whinny. It was answered back, and in a moment, two men on horseback appeared on the shore. They were well dressed and rode fine mounts with English saddles. They rode over and started to visit. The one man owned the lumber mill. The other was a banker.

I told them, "My foreman at the ranch told me of this place. He said, when he was here four years ago, there were no people here. Now I see your mill and farms springing up all over the valley."

The one man answered back "Well, I don't know how your friend came through, but the mill and our small town have been here for years. If your friend were to come back in four more years, he won't recognize this area at all. The railroad will be here next year. Then we'll have a bigger town, and all the fields will have farmers."

We spent near an hour talking of the future of this area, the ranch, my home in Oakland, and the future of the Indian Nation lands. We spent part of our time talking of the beauty of this area and the number of deer that local hunters got from here. They watered their horses and bid me farewell.

This whole shore area had been shaded since midmorning, but it was still hot. I found a little backwater and took a swim. I guess I didn't know what else to do but just sit and take in the scenery. I fixed a supper of rabbit and just enjoyed being in such a place.

After a breakfast of fish, I packed my gear. On the second try, I got it right. We climbed back up the ravine path and stopped for one more look off the rock shelf. What a magnificent view. I followed the path to the top, then down the hill that I came up. At one point, I had a better view, and sure enough, there was a small town by the lumber mill.

The ride back to the ranch was uneventful. On the way there, I was full of anticipation.

I'm so glad I got to see that area. I'm glad I got to see some of the West before it's gone. Those men said all of the land west of Omaha Creek will be farms in three or four years. I hope they don't cut all those trees back where I just came from. That would be a sin. I wonder what these grass-covered hills looked like with buffalo herds covering them?

I made good time getting back. I was back in time for dinner and an afternoon of pitching hay.

THIRTEEN

In the grub shack at supper, I had trouble eating. All the men came by and asked how my trip was. It seemed like I told the story over and over. Ernie sat across from me and smiled each time I told it.

"Isn't that spot like heaven after looking at these hills day after day?" he asked me.

"These hills look like heaven to me. Ponca was like paradise," I laughed.

By the time I finished my seconds, all that was left in the room was me and Ernie. John came and sat with us, and I told them of the gentlemen I had met at Ponca. I told them of the railroad coming and that they said this area was to be opened up for farming.

Ernie got a sad look on his face. "This ain't news to me. Tom has known of this for a long time. His lawyer in Lincoln has been fighting it. The railroad won't hurt nothing. Maybe shipping cattle would be easier. Tom's pissed off, at them selling off the Indian land that he had leased. Them Injuns are too dumb and drunk to oppose. But Tom can't fight all them bankers that want more farmers here beholden to them. The West is dying."

Ernie sat silent, slightly shaking his head.

John looked over at Ernie and grinned. "Ernie, you always say, 'Da west is dying, da west is dying,' ever since you caught da last wild longhorns in Texas. Da times, dey is a-changing. One ting dat don't change is John's catfish bait. I'll bet Emil ate catfish from da Missouri River."

I just nodded my head, and we all laughed.

Ernie said, "Well, I guess your next trip will be home. 'Bout anuther month till September first."

"I guess so," I answered.

The summer was passing fast. Ernie and I got up and left John to his cleanup. As we were heading for the bunkhouse, I thought I should write a letter home. Ernie let me use his desk, and I sat and wrote.

Dear Ma and Pa,   August 3, 1888

I hope you are all good. I hope Able is healing fine. Last month I made a trip to Winnebago Agency and was so disappointed with the plight of the Indians. Along with my troubles at the ranch with a bully, I was ready to come home. I know that you are counting on my wages, so I turned around and came back to the ranch. I was so glad I did. The Fourth of July was great, and the bully was caught slacking at his job and sent packing. I just returned this day from a place up on the Missouri River called Ponca. It is the most beautiful place I have ever laid eyes on. There are rocks and timber, such beauty. Pete is becoming a very good cutting horse. I bet he will not want to be a workhorse again. I will probably not write again, as I will be coming home soon. I love you all.

Your son Emil

I sealed the letter and took it up to the mailbox in the grub shack. John was just sitting there smoking. He quickly grabbed the checkers when I offered. We played and talked until bedtime.

The next morning I was put back on the mower. Just by looking, I thought that in less than two weeks, mowing should be finished. The job had not improved. It was monotonous, with lots of time to think. I had so much to think about: shooting a wolf, Indians at the agency, Helen Deshler, Ponca. The thought of the poor Indians sickens me to this day, and I think they always will. I still see the Indians in the lean-to in my dreams. My girl and her young man lying there in their condition still makes my stomach crawl. Helen. She was the prettiest girl I had ever seen. I could tell by talking to her that she lived such a fine life, that I could never match up to give her the life she was accustomed to. I just couldn't see her with a fine dress and curly hairdo, out in the yard, chopping heads off chickens for supper. I knew that Tim had been up in Sioux City with her these last few days and had probably coaxed her into kissing him. I thought Tim was just telling me a story about touching her breast. She was too nice to let anyone do that. That Tim would stretch the truth to his advantage.

According to Ernie's calendar, the moon would be full in two weeks. *I sure would like to shoot another wolf. That excitement of seeing them closer and closer is something I'd like to have again. I can't wait.*

The morning passed, and as I was heading in for dinner, I saw the Ryan's fine buggy and team coming home. After dinner, Chuck went to raking, and Mike and I each started mowing another section. About an hour later, a horseman galloped through the field. I did not recognize him as he passed me and rode over to Mike. I was on the far side of my section. I saw the rider pull up to Mike and slide from his saddle as Mike pulled up his team and flew off the mower seat. The rider grabbed Mikes hand and pulled him to him in a friendly embrace. They were talking as I got to the side of the section I was mowing that was near them. I pulled up my team, and as I was getting off the seat, Tom Ryan and Ernie raced up. We all gathered in front of them.

Mike said, "This is my brother. He came to get me. My pa is most likely dying. Pa cut his leg on a scythe. The doc stitched it, but he lost too much blood. Now it's infected, and Doc don't give him much of a chance to make it. I should maybe go home."

Tom told him, "Yes, Mike, you go get packed and get home to your family. I'll get your pay. I don't think you need to come back this summer. We only got a week or so left of haying. You've been good help. You write me and let me know how things turn out. And there will be a job here for you next year if you need it."

Ernie grabbed Mike's hand and helped pull him up on the rear of his horse, and they headed for the bunkhouse with the brother following. Tom raced over to talk to Chuck, then raced back to the ranch house.

Chuck had another man take on the hay rake, and he took over Mike's mower. About a half hour later, I could see two riders cross Cow Creek and head out southwest over the hills at a good pace. Within a short time, the excitement of the day passed, and the *chich chich* of the mower lulled me back to my thoughts again, and the afternoon crept by.

The next week, I had my turn at the night watch. The herds kept moving farther and farther from Cow Creek in search of new grass. It was after dark when I got to the three cedars. Bob was my partner this night, and he was later than me. He spent the night telling of his last trip to Winnebago, his luck at the poker table and all the squaws he could afford with his winnings. As he was telling me about the time he spent with the young girl in the blue dress, I tried not to hear him. Instead I looked at the crescent moon and thought of my time with Ernie and the cow moon. I kept repeating to myself "The Boy Stood on the Burning Deck" until he was done talking. Bob took the first nap.

I sat under the stars and crescent moon, left to my thoughts. I had tried to shut out Bob's story, but I heard it anyway. He told of her beauty and eagerness to sin. I had been so close to falling into sin with her.

There were times as I grew older, there were things as I grew older, that it was hard sometimes to figure out right and wrong. There were times when wrong felt so right, and I knew it was still wrong. At those times, I wished I still had my Bible, the one I threw in the creek. I had spent my summer falling away from God. When I returned home, I'd be extra fervent in my devotion to Him. I sat there awhile longer, and soon my mind went back to the girl in the blue dress. I hated this. As soon as I thought of her, her smile, her question—"Would you like to see me naked?"— my mind flashed, and all I saw was her lying in vomit with a fly climbing out of her mouth to join the other flies dining on the snot running out her nostril. It still sickened me.

I would like to think of her pretty. Or me seeing her naked. As soon as I start to see myself in these situations, I just get the vision of the lean-to. It's just like every time I hear the crash of something into boards, I see Able flying in the air, lifeless. Is this my payment from God for thinking of sinning with that girl? For being glad Able got hurt so I could have this adventure to myself to tell my grandchildren about?

Other than my trip to Ponca, there ain't a part of this summer that I would tell the little ones about. Even on the Fourth of July, I had sinful feelings about Helen. I really need to return to God.

I woke Bob and took my turn to nap. I lay there and looked at the crescent moon and stars, and tears ran down my face. *God forgive me.*

***

Two rain days slowed the mowing, but it was getting close to the end, maybe two more days. Tomorrow night, Ernie and I had night watch, and the next day I had off. I started the first cut in the field. I would have liked to have the last cut. Chuck came over as I finished the day's mowing, and we looked over what was left of the field. He thought the same as me: six sections, tomorrow or the next day. I somehow didn't see Mr. Ryan kneeling in the field, praying like Pa did when we finished planting corn.

I headed in and after supper was lying in bed day-dreaming. The bunkhouse door opened, and Mr. Ryan came in and hung the letter on the wall near Ernie's desk. The men gathered around it. Most walked away laughing. As the crowd thinned, I hopped from bed and looked to see what was amusing the men.

Dear Mr. Ryan,   August 14, 1888

Thank you for the work this summer. My brother and I got back to Pender before dark. Pa passed away just after dawn the next morning. Ma is not taking it well. My brother started farming his own place two years ago. I must take over for Pa. I am planning to marry this fall and was planning to start farming on my own. Now this is certain. I doubt very much I will come back to the ranch for work. If circumstances change, I will contact you.

Four days ago Murphy met his fate. He was found a half mile out of town with a load of buckshot in the back of his head. He had mercilessly beaten a man in the saloon the night before. The sheriff says that man had an alibi. So the sheriff has no leads. I don't think he'll look too hard. Murphy caused the sheriff more grief than the whole rest of the town.

Thank you again for the work.

Mike

I walked away laughing just like the other men. And just as I was thinking it, I heard someone across the room say it.

"That bastard got what he had coming."

FOURTEEN

Last night, while I was sitting outside, I could hear at least three different wolves howling. None of the other men had gotten a shot at any. Hopefully Ernie and I would get a whack at some tonight. Thinking about the wolves made the day pass. My last day on the mower! Less than two weeks and I could go home. There were times that this summer felt like it lasted forever. There were times it felt like it flew by. When I first started mowing this field, the grass was lush, and the seed stems were just starting to open. Now the summer's heat had the grass shrunk back and kind of yellow. The seed stems were just empty sticks pointing in the air. The hay dried faster now. The guys on the pitching crew were only two and a half days behind the mowers. With tomorrow off, I wouldn't get to cut the last of the hay. But I bet I'd get to pitch the last of it. The field had narrowed due to the eastward bend of the big creek. In the afternoon, I cut a smaller section that bordered the creek.

I finished early and headed in. I met up with Ernie and had an early supper.

John gave us our lunch sacks and me a pat on the back. "You git you a wolf tonight, Emil."

I answered John as I walked out the door, "If one gets close enough, he'll lose his ears."

We saddled and headed out. Ernie headed west. I headed across Cow Creek to check the southeast sector. It seemed like I always checked this sector. The times I checked the northwest sector, it was about the same. On the west edge of the ranch, the hills weren't quite as steep. But it was pretty much the same hills, grass, and cattle. I checked around to the east and then moved to the south. The cattle had moved a little farther in the last week. I had such a good feeling all day that we'd get a wolf tonight. I stopped and pointed at a couple jackrabbits that flushed from near Pete's hooves only to run about forty yards and stop and watch. I didn't know why those wolves would try a calf. These jackrabbits were thick as fleas on a dog's back. In my mind, I kept seeing that wolf roll back when I shot him. I could feel my heart race every time I would think of it.

The heat of the day had forced the cattle to gather in herds of a circular shape and just stand there. I don't know why cattle do that. I would think it would be cooler to be off by one's self. But the cattle stood there chasing flies with their tails, and wiggling their skin the way they do to chase flies. Flies drove the cattle crazy at this time of the year. If one got cut and we didn't get it treated, the flies laid eggs in the cut, and the maggots got them. Once that happened, all we could do was shoot them and put them out of their misery. When the cattle were in groups like this, it was easy to check them. I was over at the three cedars before sunset. Ernie must have had the same luck, as he arrived at the cedars within ten minutes of me. We set out our saddles and put the horses out to graze.

Ernie and I talked of the herd check and watched as the sun set. The white haze of the day just hung in the air. The breeze hardly moved the grass. It was hot and dry. The sun simply dropped over the far hills with no change of color, just a white haze. It was still hot. I looked over at Ernie, and he was nodding off.

Finally, Ernie just lay back. "I'm gonna snooze a minute, Emil. You may as well do the same."

I went ahead and lay back on the ground. As excited as I was, I still knew it would be well after dark before we would see anything. Soon my eyes were blinking, and I dozed off.

Something woke me. I had drool running out the corner of my mouth. I wiped my chin on my shirt sleeve. It was not totally dark yet. I must have only slept for ten or fifteen minutes, but it did refresh me. I sat up and watched the hills darken and the moon start to rise in the east. Off in the distance to the north, a wolf howled his greeting to the moon.

I saw Ernie open one eye and not move a muscle. After a moment, he spoke in a low voice. "Sounds like those critters are waking up."

When we spoke, we spoke in low voices. We moved over and sat with our backs against the tree trunks so as to obstruct our silhouettes. Ernie told me that there had been twelve wolves shot off the ranch this year.

"Maybe they're getting thinned out?" I asked in a low voice.

Ernie answered back in a near whisper, "No, they move around. There are still plenty of them. You remember from last time, if they ain't howling, they can be standing next to you, and you don't even know it."

We sat as the moon climbed in the sky. Every so often a wolf would howl in the distance, and Ernie would look over at me and wink. It was hard to judge, but I don't think I heard a wolf howl within three miles of us. The excitement of the day was starting to wane. Last month we sat here all night and never had one close. I was starting to resign myself to an unsuccessful hunt. The hope, and memory, of success kept me alert till at least midnight.

"Did you hear that?" Ernie said in a whisper.

I strained my ears. I could hear nothing. Suddenly I could hear the very faint sound of a cow in distress. Ernie could tell by the look on my face that I heard it.

"Right straight over that hill, don't you think?" Ernie said, this time with his arm outstretched and finger pointing.

I nodded my head. I saw Ernie's hand reach down in the moonlight and grab the Winchester.

"Be quiet now. Let's saddle up," Ernie said as he carefully rose to his knees, looking in all directions, and then carefully rose to his feet. He stepped like a cat and never made a noise. I did my best to follow his moves. I had seen this look in Ernie's eyes before. The look was total concentration, a look that was so intense, like the look of a cat in the haymow just as it jumps on a mouse that you could not see. This was the look he had the day he faced Murphy.

We saddled the horses. We remained as silent as possible.

Just as we mounted, Ernie said to me in a whisper, "Emil, you stay back at least twenty yards. You follow my hand signals. You keep that horse right in my hoof prints."

He looked at me as he spoke. His eyes still had that intense look. His face was stern. Ernie was going to put all his hunting skills to the test. Last time those wolves just walked into us. It was easy. This time we were going after them.

Oh, this is so exciting. I'll learn a lot of hunting tonight.

Ernie's big cutting horse must have done this before. As we walked over to saddle the horses, Ernie reached out his hand, palm down, and pumped it up and down, like a schoolteacher trying to quiet a class. When Ernie turned his palm up and motioned for his mount to come, he did so without making a sound, voice or hoof. Pete must have known that we were to be quiet. He followed at the deliberate pace that Ernie was setting. His ears were cocked forward and alert. We carefully walked down the hill to the east and up the next one.

As we approached the top of the next hill, Ernie motioned for me to stop. He moved his horse up near the top of the hill. The horse took such tiny steps.

Ernie took his hat from his head. I could see his plan. He just barely put his head over the top of the hill so the wolves would not see him if they were in that valley. Ernie backed his horse down slightly, then traveled around the hill so as to keep us out of sight. He motioned for me to follow. We slowly worked the hilltops, looking both north and south but moving east. As I watched Ernie hunt, it kept reminding me of a cat sneaking through the tomato vines of the garden hoping to pounce on an unsuspecting sparrow. This was a slow process as we worked our way east. By now we must have been at least two miles from the cedars.

The moonlight was very bright now, and my eyes were quite used to it. Ernie topped a hill, and I stood silent below. He backed down and walked around the ridge. Before he started around the ridge, he motioned for me to stay still. I watched as he carefully climbed to the top of the hill again and studied the situation. He carefully descended and motioned for me to follow. He must have seen something. This time, we turned to the north and went all the way to the bottom. Ernie took the Winchester from the scabbard. He motioned for me to do the same. I did. He cocked the lever to put a cartridge in the chamber and set the hammer in the half cock position. I did the same. Then he moved farther down the valley and to the northeast. I could hardly hold still.

He found the wolves. We're gonna get them.

Slowly he turned back to the south and stopped. Ernie motioned me to come up as he dismounted. I dismounted and readied my rifle.

Ernie walked so quietly over to me and whispered in my ear, "Stay here. I'll go check it out. Be quiet. We're real close, I think." Ernie walked to the rise of the low hill we were behind. As he walked, he pointed at the bleached bones of an unfortunate cow. The white bones glowed in the moonlight. Ernie stopped. Then he took his hat off and laid it on the ground and crawled to the top. I could see him slowly raise his head and peek over. He carefully slid back down and motioned me to come. My heart was starting to pound just like last time. This time we hunted them down. As I neared Ernie, I could hardly control myself. He leaned his mouth toward my ear.

He whispered so low I could hardly hear him. "We did it. You'll have something to tell your grandchildren about now."

Oh boy, we're gonna kill some wolves now, I thought. Ernie motioned for me to follow his lead. He carefully crawled with his rifle in his right hand. Then he shinnied on his belly like a snake. My heart was pounding. I shinnied up next to him and stopped. Ernie motioned for me to raise up and look. I did.

Oh my God!

I couldn't believe my eyes. It wasn't the wolves I had expected. It was an Indian.

He was standing in front of a dead steer. There were two arrows projecting from the steer's forward rib cage. The Indian had his hair down, but I could make out the waves from it being in a braid. He was totally naked. He had a pole in his hands. He raised the pole and put the butt end of it on the carcass

241

about where the heart should be. He straddled the carcass so he was pointing north. There he stood with the pole on the beast's heart, facing north. He began to sing in a loud voice a rhyme of sorts in his language.

I ducked my head down. I didn't even notice that Ernie had raised his head. When he saw me duck, he did the same. I think he saw the fear in my face.

Ernie put his finger to his mouth. "Shush. If we take him now, we'll be chasing that damned pony all the way back to Winnebago. It takes 'em 'bout twenty minutes to do this praying."

I can't imagine the look on my face. I must have looked terrified.

"You'll do fine, Emil. It's about the last chance you'll have to get an Injun," Ernie whispered.

Oh my God, he wants me to kill this man.

Ernie whispered again, "Don't worry. It ain't much different than shooting a wolf. Both damned cattle thieves."

I couldn't justify shooting a man. My mind was so confused. I was shaking. The Indian's voice stopped, then started again. I peeked up, and he still had the pole on the steer, but now he was facing east and singing.

Is this one of the few trying to keep their religion? The ones that Father Mike told me about? I cannot kill him. I just wanted to work on the ranch. Be a cowboy. I had no idea that I would have to kill an Indian.

I looked over at Ernie. He was watching the Indian, too. He still had that same expression on his face.

This Indian is going to die. If I don't do it, Ernie will.

The tone of the Indian's voice changed.

Ernie motioned us down. "He'll be praying to the west next. We best stay down—he may see us. Ain't this exciting, Emil?"

I chased a lump from my throat and whispered back, "Ya."

No cowboy in the dime novels ever balked at killing an Indian. He is, after all, a cattle thief. I may as well shoot him. He'll just end up a drunk like the rest of them. Thievin' damned Indian, I'm gonna shoot you.

I tried and tried. I couldn't justify killing him. What could I do? Ernie could shoot a running wolf. If I would yell a warning, Ernie would shoot before he could run far. Ernie would be mad at me, maybe send me packing. I would not kill a man. God would not forgive me, even if this Indian were a pagan.

What can I do? Oh God, help me.

I lay there with my heart still pounding. My head was spinning. I needed a plan. The singing started again. Just as I raised my head, it hit me.

I got it! I got it! I'll tell Ernie that I'll do it. Then I'll miss him, and he can run. This might work. I'll just be blamed for being a poor shot. This will work.

I felt such relief now that I had a plan. The Indian was now facing south with both hands on this pole. A few years back, he would have been standing over a buffalo, thanking his god for a good hunt and food for his family. But the government let the hunters kill all the buffalo. Now all he could kill was Mr. Ryan's cattle. I felt sorry for both men, Tom for losing a cow and the Indian for having to use a cow

243

instead of a buffalo. The song of prayer was solemn and sad.

What if this is the last Indian that knows the prayers? Indians don't write. They must have to teach one another. What if this is the last Indian to know this ritual?

The Indian finished praying to the south. He laid the pole the length of the steer and stood by the head. He outstretched his arms and arched his back. He arched so far his face was looking straight up. He started to say something in a low voice. Then he repeated it a little louder. Each time he repeated it, it was louder. Louder and louder, until it was as loud as he could yell. Then he folded his arms in and straightened his back. He moved in one steady motion down to one knee on the ground and a crouching position with one knee up and his head resting on it. He fell silent for several moments. He rose to his feet, picked up the pole, and walked over to where his pony was waiting. I had no idea what he was saying. His reverence to his god was more devout than anything I had ever seen. It moved me more than the preacher at the tent revival that came to Oakland last year. His god, his ritual, his devotion, all staged in the bright moonlight.

Ernie whispered, "It won't be long now."

The Indian put on his native trousers and moccasins. He got something out of a pouch that hung around his pony's neck and went to the carcass. He pulled the arrows out of the steer and held them up to the heavens. Then he put the arrows over by the pony. He took out a knife and began to cut the hide off the steer. I couldn't tell exactly what he was doing in the dim light, but he worked his way around the carcass. He moved up around the neck and cut and pulled on the hide until he had worked a flap of hide loose. It looked like he had a stake or pin of steel or something that he stuck through the flap of hide. I felt Ernie's foot hit mine. I looked over, and he tipped his hand up and raised his index finger. It must be time soon. My heartbeat had slowed during the ritual. Now it was pounding, and I was soaked in sweat.

Oh God. I closed my eyes and prayed like I had never prayed. *Dear Heavenly Father, deliver me from this trial. Let this man of God escape. I don't know if you are his god. But you are my god, and please let him escape. Through Jesus's name. Amen.*

I opened my eyes, and the Indian was by his pony. He had a lariat around his neck. He led the pony over to the rear end of the carcass and took the loose end of the lariat and tied it to the pin that was stuck through the flap of the hide. Ernie tapped my foot with his again. I looked over. Ernie's face looked so stern. He looked like a different man. Ernie always wore his hat, and the crease from the hatband was pressed into his unkempt hair. The moonlight coming over his stern face made him look almost scary.

Ernie put his mouth near my ear. "Next time I tap you, take him. Take aim."

I raised the Winchester. It felt like it weighed fifty pounds. I brought the barrel down on the Indian, then off to the side. My barrel followed him as he went to the steer's head. The Indian straddled the head of the steer. He pulled the chin straight up, forcing the horns of the steer into the ground. The Indian dug his heels into the ground and pulled back on the chin of the steer. As he did this, he yelled something to his pony. The lariat tightened as the pony pulled on the hide. As I dreaded, I felt Ernie's foot tap mine. I pulled back the hammer, made sure I was off to the side, and touched the trigger. A piece of sod flew in the air as I heard the explosion of the gun. The Indian stood up and fell to his side, then rolled to his back. He was screaming in pain. His arms and legs were flailing. I looked over. There was smoke drifting upward from the end of the barrel of Ernie's rifle.

"You got him, Emil!" Ernie sprung to his feet and put his hat on. "Did ya see how I used those bleached bones to mark the spot where we needed to get to? Good job of tracking, even if I do say so myself. Thievin' damn Injun didn't know what hit him. Ten-dollar bonus for you."

What was going on here? I didn't shoot him. I didn't do it. I couldn't move. I couldn't get up. Ernie was up, happy, and nearly dancing, just like it was when it was a wolf. This was a man. A man. "Thou shalt not kill." What was I a part of? These poor people. A pint of whiskey an hour for a woman, and ten dollars for a dead man. Now I was a part of it. I felt sick.

I got up to my hands and knees and took one more look as I was getting to my feet. The pony was pulling for all it was worth. The hide was about a fourth off, and the pony had dragged the carcass about ten yards. The Indian was quiet now, just his arms flailing. Our horses must have spooked at the report of the guns. They were still not far off. Ernie gave a whistle, and his horse came prancing, with Pete following. We grabbed the reins and walked over the rise and down to the scene of the crime. Ernie led the way. He walked over to the Indian and spit on him. Ernie put his rifle in the scabbard.

"He's gutshot. He won't last long. He ain't worth another bullet."

I did not go too close. I had never seen a man dying. The only dead man I'd ever seen was Johnny's grandpa. He was old. Ernie went to work making a halter from a lariat to hook to the pony. I didn't want to look at the Indian, but my curiosity got to me. I put my rifle in the scabbard, let go of Pete's reins, and walked over.

He was lying still now. The moonlight was reflecting off the puddle of blood he was lying in. He had a hole the size of a dollar, maybe a little bigger, just below his rib cage, just a little to the right of center. There was a piece of intestine or something sticking out of the hole oozing a yellow substance that was mixed with blood. The liquids ran down his belly, filled his belly button cavity, then flowed over his left side and into the puddle. His chest was heaving in and out, and a slight gurgle could be heard with each breath. Right in the middle of his chest, the moon reflected off Ernie's spittle. I looked to his face. A little blood tricked out of the corner of his mouth. His eyes. His eyes were so dark brown, black in the moonlight. He looked into my eyes. His eyes did not look angry. His eyes pierced mine. I could feel his fear. I could feel the fate he knew was his. I felt sick, and the smell of his body fluids and that of the steer put that familiar lump in my throat. I ran off to the side and vomited.

"These are hard things for a young man to see. Lots of young men had trouble in the war. Don't worry. You'll get over it." I didn't realize that Ernie had walked over to where I was leaned over. He put his arm over my shoulder and guided me over to the steer. "Let's finish up here. You get the head just like the Injun did."

My stomach was not up to this job, but I did not vomit again. I held the steer's head, chin up and horns to the ground. On command, Ernie's horse led the pony to pull the hide back as Ernie helped by cutting along the way. Soon the hide was off. Ernie laid the hide out meat side up. He handed me the Indian's knife. It was a steel knife with a bone or wood handle wrapped in rawhide straps. It was well-worn but sharp. I was sure it was his prize possession.

Ernie said, "You get a souvenir. Use it to cut four straps about an inch and a half wide off that hide as long as you can make 'em." He went to his saddlebag and got another butcher knife. He started cutting the back loins from the carcass. I started cutting the rawhide straps like Ernie told me. We worked in the silent moonlight.

The gurgling sound of the Indian's breathing got louder and closer.

Suddenly the silence was broken. "Hey ya, hey ya."

I looked over, and the Indian's arms were reaching up. He was shouting as loud as he could manage.

His words were familiar. They were the same words the young Indian man on the streets of Winnebago had screamed—or cried.

I worked at my task, trying to keep my mind off what was unfolding about me. The Indian kept this chant up for a couple minutes. I looked up. As his voice weakened, his arms collapsed. His left arm fell to his side, with his forearm and hand splashing into the puddle of blood, his right arm over his chest. He was silent. I looked over at Ernie. He was looking at the Indian. His mouth started to open as if he were going to say something. The gurgling noise started again. Ernie went back to work. The breaths of the Indian were very slow now. Then they stopped. I looked up at Ernie. He looked over at the Indian, then back to me. When our eyes met, he just nodded his head and went back to work. I went back to work too. I just watched my hands work. I wasn't there. I didn't know where I was. I was cutting hide.

But this whole scene is so unreal. Am I really doing this? Is this a bad dream? Or will it be a bad dream?

I finished cutting the straps, and Ernie was laying big pieces of meat in the hide. I just stood silent as he finished.

"Well, that's the best of what we can save," Ernie said as he straightened up and arched his back as if to stretch his back muscles.

He walked over to the Indian and grabbed a big hunk of hair from his forehead. He pulled the hair tight and took his knife and cut the flesh of his forehead down, removing the piece of scalp that was hooked to his handful of hair. He held it up and looked at it. Then he threw it to me. I didn't reach a hand to catch it, but put my hands to my chest. The scalp hit my upper thigh and fell to the ground. Ernie walked over picked it up as I stood frozen. Ernie didn't look at my face. Maybe he already had. He just turned and started for his horse. He took a couple steps, bent down, and wiped the blade of his knife on a clump of grass.

"Ya, we turn these scalps into the agency next delivery, and we get paid for the head we lost. We used to get quite few of 'em. We ain't got one since early spring. I guess them Injuns are learning their lesson."

Ernie went over to the pony and led him over. He was still tied to Ernie's horse, and he followed over at Ernie's command. Ernie led the pony over in front of the Indian, then pushed on the pony's side to make him move back over the Indian's torso. The Indian lay directly under the pony at right angles.

"Emil, get over here and hold this pony."

I couldn't bear to do it. But I watched myself walk over and do it. Ernie went over to Pete and got a rope out of my saddlebag and came over to the Indian. Out of the corner of my eye, I could see the Indian's arms flop over. I didn't look down. I could hear the sound of Ernie tying with the rope. I looked down. The Indian's mouth was partly open. The blood that ran down from both corners was starting to coagulate. His eyes looked straight ahead in a blank stare. The hole from the missing piece of scalp exposed his skull bone. It was ghastly. I felt that lump in my throat. I tried to breathe in to stave off the vomit, but the stench of death was all I breathed in. I had nothing left in my stomach. That was all that kept me from vomiting.

Ernie apparently had the Indian's hands tied because he set the coiled rope on the pony's back. He went and got Pete. Ernie tied a harness loop in the rope and put it over Pete's head.

"Hold that pony still now."

Ernie led Pete until the rope tightened. Pete leaned into it, and the poor Indian was pulled up and over the side of his pony. Ernie untied the rope from Pete and the Indian's hands and put it back in my saddlebag. He went over to the carcass and got two of the rawhide straps. He started under the pony to tie the Indian on.

"Pull that pony ahead so I ain't in the blood," Ernie continued. "This here is our mark. Injun comes back to town tied up with green rawhide, they know he was cattle thievin'. Agent won't do nothing but budget a little more money when the next month's order comes in and he gets the scalp. He gives Tom the price of the missing critter plus ten dollars for the scalp. I heard some guy from Sioux City buys them scalps from him for thirty dollars and then sells them back east for big profit."

While Ernie was talking, I noticed the pouch tied around the pony's neck. I pulled the Indian's knife from my belt, took one more look at it, and put it in the pouch.

Ernie stood up, grabbed the Indian, and shook him to make sure he was securely tied. He went to his horse and untied the lariat. He came back to the pony and undid the makeshift halter.

Ernie finished coiling his lariat as he walked to the rear of the pony. "Cut him loose."

I let go of the pony as Ernie swatted him on the rump with the coiled lariat and let out a big "hya, hya."

The pony ran off to the east with his passenger's hair, or what was left of it, blowing in the breeze. I just stood there watching as the pony disappeared over a distant hill. Ernie sat on the ground and rolled a cigarette. I just stood there. I was drained. I could smell Ernie's tobacco smoke. He never spoke.

"Let's load her in," Ernie said as he got to his feet.

He went over to the hide and somehow fashioned two big saddlebags filled with meat out of that hide and the straps I cut. I helped him lift them over the rump of his big cutting horse, and he secured it.

"Looks like it's breaking light. Let's head in."

I never answered. I just mounted and followed Ernie.

I had no idea where we were. I just followed Ernie as he was stalking his prey. Ernie headed north. Soon, I recognized a familiar hill. We were only a couple miles south of my starting point that evening. I was just drained. As before, I was going through the motions. It felt like I was just watching myself, like I had no control. I was just doing what I was supposed to do. I had a bad taste in my mouth. Probably from the vomit. Probably from not opening my mouth. I don't think I'd said a word since I saw my prey was an Indian. We were making good time, and I didn't realize it. We were nearing the creek.

Can I talk? I don't feel like I can. I must be able to.

"Come on, Pete. Cross the creek, Cow Creek."

FIFTEEN

By the time Ernie and I got to the ranch yard, the men were heading for breakfast. Ernie rode up to the grub shack with the meat. I went to the corral with Pete. I put my tack away and carried the scabbard and rifle back to the bunkhouse. I couldn't eat. The smell of blood was on my clothes. I had to bathe and wash my clothes. I went to the washhouse and heated water.

T.T. stuck his head in. "Hey, lucky night."

It wasn't luck. I thought back on it now, that look on Ernie's face. He knew we were going after an Indian the first time he heard that cow beller. The Ten Commandments. "Thou shalt not kill." That one never bothered me. I'd never kill anyone. Now I had. What could I have done to stop it?

The thoughts of the night kept going through my head as I bathed and did my clothes. I hung my clothes and went back to the bunkhouse. Ernie had washed up and was lying on his bunk snoring. I was exhausted. I fell into bed and fell asleep.

The Indian in the street had his arms outstretched, his back arched, arched to the point his face was looking up to the heavens. I was on the street this time. I was right behind him. He was crying his prayer. He spun around and looked right in my face. His face—oh my God—his face was that of the dying Indian.

"Emil, you killed me."

"No. No."

I jumped from my bed. He was still there.

"Emil, you killed me."

I dropped from his view, onto the floor. I couldn't see him now.

He still yelled, "Emil, you killed me!"

"No, I didn't. No, I didn't."

He grabbed me. "I got you now." He was going to kill me.

"No, no, please don't. I didn't do it."

He grabbed me so hard it felt like he was crushing me. "I'm going to kill you."

I looked up. The Indian was gone.

"I'm not going to kill you." It was Ernie's voice. It was Ernie. "Are you all right, Emil?"

I turned and looked up at Ernie's face. He looked scared. I'd never seen him scared. He knelt down beside me and hugged me into him. "Emil, you had a bad dream."

I was trembling. It may have started with a dream, but when I woke up, that Indian was right here, right on the other side of the bed.

"Stand up, Emil," Ernie said in a voice so gentle I couldn't believe it came from him. He helped me to my feet. "You'll be OK now."

I was still trembling, and all of my silence through the whole ordeal ended as I began shouting. "I didn't kill that Indian. I wanted no part of it. I was going to scare him off. You did it, not me. You knew we were hunting Indian. You never asked me if I wanted to be a part of this. All of a sudden we were there, and I couldn't get out of it. You act like we shot a wolf, cut the scalp for bounty. I think we killed a man. If you told me back at the three cedars we were going after an Indian, I would not have gone. It's you that wanted to kill that man, not me. I wanted to yell him a warning, but you would have shot him anyway."

Ernie looked like he'd had the wind knocked out of him. "I shot that Injun. You missed. I didn't say anything. I just thought I'd surprise you. I thought any young man would like to shoot an Injun. The West is dying. A man won't get many chances to kill an Indian anymore."

I fired back, "You act like it's nothing, like smashing a bug on the floor. It was a man damn it, a man."

I was furious at Ernie, but his arm around me felt so comforting. We sat back on the edge of my bed and just sat there in silence.

"Come on. Let's go see if there's something to eat at the grub shack. You ain't ate since supper yesterday, and you lost that. Sometimes if you go without food for too long, your mind can play tricks on you," Ernie said as he tugged me from the bed.

We left the bunkhouse and headed for the grub shack. Maybe Ernie was right. My legs seemed like they could hardly hold the weight of my body. I even stumbled and nearly fell.

The grub shack was empty and silent. Down the hall I could hear the clatter of pots and pans from the kitchen. Ernie told me to sit, and he went down the hall to get me some food. I sat at the table just blank. I was staring, but I don't think I saw anything except a fly crawling from her mouth and joining his friends, eating the snot that ran from the girl's nose. The whiskey bottle that was dangling from her man's fingers hit the dirt floor, and a few drops of whiskey ran out. It must have woke him. He raised his head. It wasn't him. It was the dying Indian. He looked me in the eye.

He looked so sad. "Emil…why did you kill me?"

"I didn't kill you. Ernie killed you!" I fell to the floor, onto my knees and elbows, and buried my face in my hands. "No. No."

The Indian grabbed me. He was going to kill me.

I fought. "I didn't kill you."

"Easy, boy, I ain't gonna hurt you."

I looked up, and the Indian was sneering at me. Then he just vanished.

I looked down to see the big brown arms of John around me. He had picked me up from the floor. He was behind me holding me on my feet with those powerful arms.

"Emil, you sure did have you a hard night. You let yourself get too hungry, boy. I got a few eggs and biscuits. You sit up and eat now."

I was still in the grub shack. John helped me back to the bench. He set a steaming plate in front of me, then reached back and set down a hot cup of coffee and a fork.

John just stood behind me with one hand on my shoulder and spoke in a soft voice. "Don't dat food smell good?"

I didn't feel like eating, but the food did smell good. I tried a bite. It did taste good, and I started to eat. I felt John's hand leave my shoulder. He walked from the room and down the hall where Tom Ryan and Ernie were standing. They were talking, but I couldn't hear them. By now I was starting to shovel the food in. It must have been that I'd been too long without food. I was starting to feel better.

Ernie came back out to the room. "I expect you want more to eat?" he said.

"Ya, I could eat a little more," I said. "I am feeling better."

Ernie grinned. But the rest of his face was sad. "John says you shouldn't eat any more right now."

I didn't know why he didn't want me to eat any more. I pushed the last biscuit into my mouth. Ernie just stood there as I finished my coffee.

He said, "Come on," and we headed back to the bunkhouse. As we passed the washhouse and outhouses, Ernie said, "You gotta use the privy?"

I guess I did. When I came out, Ernie was standing waiting for me.

"Tom wants to talk to you."

I'm going to tell Tom I don't want any part of that bounty, I thought as we walked back to the ranch house.

We went in the side door of the house and up a few stairs to the doctor room Able was in. It seemed like ages ago. John and Tom were in the room.

Tom said, "Emil, you had a hard night last night. You won't feel better until you get some sleep. John will give you something to help you sleep. When you wake up, you'll feel better and think better."

John on one arm and Tom on the other arm, they directed me to the bed and sat me on the edge. John went to a white cabinet and got down a big brown bottle. He took out the cork stopper and poured a tiny glass with a yellowish liquid. He handed me the glass to drink. It had a strange taste, and it did not go down easy. John untied my shoes and took them off. He swung my legs up and eased my torso back on the bed.

"You'll sleep now," I heard John say as the room started to spin. I felt a little sick to my stomach for a minute.

I woke up. The room was in the shadows, and Billie was sitting in the room with me.

Billie said, "Emil, you jus' wait there a minute."

Billie left the room, and in a moment, Tom was in the room with me. "How you feeling?" I answered, "I don't know. Whatever John gave me sure put me to sleep."

I just lay there, trying to stretch my eyes open. John came into the room carrying a tray with a silver cover

over it. John and Tom helped me from bed to a chair. Once I was upright, I felt kind of dizzy.

"You just sit there a minute and smell this beef stew and let your head clear."

The beef stew did smell good, and so did the bread. Tom and John talked of finishing mowing hay and cattle orders while I ate. They helped me to the chamber pot and back to bed. John poured another glass of medicine, and I fell back to sleep.

This time when I woke, Ernie was sitting in the room. "John said you'd be waking soon. We'll be getting you up shortly."

The sun was shining in the room. It must have been morning. I'd never slept this long. Tom walked by the door. He looked in as he passed, and in a few minutes, John came in.

"Well, Ernie, let's get dis boy some breakfast and back out on dat ole horse of his."

They steadied me to the chair and helped me put my shoes on. I stood for a few minutes, and my head started to clear.

We walked down to the grub shack. All the men had gone off to work. John had pancakes for Ernie and me. As we were eating, Tom came in.

He sat down across from me and said, "Boy oh boy, you sure had a bad case of hunger and lack of sleep. Let's see how you feel after breakfast. I could use you to ride with me today. We're going to try to move some cattle."

Tom told me to walk around while he did a few things, and then we would head out. I went to the outhouse and back to the bunkhouse. Ernie must have taken my clothes off the line because they were all folded on my bed. Every minute I felt better, and by the time Tom came by for me, I had Pete all saddled and ready.

We headed out to the west. Tom told me we had an order for four hundred yearlings going to West Point. He thought maybe we could move some of the cows that were farther out back in. Then it would be easier to cut out four hundred tomorrow. I felt kind of shaky at first, but the air was still cool, and the fresh air cleared my head.

It was exciting. I had never worked with Mr. Ryan, just me and him. I had worked the whole summer on the ranch and learned a lot. So had Pete. Now I could show Tom what we'd learned.

As we headed west, I noticed the grass closer to the ranch, which had been chewed off, was green and growing from the recent rains. The cattle were still pushing off to new grass. The first time I'd come out to the northwest sector, the cattle were no more than a mile, mile and a half out. Now they were out nearly three miles. In the cool air, the cattle were spread out and grazing. We started working around them. We had to stop and doctor a few of them, but for the most part, we just kept pushing them back. They were reluctant at first. When they realized that the new-growing grass closer in was to their liking, they moved much better. It was such a joy to watch Tom on that big black. Those two worked as one, not as man and horse but as one cow-herding animal. Just like Pete and Ida

261

turning the cultivator at the end of the field. No team on this ranch would turn as smoothly as Pete and Ida turning with Pa driving them. Pete had learned so much, but still we couldn't do near the work of Tom and his black. Pete and I weren't that good, but it was still fun being a cowboy. I had even developed my own yell over the summer.

"Let's get 'em, Pete. Heya!"

The day was heating up, and the cattle were starting to bunch into their circles to wait out the heat of the day.

It was nearing noontime when Tom rode up to me and said, "Let's move this bunch and stop for lunch."

I answered, "I forgot to get a lunch sack."

Tom grinned. "I thought you'd forget. I got one for you."

Boy, was I ever glad he did. I was getting hungry. We moved the cows in a mile or so and stopped by a creek to eat. We got down and let the horses go to the creek to water, and Tom and I sat. Tom was the boss, but he was always so easy to talk to.

"What's Tim doing today?" I asked.

"He's stacking hay. He thought he should be with me today, and he wasn't too happy about working hay. It's about time he learns the responsibility of running a ranch. You needed to be with me today."

I wasn't sure why I needed to be with Tom today, but I was glad I was. I'd polished enough pitchfork handles this summer.

"Ya, I gotta put my foot down on Tim. All he wants to do is have a good time. Emil, you can tell that we live well. But if we don't get out and work with you men and the cattle, we can't be in touch with what makes our wealth. Hands-on or handouts. Tim asked if he could have friends out this week. I told him this was a busy week, and he invited them anyway. Damned kid."

Boy, could that statement ever start a conversation! We sat silent for a few minutes eating our lunch.

"When I rode to Ponca, I met two gentlemen. They said the railroad was coming and all this land was going to be sold for farming. Is that true?"

Tom looked up, not at me. He just stared ahead. "Ya, it's true. The railroad will be good, I think. But this land—I had a lease on this land, and the damned government broke it. Our government is damned good about breaking treaties. Ask any Indian. My most important employee is my lawyer in Lincoln. If he didn't figure out a way for me to get this scrib, I'd be out of business. Now I'm in debt. If I have a good year or two, I can add some adjoining land. Then I'll have to fence my land. Then the sodbusters will want roads through here. It's going to change, not for the better. Not for me. The only good thing is they're gonna divide the reservation—forty acres per Indian. Them Indians don't understand owning land. They think it should belong to everyone. When they deed that land to the Indians, I'm going to bring in some agents and grab as much as I can. Some of those drunken fools will sell their forty acres for a case of whiskey. At any rate, land east of Omaha Creek will be a lot cheaper than west of the creek. The plan is, give the Indians the land, and the government won't have to buy cattle from me to feed them. That won't work. There'll still be starving Indians hanging around the agencies, and they'll still have to feed 'em. I'm not going down easy. Not me, I'm not going down easy."

Tom never looked my way the whole time he talked. He just stared straight ahead, and as he talked, his face grew sterner and sterner. Tom had shown me he was a man of determination, the kind of man I had never met before. We finished our lunch, visited about the cattle, and were soon back in the saddle. We found a bunch of cattle and pushed them back closer to the ranch. As the day heated up, the cattle became more reluctant to move. They just wanted to stand and swat flies.

It's plain to see, no matter how nice Tom is to work for, he is determined to keep his empire. He's going to keep this ranch. He will cheat and steal. Anything it takes. These poor Indians don't have a chance to match wits with men like Tom, or agents he hires to cheat them. That asshole of an Indian agent will just let it happen. These poor people will end up with nothing.

A dark feeling began to creep over me. Three head pulled out trying to escape back to their old haunts.

"Come on, Pete. Let's get 'em. Heya!"

I got them turned back into the herd. We moved them into a valley and left them. We crossed Cow Creek, went into the southwest sector, and did more of the same. Late in the afternoon, we met up with the guys working the other half of the ranch. We pushed the last of the cattle in closer and headed back to the ranch place.

The hay crew was still out, and the bunkhouse was hot as hell. I decided to go down to the big creek where John and I fished. I climbed down the steep bank. The creek bank was so deep that the sun was shaded, and it was a lot cooler down here. I sat in the shade. I started to feel drowsy. I closed my eyes, and the sound of the running water started to gurgle.

With every breath, the gurgle grew louder, and the Indian raised his arms and sang, "Hey ya," louder and louder. Then he turned to me. "Why did you kill me, Emil?" He kept repeating it over and over.

I yelled back, "I didn't do it!"

I sprang to my feet and climbed the bank of the creek. I got to the top of the creek bank and turned around. He was standing at the bottom of the creek still yelling at me. I fell to my belly and buried my face in my hands. He was gone. His words faded, and finally I couldn't hear him anymore. I lay there for several minutes. Did I dare look up? Would he still be there? I was so fearful to look up.

I don't want to see him again. I don't want to look up. I don't want to see him again.

I was shaking. I raised my head and looked down the steep creek bank. All was as it should be. The wide creek was gently flowing with hardly a sound. The sun that was hitting part of the water made it sparkle in a peaceful way. I was still scared. But peacefulness came over me.

I got to my feet and started for the yard. The men were coming from the grub shack. The hay crew must have come in and the supper bell rang. I didn't hear anything. I went to supper and sat alone and ate. The few men that were left in the room just seemed to ignore me. If I looked up and caught their eyes, they would look the other way. *Do they think I'm crazy? Do they think I lost my mind?* Even T.T., who stopped in the washhouse yesterday, said nothing to me tonight. *What's wrong with me?*

John came over. "How you doing, Emil?"

I just shrugged my shoulders and never said anything.

"Why don't you jus' go sit in da yard till I clean up. Den we'll play checkers."

I finished eating and went out in the yard to sit.

I could hear some yelling from the big house. It was Tom's and Tim's voices. I could only make out a few words. In a few seconds, I heard a screen door slam. I turned to see Tim stomping from the side door of the house. He went partway out in the yard and stood just staring to the south. His arms were at his side with his fists clenched. He stood there for at least five minutes.

Tim turned and stared at the house. "Oh, I didn't see you sitting there, Emil." I didn't know what to say, but he continued, "That goddamned old man, I told him two weeks ago my friends from Sioux City were coming for a few days. Then I get the letter that they are coming tomorrow, and he goes off his damned rocker. I know there's work to do around here, but how's it get done when I'm at the university? Damn it, I need time with my friends. I won't see them till next summer, and I'm going to spend time with them. These goddamned cows can rot, for all I care."

Tim just headed back for the house, and I never did say a word to him. *I guess I'm not the only one with problems.*

Ernie walked up to me. "Bob said he saw you up here. I was looking for you. How did it go today? Why you sitting here?"

I answered, "John said to wait out here and we'd play checkers. It went good today. We moved the cattle in closer. We're going to sort an order tomorrow."

Ernie grinned. "Tomorrow will be a big day. The last of the hay will come in, and a big order to sort. Let's go see if John is ready for some winner challenge checkers. We can start without him, and he can play the winner."

Ernie and I went into the grub shack. He got out the checkerboard. We played, and Ernie won.

John came out from the kitchen with a bottle of whiskey and a big tin cup. He set the whiskey between him and Ernie and put the cup in front of me.

"Here, Emil, you drink this."

I picked up the cup. It looked like lemonade but smelled like whiskey. "I don't drink alcohol, John. You know that."

"I know, but dere's a medicine virtue to alcohol, and you need it. Did you have any dem visions today?"

They know. They know I'm going crazy.

I answered John. "I started to. I felt it coming on, and some cows tried to stray, and I chased them, and it went away. Then down at the creek, that Indian tried to get me. John, am I going crazy?"

John came around the end of the table and put his arm around me as he sat next to me. He spoke softly. "Emil, you got sompin' wrong, son, but you ain't crazy. You got da shock."

I answered, "What is the shock?"

"Well, I ain't never seen anybody get it out on da ranch. In da army sometimes, every so often when we would get into a bunch of killing. Every so often a man would come down wid da shock. I gave you laudanum, and it let you sleep. I can't give you dat anymore, or you'll be an opium addict. A little whiskey will help you sleep. After you have dis shock for a while, you'll feel it coming on like dis morning and you chased dose strays. Well, when you feel it coming on, you'll learn to do something or think of something, and da visions won't come on. You'll learn. And in a year or two, it'll go away."

Ernie spoke then. "John's right. I saw the shock in the war. I never dreamed that you would get it from shootin' that damned Indian, or I'da left you at the cedars. I'm so sorry, Emil. John's right. In time, it'll go away."

I just sat there. *The shock. I never heard of this. They say I'll get over this. At least I'm not crazy. Or are they just saying this to me? I don't think I'm crazy.*

"I hope I'm not crazy."

We sat and played checkers all evening. I drank five of those drinks John made. They made me light-headed and pee a lot. Ernie and I went back to the bunkhouse. I slept all night.

SIXTEEN

My eyes opened. The bunkhouse was filled with the pink light of the sunrise. I didn't hear anyone stirring yet. I just lay there, that time when you wake and try to remember your dreams before they fade away. The only dream I remembered, was herding cattle, and it was a good dream. I had to pee, so I went out to relieve myself. I tried to be quiet so as not to wake anyone. The air outside was heavy, and the horizon to the east glowed red. Not a good sign. It could storm today. I felt good this morning. I thought of my dreams, "visions," or whatever you would call them. I didn't even want to think of them. John told me not to think of them, and in time, they wouldn't come back.

I'm not going to think of them. I'm only going to think of one thing today. Being a cowboy.

I must not have been up too early, as the breakfast bell started ringing. As I walked in, Ernie was still lying in his bunk. He looked up and studied me with a concerned look on his face. I smiled and winked, and he grinned.

"Gonna cut some yearlings today, Emil?"

I didn't answer, just gave him a thumbs-up. I was extra hungry and raced to dress for the day. On the way to the grub shack, and at breakfast, the men seemed to be friendly and talking to me. I felt good.

Tom and Tim rode up to the rest of the cutting crew that was waiting by the corral. Tom told us that we would work the northwest sector first. We all mounted and followed Tom and Tim off to the west. I watched from behind. Tom and Tim had not patched up their squabble yet. They rode side by side not even looking at each other.

Tim finally pulled up and waited for me to catch up. "Emil, do you remember my friends from Fourth of July?"

I nodded yes.

"Well, that's who's coming today. They're bringing Mary again. They said they'd be here around noon, and I'm going in. The old man says I have to work all day. I'm not going to. I'm going in at noon."

I didn't know what to say. I had to think quick. "If Tom were my pa, I don't think I would want to piss him off. I saw what he did to Murphy."

Tim looked over at me. He had a determined look on his face. "I'm going in at noon. If we have it out, we do. I'm ready to try him."

Gilbert doesn't want to be a farmer. He doesn't want to tell Pa that for fear Pa will be disappointed in his decision. I don't see Pa and Gilbert having a fistfight on the day that Gilbert has to tell him. I just can't see our Christian, churchgoing family having a fistfight. It's only a day's ride, but this is a different world. Much different.

Tom picked a draw to gather the yearlings in, and we started looking for cattle to sort. I remembered seeing a bunch of cattle hanging by a slew yesterday. They were just over a couple hills to the north. I motioned Tim, and we went looking for them. They were still there. It was a nice bunch of about a hundred. Just by looking, I thought there were at least thirty yearlings in the bunch. Ernie told me this was the last time we would sort in the hills. In September, they would have another roundup. At that time, they sorted the yearlings and separated the calves from the cows to wean them. Ernie said you can't sleep for three days for all of the bellering. The cows needed to shrink their udders so they didn't freeze their teats in the winter snow.

Pete once again was shown up by a fine Ryan horse. Tim had four cut out and was heading over the hills before I had even three cut out. We worked this bunch until we had all the yearlings out, then found another bunch. There were only eight yearlings in this bunch. We cut them out and pushed them back to the draw. Both Tim and I pushed this eight head back. As we topped the last hill, Tom came riding by. He pulled up his big black.

He looked furious as he yelled, "Tim, what the hell? Are you blind, or don't you care about this ranch? You have a select heifer in there. Goddamn it, you pay attention."

Tom moved in and cut the heifer out. Sure enough, she had the extra bar on her brand. I don't know. I may have sorted her out myself. This I do know: Tim caught hell. Tom had that furious look on his face as he rode away.

By late morning, we had around two hundred head sorted.

Tom gathered the riders. "Let's move these in. Jack, Ben, Emil, you take 'em in. Emil, you bring back dinner. We'll be by the Three Fork Creek in the southwest."

Tim was boiling. I could tell by the look on his face. We all started the herd moving, and then the others dropped back. Tim didn't. He kept riding a short distance off to my right. He had a determined look on his face.

"*Tim!*"

The sound roared above the sound of hooves. Tim gritted his teeth and wheeled around to join the other riders.

The cattle moved easy, down the small valley that led to the big valley north of Cow Creek, and over to the corral. Ernie and a couple of other men were waiting at the sort corral, and the cattle went right in just like they were supposed to. Ernie pushed the gate closed, and we all gathered.

Ernie looked to the east and laughed. "Look at them damned fools."

The rest of us looked to the east. It must have been the last hayrack coming in because all the field crew was riding on it. They all had their shirts off and tied to their pitchfork handles. They were waving them like flags. The guys in the hay lot had done the same. It was a good day.

Jack and Ben headed back to the southwest. Bob and Jerry went into the corral to finish pushing the cattle into the right pen. Ernie and I rode toward the ranch yard.

"How you doing, Emil?" Ernie asked as we rode.

I just rode and gave him a grin and a thumbs-up. Ernie pulled into the hay lot, and I waved to the men as I headed for the grub shack.

I looked around as I got to the grub shack. I didn't see Tim's friends' surrey in the yard. John had dinner packed into the tin saddlebags. He was grinning as usual, and we put the containers over Pete's rump.

"How you doing today, Emil?"

I smiled and nodded. "Good, John, real good—but Tom and Tim ain't. Tim wants to come in, and Tom wants him to stay out all day."

John shook his head as he said, "Dem Ryan men are hardheaded. For one to give in won't be easy."

We finished securing the load, and I headed out of the yard. I rode past the hay lot. They were nearly done stacking the last rack and cheering with every pitchfork full. I crossed Cow Creek and headed southwest for the Three Fork Creek. When I got there, the men had a few head in a group already. I picked a good spot to set out dinner, and the men started coming in. I had fixed my plate and was sitting already when Tim came in.

Tim fixed a plate and sat next to me. "Are my friends here yet?"

"No," I answered.

"As soon as I eat, I'm leaving."

The Ryan's had always had very good table manners, but Tim was shoveling his food.

I poked Tim with my elbow. "I think you have time to chew."

Tim looked over at me and grinned for a moment. Then his face looked very determined, and he kept shoveling his food. Tim and I were sitting apart from the other men. Tom was over with them, talking to Ben. Tim was done with his plate. I went for some more. I came back and sat with Tim. He just sat there glaring over at Tom. Tom looked and saw the glaring look on Tim's face. He shot to his feet and stomped over to where we were sitting. Tim started to stand, and before he got his legs straightened, Tom grabbed him with a handful of shirt and slammed him into the rear quarters of Tim's roan. I was close enough to hear.

Tom's face was only about four inches from Tim's, and Tom yelled in a whisper, "This is a family matter, and I don't like settling it in front of the men. You get the hell out of here." Tom loosened his grip on Tim. Then he tightened it again. "You take in the dinner tins and send Ernie and some men out so we can get these damned cattle in before it storms."

Tom let go of his grip that he had with his right hand. The whole time he talked, his left hand was raised in a fist. Tim just stood there with that determined sneer on his face. I could tell Tim wanted to try his pa. I think that he was shocked by the ease with which Tom flung him into the horse. He just stood and sneered and trembled.

Tom stomped over, jumped onto his black, turned him, and kicked him so hard you could hear the thump. All the men stood. We all looked wide-eyed. I put my plate and cup in the tins, and all the men followed my lead. Most of the men fixed themselves a smoke. The others watched Tom race across the hills, just kicking the shit out of his horse.

We all saddled and went back to work, and Tim just stood there. From a distant hill, I saw him load up and leave with haste.

I was working a few head back to the draw when Ernie rode up with three other men. I could see him motion, and the other men took off to work some cattle. Ernie came my way.

"What the hell happened out here?" he yelled as he got close.

I told him about Tom and Tim.

Ernie shook his head., "If Tom gave in, he won't be fit to be around for two days. We better get a move on."

I looked where Ernie was pointing. A black line was lying on the horizon. Ernie rode with me. We pushed these few head into the draw and went back to the bunch I was cutting from. It was hot, and the cattle were bunched in a circle like they do in the heat. When they got like this, it was hard to cut any out, for me and Pete anyway. Ernie's big cutting horse walked into them and seemed to dance them out. I just let him do the cutting, and I held them at a distance. We found more bunches to work as the afternoon sweltered on. The black line of clouds slowly moved at us, but the herd in the draw grew and grew.

Ernie and I were pushing ten head into the draw. We could see Tom and Ben counting. Ben started to wave at us. After our few joined the herd, we joined Tom and Ben.

Tom said, "Let's see if we can get them in before this damned storm cuts loose. I think that this makes four hundred seven. Ben has four hundred nine. And Bob and Jack are still out. They can catch up. Let's move 'em."

We all spread around the herd and gave our yells. As they started moving northeast, I could see two riders pushing a few head off to my right. *That must be Bob and Jack. We're all here now and moving.*

I noticed I wasn't the only one watching the sky. The sky looked just like it did the day Able and I left Oakland and had to take shelter under a Conestoga. We were only a quarter mile from Cow Creek and pushing hard. All of a sudden, I was blinded. Pete was rearing on his hind legs, and I nearly fell off. A bolt of lightning had struck right in front of the herd. Blinded cattle were running everywhere but forward. I had never been in such a situation. I could see men racing, trying to get around the terrified cattle. Pete was regaining his sight, and we moved off to the east.

Tom raced up to me. "Stay down here to help me hold 'em. What the hell else could go wrong today?"

Tom no sooner got the words out of his mouth and pulled away than it poured. By the time I turned to get my slicker out of my bag, it didn't matter. I was soaked to the skin. It did feel good.

Three of us stayed with the ones in the little valley. Some of the men were so quick on responding to the stampede that most of them stayed in the valley. It was raining so hard I could hardly see the other side of the herd. It had not been more than ten minutes, and Tom and Ernie felt we had them all back together. We started to move them toward the ranch. I was afraid we were in trouble. The little trickle creek in the valley we were in was now four feet across and spilling out of its banks. It was raining so hard I couldn't see the front of the herd. Now they stopped and crowded each other. Some of the cattle tried turning back at me.

Ben came racing around the rear of the herd. "We gotta hold 'em here. Cow Creek is plum full and roaring."

The cattle settled down, but the rain kept coming. It must have rained this hard for an hour and showed no sign of letting up. The lightning made the cattle nervous. Tom came by after a while. As he talked, the water running off the brim of his hat made it look like he was behind a waterfall.

"If that damned lightning hadn't hit, we'd of got them in. We're going to be here a long time."

There was nothing to do but sit and get soaked. Another hour passed. Maybe not that long, it just felt like it. As suddenly as the rain came, it stopped. I could finally see. I walked Pete over to the west side of the herd. The tiny creek that flowed down the valley we had come down was out of its banks and dumping into Cow Creek. Cow Creek must have been twenty-five feet wide and just racing. I had never seen this before. The water in the middle of the creek looked to be a foot higher than along the banks. There was nothing we could do but sit and wait and watch. Tom acted like a caged cat. He rode two miles west looking for a place to cross to no avail. I didn't know how long we'd been here now, but my stomach was feeling hungry. I could feel the skin under my wet clothes getting wrinkly. The little creek we were by was starting to go into the banks, and Cow Creek was down only an inch or two, but still roaring.

I could see a rider coming from the ranch place. I could hear some yelling, but I couldn't make out what was said. Then the rider turned back. About half an hour later, Tom came back to where I was. He had Bob with him.

"Emil, come with me." I followed Tom up to the bank of the creek. "I sent T.T. back to tell John to pack us supper. If you jump in here, you should drift some and get out over there where the bank is easy. Just hang on tight. That horse will swim you right over."

I wasn't so sure of this, but Tom seemed to know what he was talking about.

I turned Pete around back about twenty yards and put my heel in his side. Pete shot forward about half the distance and set his feet. He stopped so fast I nearly flew over his neck. I hit him with my heel again.

He would not move. Tom came up and hit him on the rump with a strap. Pete reared up on his rear legs and turned his head, and I could see one of his eyes. It had a terrified look in it.

"That goddamned plow horse," Tom said as he put his heel into the black.

The big black took two strides and jumped halfway across the creek. He didn't swim. *Oh my God.* The current rolled him over and left Tom flailing in the water. Tom's hat went floating down the stream right side up. From nowhere, Ernie and Ben appeared throwing lariats at Tom. Tom was fighting so hard to stay up he didn't have wits about him to grab a rope. Ernie and Ben were off, their horses running down the bank, trying to get a rope around him. I didn't remember getting off Pete, but I was right there with Ernie and Ben. Tom's battle was futile. He slipped under the surface of the water just as he was to pass under a downed tree. His leg came up, and his foot caught in the fork of a branch.

Ernie looked at me. "Emil, get out there."

I was up on that tree without thinking. I shinnied out as fast as I could—faster than I thought I could.

From behind me I heard Ernie's voice. "Ready?"

I felt a lariat fall over my neck. I put it over Tom's foot and watched the loop instantly pull tight.

"Break the limb," came from behind me.

I put my foot down and pushed for all I was worth. I heard a crack, and then it broke. The rope flew from the water with drips of water falling off it. I looked back. Ernie and Ben were both on the end of the rope with someone else running to join them. Tom's leg came out of the water and headed for the bank. His other leg was cocked back under his torso as it floated up. His arms were back above his head. Then his face surfaced. His seldom-seen hair was laid straight back over the top of his head. His face was all blue. His swollen tongue hung from the side of his mouth. His eyes. His handsome blue eyes. His eyes looked kind of gray and were staring straight ahead...but seeing nothing. I started to shinny back to the bank. By the time I got back to having my feet on the ground, Ernie and Jack each had a leg in the air, lifting Tom's body off the ground. Tom was on his chest, and Ben was hitting his back. They kept it up for a couple of minutes.

"Guys, we're too late," Ernie said with such sorrow in his voice.

They lowered his legs and laid him flat. Ben rolled him over. He looked the same, but now his face was muddy. He had a glob of mud on his right eyeball that nearly covered his staring pupil. He was gone. I ripped my shirt off, laid it over his face, and went and vomited.

Ben came to make sure I was all right. I think I was. I was gasping for fresh air. I soon felt better, and I turned back around. All the men had gathered.

Ernie was on his knees, holding Tom's lifeless hand and repeating, "We had some good years, old friend."

I started crying out loud. I suddenly felt obvious. I couldn't stop crying. Men don't cry. At one time or another, they all looked at me crying. I could tell from the look in their eyes, a few of them wet, that they wanted to cry too. We all stood in silence around our fallen boss, friend, and a great cattleman.

I looked up, and the big black had struggled up the other side. He was standing there with his head low and the reins dragging on the ground. He started walking slowly for the barn.

I looked over, and Jack was looking at the black also. "It looks like Baron took some water. He might be done too."

I looked at Jack. "Was that his name?"

Jack answered back "Ya. Baron—the finest horse for the finest man."

Somebody must have had a bedroll on their saddle. They picked Tom up and laid him on it. Ernie used my wet shirt to wipe the mud from him. Ernie covered him with the bedroll and gave my shirt back to me. I threw it in the creek.

I don't know how long we stood there in shock, sorrow, and silence. We looked up to see a rider coming full-out around the sort corral, heading our way. By the time he got close, we could see a buckboard and a surrey coming their teams at a gallop.

T.T.'s horse slid to a stop as he yelled, "What the hell happened?"

Ernie yelled back, "We lost Tom!"

Billie and John were on the buckboard. Mrs. Ryan and Tim were in the surrey. T.T. went and told the bad news. John got out of the buckboard and fell face-first on the ground and pounded the heels of his fist-clenched hands into the muddy soil. Tim and

Mrs. Ryan sat on the seat of the surrey and wept. Even the wild range cattle stood and paid their respects. No one was left to watch them, and they didn't move.

After another hour, the creek started dropping as fast as it had risen. John walked in and crossed. The water was belly deep. He came over to our side. No one said a word. John picked up Tom's body wrapped in the bedroll. He carefully carried his friend back across the creek and set him gently into the buckboard. The wagons turned and slowly headed home.

By just before dusk, the creek fell to the point we could push the cattle across. The cattle didn't even beller. They just did what was expected of them. Like a silent processional, they walked to the corral and in. We all went back to the bunkhouse and put on clean clothes.

The front door of the ranch house was open. Tom was clean, dressed in the suit he wore on the Fourth of July. His color was still bluish. His mouth was closed, and so were his eyes. He was laid on the dining room table. I took a quick look and left the room.

Ernie took my arm. "Go to the grub shack and eat so you don't get sick."

I wasn't hungry, but I knew Ernie was right. They didn't need me getting sick, or whatever you wanted to call it, tonight.

The tins were set on the table, and two other guys were in the room eating. No one talked. I did feel better after eating and went back to the bunkhouse. The men were passing the bottle around, toasting the life of Tom. John came down and joined us. He brought a pitcher of lemonade and a tin cup for me. I joined in the toasting.

Ernie pulled me off to the side. "Emil, do you remember how bad you felt the day you couldn't make yourself help with Murphy?"

I nodded my head.

"I told you that you would be a brave man when the time comes—well, today was that time. You did what needed to be done. We were just too late. I'm proud of you, son."

The toasting didn't last too long, but I must have had enough to drink. I was exhausted and emotionally drained. I fell into bed and slept as sound as I ever had.

***

The next morning there was no breakfast bell. I walked up to the grub shack. There was a pot of oatmeal and coffee. No John. Ben told me John wanted to dig the grave. A silence hung over the ranch. I went back to the bunkhouse and put on my church clothes. All the men were putting on their best clothes. Around mid-morning, the bell rang very fast. Then it stopped for a couple of minutes. Then it tolled. We walked up to the house. John was dressed in his best servant's suit. He had a hammer, and he was tolling the bell forty-eight strikes, one for each year of Tom Ryan's life.

John went in the house. All of us men waited in the yard. Chuck, Ben, Ernie, and John carried the pine box that Billie had spent the night building. Mrs.

Ryan and Tim followed, with Tim's friends following behind. All the men followed in silence. We went around to the family plot just north of the house. The men set the pine box down on the ropes John had laid there. They took up the ropes and lowered the box into the grave. John came around to the head of the box and stood silent for a while. Tears ran down his face as he said the Lord's Prayer.

Then he followed with, "Remember, man, dat you are dust, and to dust you shall return."

We all stood in silence for a few moments. John took up a shovel and put a scoop of dirt on his friend's body. He handed the shovel to Mrs. Ryan and burst into a loud sob. She put a scoop of dirt on the box and handed the shovel to Tim. Tim put a shovelful on the box. He handed the shovel to the next person and helped his mother back to the house. We all took a turn at the shovel and left, leaving John standing there with tears running down his face—tears for a friend.

SEVENTEEN

John finished covering the grave and returned to the house. A short time later, Tim's friends left. Ernie and Ben joined the Ryans and John in the house. No one worked this day, except a few men that helped remove Baron from his stall, where he had perished overnight. Men just sat around the bunkhouse or grub shack. I heard some men talking. They were worried the ranch would go out of business and they would lose their jobs. I had only known Tom Ryan this summer. The other day when I worked with him all day, I learned he was a ruthless businessman. But he had respect for the men that worked for him. The men that had been with him the longest considered him their best friend.

Poor John. Will he ever have his warm smile again? This is my first job. I have been blessed to have such a fine boss. Otto Johnson, who works for Ulmquist, doesn't feel that way. Pa said he heard Otto say that the night after Ulmquist dies, he'll go dance on his grave, then pee on it.

I felt so sad when I heard Tom's big black died. That was all right, though. No one else would have looked right riding him.

I spent the rest of the morning just walking around the yard thinking. I did walk by the kitchen. Billie was cooking.

The way Pastor Nielson sees it, Tom doesn't have much of a chance to be in heaven. Mr. Ulmquist is in church every Sunday. That don't seem right, that he would get in and not Tom. When I get back to Oakland, I will always be faithful to God. I want to get in. I want to see if either of them are there.

The dinner bell rang. The men started heading for the grub shack, and I followed. The inside of the grub shack had been rearranged. There was another table and chairs in the room. John stood by the door and held us back. Ernie, Ben, Tim, and Mrs. Ryan came down the hall and filled their plates first, and then John joined them. All the men filed through and sat down. There was no buzz of conversation. Just silence. After everyone finished eating, we just sat. Finally Mrs. Ryan stood up and spoke.

"Tom Ryan worked his whole life carrying on the work his father started."

She looked down with a loving look at John, Ben, and Ernie.

"Some of you have been with this family for two generations of Ryans. If you are willing to stay for a third generation, this family will not let you down. I will continue to keep the books and manage the finances. Ernie and Ben will run the day-to-day work of the ranch until Tim finishes at the university. Your support these last couple days is so very much appreciated by Tim and myself. Thank you very much. You have our word that things won't change here. I hope you all at least stay on long enough to see that I mean what I say. Tom will be sorely missed. As long as this place stands, he will be here. We are the Ryans, and this is Cow Creek Ranch."

EIGHTEEN

Ernie stood and shook Tim's hand, then Mrs. Ryan's hand, and then he left the room. Ben and John followed, then each man in the room, single file. If Tom was the king of this empire, now Prince Tim would be king.

Mrs. Ryan's talk seemed to lift the dark curtain that had been hanging over the ranch. The men were in small groups laughing and talking, mostly telling stories of Tom Ryan. I sat with Tim for a while. He felt so bad that he had fought with his father the last he saw him alive.

Ernie overheard us talking and came over. He put his hand on Tim's shoulder and spoke. "Tim, you're a Ryan. If you don't have your own mind, you wouldn't be a Ryan. That little squabble you had with your pa ain't nothing. That wern't nothin' compared to what Tom and his pa had. Shit, Tom wouldn't have wanted it any other way."

Tim sat for a few minutes in silence with a grim look on his face. Slowly his face returned to normal.

Then he got a mischievous smile and pulled close so no one would hear. "The old man picked a piss-poor time to die. I had Mary here. I could have had a good time in the haymow last night." Tim slapped me on the back and walked away grinning.

I liked Tim.

I walked down to the corral to see Pete. He came over to have his ears scratched. One of the horses in the corral kicked up its heels and struck a fence board. Able went flying lifeless in the air.

"Hey, you dumb Swede. Why didn't you leave with your brother? No, you wanted your own adventure."

I turned, and it was Murphy sneering at me. His face was all blood spattered.

"All you did is mess things up around here. You wished me dead. Now look at me."

Murphy turned around, and the back of his head was missing. All I could see was meat and bone with brain matter oozing out.

"Looks good, don't it? You came here and ruined everything. Now I'm dead. Tom's dead. And you killed that Indian. That Indian wants revenge. And so do I. I'll break you as easy as you broke that tree branch that held Tom underwater."

Murphy was looking at me now.

"You wanted a piece of me, but you were chicken shit. Come on. Try me now."

Murphy's eyes looked bloodshot. His face was full of rage just like when he was on the floor of the grub shack.

"You gonna try me, or will you just stand there and let me pound the crap out of you while you cry like a baby?" Murphy's fists were clenched. He was ready.

I can't do this. I'll run and find Ernie.

I ran for the bunkhouse. Murphy was right on my tail. I ran into the bunkhouse. Ernie wasn't there. It was hot in there. No one was there, and Murphy guarded the door. I looked to the rifle rack. *He could get me before I could load a rifle, and he's dead anyway.* I crouched in the back corner. Murphy never moved. He just stood in the doorway with that look of rage on his face and making the same growling noise he'd made in the grub shack.

He's going to kill me. It is so hot in here. I'm sweating so hard my clothes are soaked. I have to get out of here. I have to find Ernie or John. How can I get by Murphy? There it is. There's my escape.

I sprang to my feet, ran to one of the bunks on the west wall, jumped on the bunk, and dove out the window. The screen and frame shattered as I hit it, and I fell hard on the ground outside. Murphy came around the corner of the building.

"You ain't getting away. Not this time," Murphy shouted as he ran toward me.

I jumped up and ran for the yard outside the grub shack. *Ernie must be there.* I ran as fast as I could, but Murphy was getting closer. I could hear his growling noise now. I ran for all I was worth. I couldn't get away. He grabbed me.

"Don't kill me."

"Why not, you afraid of going to hell?" he answered. "You turned from God. You threw your Bible in the creek. Now you're going to hell."

His grasp on me was harder now.

"Don't kill me. Don't kill me."

He threw me down and straddled me, pinning my hands down with his knees. I closed my eyes and waited for the blow that would end my life.

It never came. I waited. It never came. I feared to open my eyes. I had to peek. I opened one eye, just enough to let a little light in.

It was John on me. "You're all right, Emil. I got you, son."

I felt the pressure on my hands ease. I opened both of my eyes. I was in the yard. Tim was standing on one side of John, Ernie on the other. I lay on the ground. My eyes looked around as far as I could. All the men were standing there. They all had a sad, shocked look on their faces.

"Do you know where you are, Emil?" John's voice said in such a soft tone.

I didn't answer. I thought Murphy had me.

Murphy was real. I'm not sleeping. It's the middle of the day. I saw all of this. It was real. I'm sure of it.

"Do you know where you are, Emil?"

I nodded my head yes. But I wasn't sure.

I heard Ernie shout, "You guys go on. The show's over."

I watched the men leave. It was just Tim, John, and Ernie with me now.

John got off me and helped me sit up. I could not think right.

John said, "You had another spell. You'll be fine now. You just let your head clear."

"John, it's the middle of the day. This was no dream. I saw Murphy. He was going to get me. He was going to kill me. He was going to send me to hell. It was real…It was real…or…or…I'm crazy."

"No, son, you ain't crazy. You just got a touch of da shock. Da shock will go away in time, and you'll feel fine. Emil, I promise. You'll get over dis."

I sat up in the yard chair. Ernie gave me a cup of coffee that had the taste of whiskey to it. Tim sat with me for a long time. We did not have that much in common, but he told me of all the girls he had been with and what had transpired with each one. He was such a good liar.

Ernie sat with me and told stories of the trail drive of the cattle, the cattle whose descendants populated this ranch, stories of three generations of Ryans.

After supper, John took me to the doctor room. He told me I would be going home in the morning, and I would take this medicine tonight so I would be fine for the trip. *I believe John. I trust John.* He poured me a glass of the medicine from the big brown bottle, and I drank it. *John is the first Negro I've met. What a nice man.*

When I opened my eyes, Mrs. Ryan was sitting in the room. She was reading the Bible. I didn't think the Ryans ever read the Bible.

"How do you feel this morning, Emil? You sure slept good."

I smiled.

"This is a big day for you. You get to go home. Your mother and father will be so glad to see you. Do you have brothers and sisters other than Able?"

It caught me off guard. I hadn't really thought of going home. I had to think a second.

"Yes, counting Able, I have three brothers and two sisters."

Mrs. Ryan answered, "Oh my. You come from a large family. I did too. I have four sisters and one brother. I had wished Tim to have brothers and sisters, but I guess it wasn't to be. Well, I'll leave so you can be getting dressed. John will be up in a few minutes."

She left the room. I got up. My head felt fuzzy. I got dressed and was just finishing tying my shoes when John came into the room. I got my question answered. John smiled his same old smile.

"Emil, you hungry?"

"Yes, I am," I answered.

"I swear boys your age is always hungry. Come on down. I have chipped beef and gravy on biscuits."

As we walked to the grub shack, I told John that was my favorite of his breakfasts. When I finished eating, Ernie and Tim came in. We all went out to the yard. Pete was saddled and tied to the hitching rail by the barn. We all went over to him.

Tim held out one of the blue envelopes. "Emil, here is your pay." He went over and opened a saddlebag.

As Tim was putting it in, John said, "Emil, I wrote a letter to your pa. You be sure he gets it. I put it in your pay envelope, and a lunch in your other saddlebag."

We all shook hands. I undid Pete's reins and mounted up. I pulled Pete around and let him take three or four steps. I pulled him up and turned him halfway around. I waved good-bye. So did they. John had a tear in his eye.

So did I.

NINETEEN

I pulled Pete around and put my heel soundly into his side. He shot off through the yard, and I let out a "heya" and waved to the men working as I raced by. I let Pete run all the way to Cow Creek, which now was no more than three feet wide and ankle-deep. I wanted to look off to the west where Tom drowned, but I didn't. Pete went down the creek bank and up the other side without hesitation. We turned southeast along the big creek. I took one more look back. Straight across the creek was the barren hayfield where I'd spent most of the summer. On the other side was the big valley, the sort corral off to the west, the hay lot over near the creek, and the white buildings on the far north end of the valley. I took one more look. Something told me I would never see it again.

I followed the big creek southeast past the graze line. I wanted to get home today. It was early when I left, and the days were still long. Pete was in better horseback shape now than when we left home. I understood how to work him now to get the most out of him. The ride home was the same as the ride here: hills and grass. The grass was not as green now, more yellow and brittle. The path of the monthly order to the Omaha Agency was now fairly well-worn.

My mind started to wander.

Mrs. Ryan asked of my brothers and sisters. I just haven't thought much of them. It was such fun playing hopscotch and hide-and-seek with the little ones. Playing cowboy and Indians with Able. Ma and Pa. Ma's fried chicken. Oh, I haven't had fried chicken in three months. Every Sunday, most every Sunday. I don't even know what day of the week it is. I hope it's Sunday. Get home and have fried chicken and apple pie. My own bed to sleep in again. I'm glad I'm going home. Ernie said I was a man. I came to work at this ranch a boy. I'm going home a man. And Ernie said I was brave.

Up ahead I saw something. I couldn't make out what it was. It was a black building or something. Was I on the right trail? That wasn't here when I came. A little closer and I realized the creek moved a little to the north in the valley. This was a heavy timber bridge, like the one on the west side of Winnebago. As I drew nearer, I could smell the new creosote in the timbers. They'd sure built this bridge fast. I took one trip over it, just to hear Pete's hooves clomp on the new planks.

I was here, the high trail. I let Pete run down the hills and walk up the other side. We were making good time, I thought. We topped a hill, and it was the last one. Down below was the creek that Able and I waited out the storm by. And the main trail. I had just watered Pete a half mile back. I sat on this hill and ate my lunch. When we came, it had seemed so strange to see so many hills. Now it seemed so strange to see flatlands. This land looked barren to me then. Now it looked populated. Looking off in the distance, I saw section roads and a few farms. There was a three-wagon freight train coming my way, and a buckboard going the other.

I think Ernie is right. The West is dying, and it won't be long now. That buckboard is making good time. The road looks in good shape. I should have no trouble getting home by dark.

I finished my lunch and pulled Pete away from his grass. I mounted up, and we headed down the last hill, down the creek bank. As we crossed the creek, Tom's body floated up. His eyes looked more alive. He pulled his swollen tongue in and spoke.

"Emil, you aren't leaving us in these hills. We're coming with you."

I put my heel into Pete, and he climbed up the other creek bank. I hit him again and took off down the road, passing the buckboard. Father Mike was driving it.

As I passed, he yelled at me, "You can't fix a broken man. You can't fix a broken man."

I put the buckboard a distance behind and slowed Pete to a trot.

How did Father Mike get here? Am I a broken man? Why did Tom want to come back to Oakland with me? Can't they all stay back on the Indian Nations? Why me?

We came up on a grain wagon with two men on the seat. They were both Father Mike.

"You can't fix a broken man," they both yelled.

I'm not a broken man, am I?

An oncoming freight wagon passed, and the Indian was driving it. "Why did you kill me, Emil?"

Murphy was in the seat next to him. Murphy stood and slid his index finger across his neck. As he did, he grinned his bloody teeth at me.

Am I crazy? Am I a broken man?

I heard the sound of hooves off to my side. I turned and looked. The Indian's pony was right on my flank. The Indian was strapped on still. He was looking up at me.

"Why did you kill me, Emil?"

His face looked so mean now. As he looked up, the wind blew a separation in his remaining hair, making his scalp wound ever more grotesque. I hit Pete with both heels, and he started running full-out.

As I started to pull away, the Indian yelled, "You're not going to get away from me!"

But I did. I left him back seven or eight lengths.

Pete ain't the greatest horse, but he should outrun that skinny pony. It can't be more than ten miles home. That pony can't run that far, can he?

Every wagon we passed had Father Mike or Murphy in it, and they yelled at me. And that Indian was not losing ground a bit.

Pete was sweating and breathing heavy but staying ahead of that Indian. We passed a corner I recognized. We were only two miles from Oakland, just three miles from home. Pete was in full lather now, and the foam from his mouth was flowing back and hitting my knees. The pony looked as fresh as when we started, and no more than three lengths behind me now.

I could see the main street of Oakland coming up, and Pete kept on running full-out right through Main Street. All the people turned to look. All the men were Murphy. All the women were the Indian girl in the blue dress. I turned east up the slight hill that led to our road. Pete was done for, and the Indian pony's head was even with Pete's rump now. Pete knew where he was, and he was trying his best, but he couldn't pull away.

The Indian was yelling again. "Why did you kill me, Emil?"

I shouted back, "I didn't kill you! Leave me alone!"

I'm home. There is our corn. Here comes Willie. He's barking at me.

Pete knew where he was. He turned into the yard. I pulled him up in front of the house. I jumped off and looked back. The Indian pony was standing next to Pete. The Indian was gone. I turned around. Where was he?

I turned round and round "Leave me alone. Leave me alone."

Suddenly he was right in front of me. He sneered at me. "I've got you now."

I fought for all I was worth. He was too strong for me.

"Leave me alone. Leave me alone."

He yelled back, "I got you!"

He threw me on the ground and straddled me with his knees, sat on my belly, and pinned my hands to the ground.

"Leave me alone" I yelled.

He looked down at me as mean as ever. "I got you. I got you. I got you. Ve got cha. Ve got cha."

It was Pa's voice! I opened my eyes. It was Pa. I was really home. But Pa looked worried. Pa looked scared. Ma and the little ones were standing there. Ma looked scared, and the little ones looked so confused. I was sure they had never seen Pa wrestle down anyone before.

"Are you all right, Emil? Vy did you race dat poor beast?"

"That Indian was after me, Pa. I thought I could outrun him."

"Vat Indian?"

"His pony is right there next to Pete."

"Vat pony?" Pa said as he turned to look at Pete.

I looked over. No pony. Just Able and Gilbert cooling Pete with wet towels.

"Vat is in yur head, Son?"

Pa released my hands and helped me sit up. Ma ran and got me a yard chair and then helped me into it. Ma got Nellie to run for a lemonade. Ma kissed me. I sat for a few minutes, and then it hit me.

"Pa, I have my pay in the saddlebag."

Able anxiously grabbed the saddlebags and opened them. He pulled out the blue envelope and broke the seal.

"Pa, there is a letter in here for you," Able said.

Pa went over by Able. "You read da English for me, Able."

Able started to read. Then Pa started to cry. Pa told Able and Gilbert to take Pete to the barn. Pa told Ma to take the little ones in the house.

Pa came over and knelt in front of me.

"Did you read the letter from John? I'm not crazy. I'm not. I have something called shock. It will go away."

Pa wept as he talked. "Vy didn't da Lord guide you home vin you said you t'ought of coming? Dis money you earned is not vorth da pain you vill have for a long time. Dis money is evil. Vat a man vill do for money! You must promise me, Emil. You vill never tink of dis place again. Never tink of dis place again. Dis Cow Creek Ranch."

EPILOGUE

Not to worry. Emil was able to manage his demons. At the age of twenty five he married my grandmother Ellen. They began to raise a family and he took over the family farm.

***

When Fergie challenged me to tell this story, I struggled to figure out what could have happened up on that ranch. I started thinking back on the memories of my grandpa.

This is my first memory of my grandpa.

"Emil, Emil, wake up!" Grandma called to Grandpa. "Irene and Arthur are here. Carol and Robert didn't come, just Richard."

For a man that lived in darkness, Grandpa loved to sit on the enclosed front porch. It was always sunny. Grandpa always sat in a big rocker. At least to me it was big. This rocker had wide armrests that curled into a spiral under where his hands rested. Grandpa opened his eyes. His eyes were just gray. He had been blinded by diabetes.

"Pa, it's Irene. I have Richard here."

"Well, what are you waiting for? Send him to me."

He must have been able to hear my steps on the floor. As I neared, he leaned forward and reached out his arms. He snatched me from the floor and pulled me to his lap. He reached to touch my face. He took his index finger and ran it down my chin, down my neck, down my chest, then, with lightning speed, over below my armpits for a tickle.

He laughed as hard as I did. He pulled his hand back and bumped something.

"What is this, Richard?"

I answered back, "It's my cap gun and holster. It's a Roy Rogers. When Sam gets here, we're gonna play cowboys and Indians. I got the gun. If Sam don't have a gun, he'll have to be the Indian."

Grandpa laughed.

I looked up at him, and it hit my young mind. "Grandpa, you're really old. Did you ever know any cowboys or Indians?"

"*No!*" he answered back in a gruff voice that I had never heard him use. I could feel his arms tighten around me, but in a soft way. I looked up, and his face was stern. His expression softened, and a little tear came to his eye.

He put a little smile on his face and said, "I met a cowboy once. He was from Georgia. He told me this."

The boy stood on the burning deck,
Eating peanuts by the peck.
His mother called him,
He would not go,
Because he loved the peanuts so.

***

Any of us grandchildren can attest. If you spent a day with grandpa, you heard "The boy stood on the burning deck."

***

In 1934 the State of Nebraska purchased a tract of land along the Missouri River.
The following year Ponca State Park was opened.
It is still beautiful!

***

The End

ABOUT THE AUTHOR

I was born in Omaha, Nebraska, and raised on the very north edge of town. My childhood was filled with playing along the banks and bluffs of the Missouri River. My father was an avid upland game hunter, and I believe I inherited my zeal for hunting from him. One of our favorite hunting areas was west of Winnebago, Nebraska. I have hunted for nearly fifty years in these hills, so I have an easy time describing them for readers. When Uncle Fergie told me I was hunting near Cow Creek, I took him at his word. It wasn't until my research at the Thurston County Register of Deeds proved him right. I was so familiar with the area and families that live there that research was fun and interesting. While this is a fictional story, and names other than my family names have been changed, there is record of a family holding that could have been Cow Creek Ranch.

When Fergie challenged me to tell this story, my thought was to do so in short-story form. But as my outline grew, it was plain to see that this was to be a much larger endeavor. When I knew Emil was going to the Indian Nations to work, I knew what this innocent fifteen-year-old would see. The reservation system for our native people is a failed government program. I know what Emil saw, because I have seen all these things. People were living in tin sheds along Highway 75 north of Decatur, Nebraska, in the 1950s. Prostitution for alcohol was still occurring in Decatur in the 1960s. During the 1980s, the Winnebago tribe began to offer hunting permits to hunt on tribal land. I mistakenly entered the wrong door of the tribal office building when I was going to purchase a permit. What I found myself in was the tribal flophouse, thus "Indians at their best." This was a hundred years after Emil's trip, and I described what I saw that morning. My father's special charity was the Catholic mission at Winnebago. Every time we drove through town he'd say, "Watch for your old clothes." Can you imagine how Emil felt when his dreams of seeing the noble red man that his dime novels portrayed were shattered by the reality of reservation life?

This is a failed federal program. The state of Nebraska is no better and still allows the town of White Clay to sell beer right next to the "dry" Pine Ridge Reservation. As of 2011, there are still prostitutes for alcohol. My wife covered her eyes to shield the view of drunks lying in the streets, sidewalks, and gutters. "Indians at their best." How long must we torture our native peoples?

As for cowboys, I loved growing up in the fifties. My friend and I would sneak into the neighbor's pasture, get on those old nags, and ride around playing till we'd get chased off. We had great radio and TV

Westerns to rely on. I have a great imagination, I think, from radio and reading. I love stories of the Old West.

As for my ability to tell this story, I attended University of Omaha studying engineering. I filled my electives with public speaking and creative writing classes. My life after college included marriage, my own construction company, a move to the country, three children, breeding champion English setters and French Alpine and Toggenburg dairy goats. As for writing, I never quit; I just wasn't too prolific. Bob Dylan inspired me to write song lyrics and poetry. Some were pretty good but not published. My published works were articles in dog and dairy goat publications, and public-pulse articles in local newspapers. I had a friend that was editor of a national dairy goat publication, and after he read some of my short stories, he thought I should try to publish them. I never did.

Fergie challenged me to write this story about a year before he died. I really did nothing with it for several years. In 2005, I started the research and worked on the outline. In 2006, I took an early retirement, and in July of that year, my wife passed away. In my time of mourning, I decided to write this novel. Anyone who loves to write dreams of writing a novel. By December of 2006, I began. I took off ten days for the holidays and finished by late January of 2007.

I thought when I finished, *Damn, this would make a good movie.* I felt if I could get a movie made, then the book would be a big seller. I knew a person I felt could pull some strings to get the job done. The only strings that were pulled were my purse strings. I backed off. I went the route of trying to find a publisher or agent, to no avail.

About the same time, I met Libby. A new life put this project on the back burner for a while. Just a little side story, my meeting Libby was a blind date set up by a mutual friend. I was doing some research in White Clay, Nebraska, and sitting in my car when my cell phone rang. I talked to the friend and then called Libby to set up a date. As we talked, I had a teenage girl come up and ask if I was interested in oral sex for the fee of a twelve-pack of beer. I waved her off and continued talking to Libby. That girl probably wondered why I was sitting there if sex wasn't what I was there for. She had no trouble finding a customer two cars up the street. I told Libby about it later. Then in 2011, I showed her the main street of White Clay.

Well, back to the book. I have had so many people ask why I haven't published the book. I don't want to go through rejection again. I am also not very tech savvy, but online publishing seems the way to go. I hope that you have enjoyed my story, and if you have, tell someone. As I always told my customers, "If you're happy with your job, tell a friend. If not tell, me." I will see how this goes. Should I find there is interest in my work, there is more where this came from.

Thank you for choosing my story.

Richard

www.cowcreekbook.com